Damiano's Rescue
The Famiglia (Book 1)
Leah Merrill

Red Ten Publishing LLC

To the firefighter who rescued me

"I KNOW IT'S HARD," Gina tells me. "But it's time to ditch the rat."

I shift my cell phone from one ear to the other as I step over a giant clump of snow. "He's not a rat."

"He is *literally* a rat."

I huff, looking down at the little guy zippered into my puffy coat. "He's *actually* an opossum." An adorable baby opossum who's finally recovered from a broken tail, thanks to me.

The little guy is swaddled in my ex's vintage Van Halen tee to keep him cozy and warm. Tom loved this shirt and thought I should give it back when we broke up. I thought he wouldn't stick his dick in other girls while we were dating. We were both wrong.

"Rats and possums are, like, cousins."

I know Gina won't care, but I correct her anyway. "Opossums are marsupials. Rats are rodents. They aren't related." I step over a pile of melting snow, the wet ground squishing under my Uggs.

"Whatever, Paige. He's a beady-eyed sack of fur, oozing rabies and reeking of Black Death."

"Don't listen to her, Oscar," I tell my little fur baby.

"Dump the rat, disinfect your apartment, then I'll come over. I'll even pick up takeout from Qing Xiang." She singsongs the last part, knowing I'll never pass up their Kurobuta and cabbage dumplings. Gina knows *exactly* how to cheer me up.

"Yes, please!" I step off the cleared path toward the opening in the woods I use for most of my releases. Ooh, no one's walked on this patch of snow before, so I get to make fresh footprints. The perfect crisp crunch of old snow.

"I'm going to get two orders of those because I love you to death but not enough to give you half of my dumplings."

"That's fair." They really are that good.

"Listen, Paige. If the little rat is all better now, you have to get rid of it. Don't change your mind about releasing this one."

Gina doesn't mind the turtle and rabbit I've been rehabbing for the past two months, but she completely freaked out when Oscar hissed at her. She's refused to come over ever since. "That was one time, G. One time. And I did release Charlie on my second attempt."

Technically, my third attempt. But it's not my fault that baby chipmunks are irresistible.

I walk over to the perfect tree. It has a broad evergreen canopy that touches other trees, so Oscar can pick one for his new home without climbing down to the ground. There's an access road maybe thirty feet away, but there's a babbling brook separating the trees from the road, so I don't think he'll try to cross over.

Home sweet new home for my little Oscar. I pet his supersoft, super-silky head and get a whiff of the strawberry-scented baby shampoo I used to give him a bath.

"How long until you're on your way home?"

"I just got to the release spot. I'll text you when I know for sure." I'm not going to set him free until dusk so he'll be safe. Plus, that gives me a little more time to say goodbye. "I should get home by 6:00. Maybe 6:30?"

"Okay. I don't want you out there alone after dark."

"I'll be on the road before it's dark, but I'd be fine either way. Tons of people come to Horner Park."

"Are there people near you now?"

Two joggers ran past me near where I parked, and there was a guy with his dog, but I was happy to see them going in the opposite direction so the dog wouldn't freak Oscar out. As I look around now, I don't see anyone. "I mean, there were a bunch of people here a few minutes ago."

Gina sighs so heavily, I can hear her eyes rolling. "I wish you waited until I got off work so I could go with you."

"Really? You hate this little guy. Anyway, I'm fine. Relax. I'm almost done here. I'll leave in twenty minutes." Or so.

"Fine. But promise me you won't pick up any other rats while you're out there."

"I make no promises."

"Seriously, Paige." Gina hangs up, which is good because my phone is almost dead, as usual.

Damiano

"Pronto." Ready. I answer the call through my Range Rover's speakers, knowing it's Salvo.

He's on the very short list of people whose calls I answer. Salvo, our boss Rob, and any of the girls from the Cat's Meow, our strip club. No one else. If the rest of the world wants me, they can text. Even then, there's almost no chance I'll respond.

"The girls want to know when you'll get here." We meet up at the Cat most nights.

"Aww, do they miss me already?" I was at the Cat a few hours ago to pick up the bag I'm on my way to deliver.

"Apparently." He sounds annoyed, which makes me smile.

"Tell me, which girls specifically?"

Salvo starts rattling off names, but I don't care who he says. They're all perfect—fit as fuck, friendly as fuck, and not a single one of them expects me to stick around and cuddle after. But if there's a chance to push Salvo's buttons, I'm in. And fucking with him about the Cat girls is the only thing that gets him riled up.

"What about Amber? She ask about me?" I rarely fuck around with Amber since she's Salvo's favorite, or with

Rob's favorite, Megan. The rest of them, though? They're my favorite.

Salvo huffs. "So, when the fuck will you get here?"

Not soon enough.

"Well, some of us"—meaning me—"have to handle the dirty work so that the rest of us"—meaning him and Rob—"can sit around getting your dicks sucked."

"Come on, man, you know I prefer to stand to have my dick sucked. And anyway, like you even want us there with you."

He's right. I prefer to work alone. When Rob or Salvo joins me on a job, too much of my attention is on their six, making sure they don't get in over their heads. They tell me again and again to fuck off and stop babysitting them, that they can hold their own. And they can. But it doesn't change the fact that my primary focus will always be on their safety. So it's a fuckton easier for me when they're at the Cat getting their dicks sucked while I'm out cracking skulls.

"I'm meeting Joey's guy in thirty minutes, then I'll head to the Cat." I check the rearview mirror to make sure no one's following me. No reason anyone would be tonight, but it's a habit. "We'll be there in an hour fifteen, maybe less." I cruise through a yellow light that was probably already red.

"We? Who's with you?"

"Paulie will be in two minutes. I'm picking him up now." I turn onto Lincoln and double-park next to a set of plastic lawn chairs claiming dibs on a shoveled-out parking space. I don't bother to honk to let him know I've arrived.

I'm here exactly when I said I'd be here, so he better get his ass into my car or I'll leave without him in three minutes.

"Paulie? Why the fuck are you picking up Paulie? You don't like that guy."

I don't like anyone. Except for Salvo and Rob. And the Cat girls, I like them a lot. "He wants to talk."

"So?"

"So what?"

"So since when do you give a fuck if someone wants to talk to you?"

"Since *Rob* told me to give him an hour of my time."

"Huh."

Salvo didn't know about this? I didn't think there was anything Rob or Salvo did without the other knowing.

"Any idea what he wants?"

"No clue." I crack the window open for fresh air. There's a faint smell of bleach in the car from a cleanup two days ago. I'm definitely trading this Rover out for a different one when I leave the Cat tonight. "And I don't fucking care. Rob's the boss. If he tells me to talk to someone, I'm talking to them."

"Well, if Paulie needs advice about hurting people, he went to the right guy. But if he wants advice about the ladies, be sure to send him my way."

"No one's coming to me for dating advice. You either. What the fuck do you know about dating?"

"Dating? Jack shit. But wooing the ladies? I am the undisputed heavyweight champion of woo."

I can't disagree with that. There are probably two girls sitting on his lap as we speak, another rubbing his shoulders. Maybe another one making eyes at him from across the room as she grinds on some customer's lap.

Salvo may be annoyed that some of the Cat girls asked about me, but we all know they fight over who gets to go home with him each night. Some of the girls actually worked out a rotation schedule a few weeks back to keep it fair. It's posted on the wall in their dressing room right next to the main stage spotlight schedule.

"If Paulie asks me about *wooing the ladies*, I'll be sure to send him your way."

"Grazie. You expecting any trouble tonight?"

"No. Should be a quick exchange. Don't think I'll even get to shoot anyone."

"Well, the night is still young, my man. Where's it going down?"

"Same as two times ago. Horner Park."

"I'm never fucking late, man, so hurry the fuck up." I slam the car door closed.

Paulie is dragging his ass so slow that we'll barely be five minutes early. Which means we'll be ten minutes late. The fuck is his problem?

I stand outside my Rover and stare at him through the front windshield. I watch as he pats his pockets, looks around inside the car. Opens the door. Steps one leg out. Then the other. *Finally* pushes his door shut, but then actually *stands there watching* the soft-close feature engage. He puts another cigarette in his mouth, feels around for his lighter. "Yeah, man. I'm coming."

No one, in the history of all eternity, has moved this fucking slow before. *Ever.*

This entire meetup would take all of two minutes if Paulie would just hurry the fuck up. I'll hand the Bagliateri guy a duffel bag, he'll hand me a duffel bag. Maybe we'll shoot the shit for a few minutes, maybe we won't—depends on who Joey sends—then I'll be back at my favorite booth at my favorite place with any one of my favorite Cat girls.

Paulie's taken only one step away from the car. Maybe he's scared to meet up with Joey's guy? He doesn't usually get his hands dirty, so maybe he's trying not to piss himself. I hope the fuck not. Pissing himself and then trying to get back into my Rover is going to be a big fucking problem for him.

"Get back in the car if you want, come with me if you want. I don't give a shit. But if you're coming, start hauling ass *now*." I stomp away toward the field.

Every other month, I set the location for this exchange. I like this isolated, barely lit part of the park. No cameras, no cops, no witnesses. If Paulie's coming with me, he's got to approach at the same time I do. Last thing I need is for him to creep into the meeting late, spooking Joey's guy into thinking there's an ambush. So either he gets there when I get there, or I'll zip-cuff him to the car door handle.

"I'm coming, I'm coming. Let's go."

I probably should have him hang back. The whole ride here, he was squirrely as fuck. Asking where we were going, asking if we could stop for a smoke when I wouldn't let him light up in my car, asking me to pull over so he could take a piss.

He's jittery too. And as slow as he's moving now, the guy was talking a mile a minute in weird-ass short bursts. I actually checked to see if his pupils were constricted because he sure as shit was acting like he's jacked up.

But at least he's moving now. It's a ten-minute walk from the parking lot to where we're meeting, two picnic tables and an old barbecue grill missing its grate, smack-dab in the middle of a field. Only a sharpshooter could take a reliable shot from the woods or from the parking lot on the far side of the field. If someone comes charging out of the trees, I have plenty of time to take them out.

Joey's guy is already at the picnic area, having approached from the parking lot on the opposite side. At dusk like this, I can't make out his face from this distance, and it's entirely possible I don't know him. But that doesn't matter. He's in the right spot, and there's a familiar duffel bag on the table.

Paulie's twenty feet behind me. I hate when anyone's behind me. "Hurry the fuck up."

"Gimme a fucking break, Dom. We're right on time."

Motherfucker.

"We are n—"

Wait.

His voice is too close. How is he right behind me now? I turn to look at him.

A blast *scorches* my shoulder. It throws me forward, like a searing hot battering ram struck my back.

I stumble toward the ground, knowing full well a second jolt of pain will shoot up my arm when I try to brace the fall with my right hand, but my left hand is already busy.

It's moving on autopilot.

It's pulling my Glock 41 from its holster before I even hit the ground.

It's aiming in Paulie's general direction as I roll onto my back, my right ear ringing from the familiar thunderclap.

A micro-adjustment now that Paulie's in my sight. He's wide-eyed. *Surprised you missed the back of my skull motherfucker or surprised my gun's aimed at your face?* Shame on you, Paulie. Point a gun at me and you sure as fuck better make your shot.

He missed.

I won't.

Here we go.

Bang.

His throat explodes, blood rains down everywhere.

Now both my ears ring. My .45 is a shit ton louder than the .22 that fell from Paulie's hand as he collapsed.

What the fuck just happened?

I start to push myself up with my left arm.

Pop. Pop.

For fuck's sake. Now Joey's guy is firing at me.

Pop.

There's no cover in this field. That's part of the reason I picked it.

I one-arm crawl over to Paulie, pull his limp body over, and prop it against me like a barricade.

Was Joey's guy working with Paulie and now he's trying to finish what Paulie started, or is he firing at me because he thought we were firing at him?

I watch him for five seconds, evaluate what he's doing. He's crouching behind the picnic table, gun in one hand, phone in the other. He pops up and shoots in my direction. Paulie's body jolts twice from getting hit. Paulie was useless alive, but dead, he's a decent meat shield. Thanks, man.

If Joey's guy is here to kill me, I'm a sitting duck. There's no way for me to leave this field without being completely exposed. He's fifty meters away. Back in Gruppo Operativo Incursori, Italy's version of Navy SEALs, I trained to shoot at double this distance. I can take him out, no problem.

But if he's not here to kill me, if he wasn't working with Paulie, if he's just defending himself, and I take him out? Then I'm starting a war between the Famiglie.

I need him to fuck off, alive.

Bang. Reset. *Bang.*

One shot hits the table next to his head as a warning, the other's a clean shot to his left thigh. Enough damage that he needs immediate medical attention, but I steered clear of his CFA, so he does some PT and shouldn't even have a limp. Plus, Joey Bags' enforcer, Massimo, will take one look at my shot and know exactly what I was doing—telling him to piss off and not trying to kill him. Hopefully that avoids a war.

I hold fire to see what he does.

Exactly as intended, he hobbles toward the parking lot. But then he turns back. *Pop, pop.* He's firing in my direction, probably to give himself cover so I don't shoot him again. *Pop.*

That last one grazes my side. *Fuuuuuck.* I was being nice by only shooting you a little, and this is how you thank me?

Seconds later, his SUV revs then skids in the gravel as it peels out of the parking lot on the far side of the field.

I close my eyes and take three box breaths to regroup.

In for four.

Hold for four.

Out for four.

Hold for four.

In for four.

Hold for four.

Out for four.

Hold for four.

In for four.

Hold for four.

Out for four.

Okay. Stop the bleeding. Get the fuck out of here. Worry about what the fuck just happened later. Go.

I pull my left arm out of my suit jacket. No way I'm getting my right arm out, so I rip the sleeve off. I pull the belt out of my pants, then buckle it into a loop. It's a bitch to do with only one fully functioning arm, but after a few tries, I have a field tourniquet in place, my bunched-up jacket applying pressure to my shoulder and the right sleeve wadded up against my left side, with my belt cinched diagonally across my chest, snugging both spots tight.

Now I've got to get the fuck out of here. That guy isn't coming back, but he probably called for backup, or if Paulie was working with anyone else, whoever that is might show up to try to finish what he fucked up. Paulie didn't know where we were heading when he got in my car, but he was fucking with his phone on the ride here, so he easily could have texted someone.

And Rob knew where we were meeting.

I take a few staggering steps toward my Rover.

The adrenaline is wearing off. My heart's beating a thousand times a minute. My shoulder is burning. I'm panting, struggling to take deep breaths. My hands are cold, and I'm sweating all over. I need to get the fuck out of here in case I go into shock or pass out.

No fucking clue why Rob would have it out for me, but also no clue if it was just a shitty coincidence that he told me to bring Paulie along tonight. All our Rovers have trackers so Rob, Salvo, and I can know where any of our guys are. It's too risky to go back to my car.

I turn and head across the field toward the far parking lot.

I SAID GOODBYE TO Oscar ten minutes ago. He didn't want to climb up the tree at first and kept trying to scurry down to the ground, but after the third time I turned him around, he scrambled right up and disappeared. He didn't look back, but I know he's going to miss me.

Now I'm sitting on a boulder, trying to wipe the tree sap off my fingers and trying not to cry. Just like every other release, it's bittersweet. I'm thrilled for the ones that get better, but I miss the crap out of them.

I take a deep breath and let it out. I need to get back to my car before it gets dark so Gina doesn't send out a rescue party. Plus, dumplings sound like the perfect pick-me-up. I blow a kiss up to Oscar somewhere high in the branches, my fingers still smelling like pine sap.

It's only a five-minute walk back to my car so—

Pop.

I freeze. My shoulders stiffen.

"What was that?" I whisper-ask Oscar, knowing full well he's gone and that he wouldn't be able to answer me even if he were still here.

Was that a gunshot?

Bang.

That was definitely a gunshot. I drop down to a squat to hide.

Pop pop pop.

Bang. Bang.

That's more than one person shooting. It might be more than two people shooting.

Do I stay here, or do I make a run for my car? The shots sound close but not *that* close. But how the hell do I know? I have no idea how to tell how far away guns are. I need to get out of here.

Pop. Pop.

No, I should *not* run to my car—the shots are coming from the direction where I parked.

Pop.

What the hell am I supposed to do?

That tree. I'll hide behind that tree. I get up and run over, leaning my back against it.

But this tree is really skinny and not hiding me at all.

I should run over to that wider one, stay there until the shooting stops.

But that's the tree where I released Oscar. I don't want to draw any attention there.

I drop down to the ground on all fours, my knees instantly soaked by the wet ground seeping through my thin scrubs. Sharp rocks dig into my hands, and twigs scratch my wrists as I crawl behind the boulder I was sitting on. It's tall enough to give me cover.

Maybe the gunshots came from hunters? Is there a hunting season in Chicago?

Will the hunters see me on all fours and think my tan coat is a deer? But if I take it off, I'll freeze. The inside lining is pink, maybe I should turn it inside out? If they're hunters, seeing pink would tell them not to shoot. But if they're bad guys, seeing pink might be a red flag that there's a witness. Dammit.

I'm facing the direction the shots came from so I can see if anyone is coming this way, but maybe I should turn around so I'm poised for a getaway sprint if they come this way. I turn.

But if I don't see them coming, how will I know when to run? I turn back.

I am *not* handling any of this right. What the hell am I doing?

Get up, Paige. Get up off your hands and knees and squat behind the rock. That way, I can see them coming and run. That is, if I don't have a heart attack first since my pulse is thudding so hard, it's drowning out other sounds.

Headlights glare up the access road, coming from the direction of the gunshots. Can they see me? I think it's dusky enough now that they can't. Hopefully, my jacket and mint-green scrubs blend in with nature. Thank god I'm not wearing my bright-pink scrubs.

An SUV speeds by. Did they see me? Is that the shooter fleeing the scene? Or are those the good guys running away from the bad guys? Or was it just hunters and now they're going home?

I'm just going to stay here longer. Crouching, as still as possible. For another hour. Maybe all night.

It's pitch black now.

I've been hiding here so long—hours?—so motionless, my legs are cramped. All the adrenaline has worn off and I'm shivering even in my winter coat. And I have to pee. Like painfully need to pee.

And of course my phone is long dead.

Okay. It's go time. It's got to be. I can't stay in the woods all night. I have to assume that the guys with guns left, that it was them in the SUV that sped past. No reason for the shooters to wait around for the police to come.

Why haven't the police come? They probably were just hunters and I'm completely overreacting.

I stand up and stretch my legs. Pins and needles shoot through my left foot, my toes tingly and prickly. I don't know if I can put any weight on it until it wakes up, so I shake it.

Without my phone's flashlight, it takes me twice as long to follow the path back to my car. Plus, I stopped to pee in the woods and that added a few minutes because somehow, in the middle of nowhere, in the dark, with no one around, I got stage fright.

I finally reach the parking area and there she is, my beat-up old Chevy Blazer, Jolene. I let out a long breath. She's safe and sound. As I was walking back, I had this weird feeling Jo-Jo would be riddled with bullets or on fire or something out of a movie. But no. She's fine. Just as dusty and unwashed as I left her.

But... What the hell? Her interior light is on.

Why is her interior light on?

Dammit, my battery. But I guess it hasn't drained all the way since the light is still on, so it should be f—

The rear passenger door is open.

My entire body tenses. My shoulders hunch up. My breaths are shallow puffs of cloud.

I definitely did *not* leave the back door open. I didn't use that door at all.

I'm going to hyperventilate.

Someone messed with Jo-Jo. Someone invaded my private space.

My feet are frozen in place, afraid that if I move, someone might see me. I slowly twist my body to look around again.

There's no one in the parking lot. Just the one dim streetlight, my Jolene, and me. No unusual noises either. Just normal forest sounds, the drone of the highway in the background.

Did someone break into the car to steal my stuff? Joke's on them, breaking into a broke girl's car.

I sneak around the back of Jo-Jo to close her door. Slowly, quietly. Am I being 'stealthy'? I've always thought that if the occasion arose, I could be particularly stealthy. Like there's a stealthy side of me I've yet to discover. Like, if ninjas attacked, I could actually take them on. Like I have a secret stealth superpow—

There's a foot.

Hanging out of Jo-Jo's open door.

A man's foot in a big leather shoe that isn't moving.

Which means there's a guy—*who might be a dead guy*—in my car.

I check my cell phone again, praying that it spontaneously recharged itself just a little, but nope.

What am I supposed to do?

Maybe I can throw a rock at the foot. If it moves, I'll run. I don't know where to. Maybe back to Oscar. I'll hide there until the morning. Gina will realize I never made it home and send the police. If it doesn't move, that means he's dead.

I pick up a golf-ball-sized rock. I'm oddly good at throwing darts, so I should be good at hitting a man's foot, with a rock, in the dark, from twenty feet away.

Except that I'm not. All I manage to do is whack the door. Sorry Jo-Jo.

But it did make a really loud bang, and the foot didn't even twitch.

I pick up a decent-length stick. I can whack the guy with it if I need to, if he's faking it and attacks when I get close.

From as far away as possible, I lean all the way forward and reach out with my stick, almost falling over, to poke the foot.

Nothing.

I poke it again.

Okay, dead. Not the most technical way to decide if this guy is dead or not, but it's not like I have my stethoscope out here in the woods with me.

There's no way I'm getting in the car with a dead guy. I'll pull him out, leave him here, then drive to the police station to report this. Then go home and crawl under my blanket with an entire bottle of wine.

It's a half-decent plan, and it's all I've got.

I take hold of the guy's ankle. It's still warm.

Dammit. If I had gotten here sooner, if I wasn't so scared and hiding behind a stupid rock, maybe I could have saved him? I might need to switch that bottle of wine to a bottle of tequila to deal with this.

I grab his other ankle from in the car. One, two, three and *pull.* He's heavy but slides toward me a few inches. Another big yank, and he'll be—

"Stop."

What the hell?

I stumble backward, tripping over my poke-him stick and falling hard onto my ass. "Holy shit. You're alive?"

"What... are you doing?" The guy's voice is strained. It's hard for him to talk. But he's obviously not dead.

I stand up, brush the dirt off my ass, and rub my left butt cheek that took the brunt of that fall. "I was pulling you out of my car so I could leave you here."

"Don't... do that... per favore."

I took Spanish in high school but didn't absorb much, but I know that means 'please.'

"Well, amigo, that *was* my plan when I thought you were dead. But you're alive. That's good. But you're in my car, which is not good. Why are you in my car?"

He doesn't answer. I take a step closer. The light is so dim inside that I can barely make him out. I reach into the pocket in the back of the passenger seat for my emergency flashlight. I can use it to light up the car, and I can whack him with it if I need to.

Except now that I have enough light to see him, I can see he looks pretty close to death. He's covered in blood. Drenched. Thank god I keep the backseat covered with a tarp for when I pick up rescue critters.

Looks like he might have passed out again. No way this guy is lunging at me.

"Hey." I tap his foot with the flashlight. "Hey? Where's your phone?"

He doesn't answer. I reach in slowly and pat his pants pockets. No phone.

But not *nothing*. I felt something in there and it was not for making calls. "Oh my god, I am so sorry about that." Holy shit, I just touched a stranger's dick.

But also, good for you, my guy. Good for you.

"Wake up. Hey, wake up!"

He opens his eyes. Wow, those are the greenest eyes I've ever seen. Jet black hair, dark tan skin and brilliant jade-green eyes.

He closes his eyes again. "I'm here." It's barely a whisper.

Yeah, no duh, you're here. Here in my car, where you definitely do not belong.

I stare at him. I know it's wrong to perv out over the half-dead guy who broke into my car and might be bleeding out, but holy hell, he's all full lips and a broad nose and enough scruff that his five-o'clock shadow has got to be intentional.

It's like an olive-skinned Tom Hardy is bleeding out in the back of my car. And even though there's the metallic stench of blood in the car that makes me want to gag, there's also a heavenly scent of oranges and cedar and musk, delicious enough that I almost want to lean in and take a deeper whiff.

He tries to prop himself up, using one arm. He's struggling to get upright in the seat. I don't really want to touch him, but he's not going to get up without some help.

"Hey, don't overdo it. Hold on. Let me help."

"Grazie." He smiles slightly at my offer. He definitely wants my help. The state he's in, he definitely needs my help.

He needs me.

Let's do this. I'll sit him up, I'll seatbelt him, then I'll take him to the hospital.

No way I'm touching any of the bloody parts of him without gloves on. Luckily, I keep my wildlife rescue supply bag on the backseat floor. I shine the flashlight down onto it. Hmph, it's open, and there are gauze wrappers on the floor. Looks like this guy already raided the bag. Well, that's what the supplies are for, I guess. I pull out a set of latex gloves, put them on.

I help him upright. "Where's your phone?"

"I lost it."

"Mine's dead. What do we do now?" I ask, more to myself than to him.

He looks me up and down with *those* eyes. "You can help me."

"Yeah, no, I get that. I'm trying to figure out how. I think I should leave you here and then go get the police and an ambulance."

"Don't." He closes his eyes again, taking long, slow breaths.

"Don't? Don't to which part? Don't leave you here or don't go get the police?"

"Both."

"But you need help."

"You... help... me."

"Yeah, by getting you someone who can help you."

"No." He opens his eyes and looks me up and down again.

Is he checking me out?

His foot nudges my supply bag toward me. "*You* can do it. Just... you."

He's passing out again. Crap. He can't wait for help.

I don't have a choice or this guy will die in my car. Holy shit, if he dies in Jo-Jo, will the police seize her as evidence or something? Would I get her back?

He cannot die in my car. And this is already taking too long, wasting precious time. And people are supposed to help people, especially helpless people. Okay, decision's made.

"Can you get your seat belt on?"

He looks confused. Maybe he's going into shock?

I climb partway in and reach over to pull his seatbelt on, click it in. I hop out and shut the door, then run around to the driver's seat. Thankfully, Jolene starts on the first try.

"Don't worry, the hospital is only a few minutes from here." I drive off the road, over some grass to get to the access road faster. It's bumpy, but the actual road from this parking lot winds and twists the long way through the woods in a big swirly loop before connecting with the access road.

"No... hospital."

"Are you crazy? You need a doctor. You need all the doctors."

"No." He's struggling to talk between breaths. "No hospital. No police."

"Yes hospital, so they can patch you up, and yes police, so they can find whoever shot you."

"Pull over. Pull over and leave me here. I can't go to the hospital."

"I can't just leave you here."

He looks at me in the rearview mirror, tilting his head, questioning me.

"Okay, yes, I *was* going to leave you in the park. But that was before. Now it's too late for that. I have to get you to the ER."

"I only need... a few stitches. You... can sew me up. You have sutures, yes?"

"The ER has to help you even if you don't have insurance." I mean, I'm still paying off the $18,000 bill from when my appendix burst, but at least they treated me.

He's shaking his head. He's definitely passing out again soon. "Please." Those stunning green eyes are begging me. "No hospital. I was barely shot."

"I don't think there is such a thing as 'barely shot.' Plus, you've lost a lot of blood. They might have to give you a transfusion."

"It's not that bad... I promise... You take care of me, or let me out here."

I mean... I *am* pretty good at stitching up the critters. Most of them survive.

Some of them survive.

This guy is no critter, but maybe I can at least patch him up so he's stable? I'm pretty sure I can. Then he can call his friends or something, and they can come get him.

He's watching me in the mirror. Waiting. His jewel-tone eyes piercing into mine. "Promise me no hospital."

"You need the hospital."

"No. Promise... me." He's about to pass out again.

I'm about to make what's quite possibly a very stupid decision. Except that... I think he's right that I'll be able to patch him up. I've gotten really good at it in the past few months.

I take a deep breath in. And out. "Okay. I promise. What's your name?"

I look back at him in the mirror.

He's out cold.

Don't worry, my guy, a promise is a promise. I've got you.

Jo-Jo hits another bump. There's a dull thud in the backseat. I look over my shoulder. There's a gun on the floor of my car.

What the hell?

Paige

"WHY ARE YOU SO late?" Gina shouts from the kitchen as I open the front door to my apartment. "I've been calling you for hours. I ate all the dumplings, by the w—what *the fuck* is that?"

"Oh, you're here."

"Don't '*oh, you're here*' me. Is that a fucking bear?"

"Shh. My neighbors will hear you. Just... help me get this inside."

I'm trying, but failing, to pull the luggage cart my apartment building makes available for tenants to use into my apartment. It's almost never in the parking garage storage room where it's supposed to be. But, stroke of luck, it was there tonight.

And it's now holding one large man, who's mostly covered by a tarp, and it does not want to roll over the slightly raised threshold into my apartment.

"Did you rescue a fucking bear, Paige? Do *not* bring that in here. Take it back to the park."

"Shh! Can you just help? And we don't have bears in Chicago."

"Of course we have bears in Chicago. Haven't you heard of, like, *any* of our sports teams?" She stops talking, waiting for me to answer.

"The... Bulls?" I ask sheepishly.

"Do *not* mention the Bulls in my presence. You know that. I was referring to the Chicago *Bears*. The Chicago *Cubs*. We definitely have bears here."

Huh. That's pretty sound logic. Do I need to worry about bears when I'm in the park for a release?

A groan from under the tarp brings me back to the moment. One final tug, and I get the cart inside with no help from Gina.

"Even if we did have bears in Chicago, there's no way I'd bring something that dangerous home."

Gina gives me a look. "Uh-huh. Except that you care more about your rescues than you do about your own well-being."

I huff and roll my eyes at her. "*Anyway*. It's not a bear. It's a guy. Help me get him onto the couch."

"Holy shit, Paige. Did you kidnap some guy?"

"Of course not. He's a rescue."

She closes her eyes and rubs her forehead. "Please tell me you're joking."

"I don't joke about rescues."

"I can't believe I'm saying this, but this was actually less insane a minute ago when I thought you brought home a bear."

Gina steps closer to the cart, her curiosity definitely piqued. She reaches for the tarp.

"Just be careful—he's completely covered with blood and somewhere under the blanket is his gun."

Ten minutes later, we've managed to get the guy onto my couch.

"Go hide this somewhere in your room," Gina whispers, covertly handing me the guy's gun that she placed on a book, like it's a tray. She used my kitchen tongs to pick it up and set it down, refusing to touch it.

"Yeah. Good idea." Not that this guy is pulling any weapons on anyone anytime soon.

Under my bed? In my closet? Too obvious. Better idea—in the bathroom, under the sink, *in* the box of tampons. Same place I used to hide anything I didn't want my brother to find. Brian may be a former Navy SEAL, but even hint at a woman's cycle, and he'll run out of the room covering his ears.

It's the perfect hiding place. Shoot, the box is almost empty. I didn't realize I'm almost out. Add that to the mental shopping list.

I grab some medical supplies while I'm in the bathroom. A few rolls of gauze, my suture kit, forceps, Betadine, a tube of bacitracin, and two pairs of latex gloves.

I also change out of the green scrubs I wore to release Oscar because, for one, I snuggled the crap out of him before letting him go. I mean, literally. He peed on my shirt a little. And for two, there was like a quart of this guy's blood on them, plus mud on the knees from crawling on the ground. I slip on my other set of scrubs. I picked these up at Salvation Army a few weeks ago for four dollars. Awesome find.

Gina is still standing over the guy. "He needs the hospital, Paige. He's—" She turns to me, her eyes dropping down to the tray I'm holding. "Why do you have all that stuff?"

"They're my rehab supplies. I have tons of this stuff."

She squeezes her eyes shut then continues. "Let me rephrase that. Why do you have all that stuff *out*? Out like you're going to be using it? Is there *also* an injured squirrel here somewhere? In his pocket, maybe?"

"No, there's no injured squirrel in his pocket. I'm going to stitch him up."

"No, you're not. I'm calling 9-1-1."

"No need. I've got this." I put the tray on the coffee table and go to the kitchen to get my good scissors. Pretty sure I'll need to cut his shirt off like EMTs do.

Gina follows me. "This is a person, Paige, not some random animal."

"Stitches are stitches. And he's not covered in fur or shell, so it'll be even easier." I walk back to the couch.

"Paige, stop." She steps in front of me. "How do I say this without being mean?"

I cross my arms. "Clearly it's going to be mean now, however you say it."

"Fine. I'll just say it then. Babe, you are not a doctor. You are not a nurse." She tugs at the sleeve on my scrubs. "You are not even a *licensed* wildlife rehabilitator. You failed the test. Twice. Half of the animals you take in leave in shoeboxes, Paige. *Half* of them." She points to my Goodbye Shelf.

I put a small stone on the shelf for each little guy that doesn't make it. A memorial, so they'll know they were loved.

"You're being an asshole, G."

"I'm being honest. This is a human being. He needs an actual doctor."

I step around her. "He doesn't want one. He doesn't. Before he passed out, he was very clear about that. He said, no hospital, no police. He very clearly asked *me* to help him."

"He needs professionals."

"The guy was in a shootout in the park, Gina. I can't call the authorities. They'll patch him up, and whoever was shooting at him will show up at the hospital and finish the job. Taking him to the hospital isn't going to help him."

"And *this* is going to help him?" Gina points to my tray of supplies.

"Yes. I may not be a '*licensed*' rehabilitator, but I know what I'm doing. Look," I point to the terrarium and wire cage on my desk.

The terrarium currently houses Tango, the box turtle whose shell was ripped open by a lawn mower. He's doing great now. I'll release him in another few weeks. The wire cage holds Romeo, a bunny that was mauled by something. He lost one of his legs, but other than that, he's doing great now too. Not sure I'll ever release him back into the wild, but we'll see.

"I'm calling an ambulance." Gina takes her phone from her pocket.

I put my hand on her arm. "I made a promise to him, Gina. A promise. He asked me to do this. So either help me with it or go home and forget you were here tonight. But don't break my promise to this guy."

She stares up at the ceiling. She's probably counting to ten or regretting our entire friendship. "You *swear* he asked you to do this, like with actual words coming out of his mouth and not just you interpreting some look he gave you?"

I roll my eyes. "Yes, with '*actual words*.'" I almost can't believe she needed to ask me that. "I swear he asked."

She huffs out loud. "Fine."

I clap my hands and bounce up and down. Then I just can't resist. In a nasally voice, "Paging Doctor Paige. Paging Nurse Gina. Your patient is ready."

"Oh my god, stop."

I quiet down, but I can't stop smiling. I hand her a pair of latex gloves.

"Let me guess, you have some special soap for before surgery?"

I nod. "Hibiclens. In the medicine cabinet. Blue bottle."

"He's actually really fucking hot." Gina's staring at the guy, mesmerized.

"Right?" We sponged most of the dirt and caked blood off his face.

"And ripped." We also removed his makeshift tourniquet then cut his shirt off.

And his pants. To check for more wounds.

We found one bullet hole in his right shoulder that went straight through, I think from back to front, and a gash on his side where it looks like another bullet grazed him. No other injuries, but lots of scars. Clearly not his first rodeo.

There was a ton of blood on his clothes, which are now in a trash bag, but the rest of him seems fine. In fact, it was a ridiculous amount of blood, considering the bullet hole is tiny and he packed both wounds with the gauze he found in my car. Seems like he completely stopped the bleeding before I even arrived on scene.

Gina lifts the guy's left hand and holds it up to me. "No wedding ring."

I roll my eyes at her. "Can we focus on fixing him? A hot, ripped, *dead* guy on my couch is going to be a big frickin' problem, whether he's married or not."

"Shit. Yeah. What are we going to do if he croaks? He's not going to fit in a shoebox."

"I don't know." I shrug my shoulders. "Chop him up?"

"*Paige!*" Gina jumps back two feet, stumbling a little.

"Oh my god, relax. I'm kidding. He's not going to croak."

"If you say so."

"I do."

Gina continues to check out the guy's very fit, very perfect body. "What flag is that?"

"Hmm?" I look to where Gina is pointing, then wipe some of the blood off his tattoo. Green, white, and red with an emblem in the middle. I actually know this one. "Mexico."

"Hmph. With the Prada loafers, his olive skin, and being in a shootout in Chicago, I would've put my money on him being mafia. Are you *sure* that's not the Italian flag?"

"I have no clue what the Italian flag looks like, but I grew up seventeen miles north of the Mexican border, G. That's definitely Mexico. And he was speaking Spanish a little. Mostly English, but he dropped in Spanish word or two."

Gina twists her lips, clearly not believing me. "Siri, what does the Italian flag look like?" She stares at her phone, then looks back at the guy's tattoo. "Okay, fine. The Italian flag is also green, white, and red, but it doesn't have a little picture in the middle like his does."

"Told ya. Now can we stop ogling this guy and get back to saving him?"

"No. Let's ogle for another minute first."

I shake my head as I grab a pill bottle off the tray. "You think I should give him something for the pain before I suture him up? Maybe crushed up Tylenol dissolved in a little water? I can pour it in his mouth, and I'm pretty sure he'll swallow it."

Gina gives me a look.

"What? Most of the little critters can still swallow some water when they're passed out. It's like a reflex or something."

"I wasn't even questioning your judgment about *that* part. I was questioning your judgment about giving him Tylenol. The man was shot twice. I think he needs something a little stronger."

"Yeah, you're right. Oh! I have some muscle relaxers. Pretty strong ones."

"Why do you have muscle relaxers?"

"Left over from last year. I would take one-quarter of a cyclobenzaprine tablet, and it was like I was floating on a cloud. We can give him that."

Gina nods her head. "Yeah, that might work. But probably a whole one. Actually, he's big. Maybe two? You know what? Crush up three of those fuckers. This guy's not going to want to remember *any* of what's about to happen."

"Good thinking. While I do that, can you grab my iPad? There's a how-to video on doing stitches saved in my YouTube favorites."

Damiano

WHAT THE HELL DID my guardian angel give me and where can I get more? My shoulder has never hurt like it did yesterday.

Was that yesterday? I have no fucking clue.

This isn't the first time I've been shot, but it's the first time I've been shot at point-blank. Fucking *scorched* my skin as it pierced through me, like a bolt of lightning incinerating my skin.

Whatever the fuck magic potion she concocted, it knocked me on my ass. It's like my head is floating a few inches above my neck. But at least the inferno burning in my shoulder is gone. So far gone that I don't even think pain is what woke me.

It's the need to take a piss.

I've never needed to piss like I do right now.

The apartment is quiet, except for clanging coming from a metal cage on the desk in the corner. I haven't heard any other noises for the past few minutes, so I think I'm alone. Which is good because I'm not ready to answer any of the girl's questions. Not until I talk to Salvo and find out what the fuck happened last night. Or two nights ago. Whenever the fuck that was.

But I have to piss now. Doesn't even matter if I can stand on my own. The need to piss far exceeds any concerns I have about falling flat on my face when I try to stand.

Let's do this.

Left foot onto the floor. *Check.*

Sitting up is going to be a bitch. I need to push myself up with my uninjured left arm, but... What the hell?

My left wrist is... tied to the end table? Come on, angel, seriously? You bring *an absolute stranger* who was obviously *in a gunfight* home and *then* you tie him to a small table? A table I could just carry around with me? Should have at least tied me to the foot of the couch.

I roll toward the end table to check this shit out. I'd reach over with my right arm to yank the rope off, but I know exactly the pain that will shoot through me if I do. Being exceptionally well-versed in the precise quantity and quality of pain an action will cause makes me particularly good at my job as enforcer for the Galliano Famiglia.

The knot tied around my wrist actually looks half decent. A textbook bowline. I'm not wriggling out of that one-handed. But the way the other end is tied around the leg of the end table... can't I just... lift up the table leg and pull it out from under? No way it's that easy.

Yeah. It was that easy. There's still a loop dangling from my wrist, but I'm detached from the table.

I push up onto my feet. Fuuuuuck, that hurts. Pain shoots from my shoulder up the back of my neck, straight to my teeth. *Son of a bitch.*

Breathe in. Breathe out.

It's only four steps to that chair. Do that. Get there.

Either get there or piss in your boxers for Florence Nightingale to clean up. No fucking way.

Step. Breathe. Step.

Actually, walking isn't bad. Much easier than standing up. Walking is almost perfectly fine, as long as I don't swing my right arm. I make my way through the tiny living room, through the tiny bedroom, into the tiny bathroom. I feel like a giant in this place.

I piss for what feels like ten minutes. Best piss of my life.

Holy fuck, this is a good piss. Euphoric. Better than a blowjob from any of girls at the Cat.

Except for Candy's. Hers are like bursts of rainbows are shooting out the tip of my dick while glitter snow-globes around in my balls.

But that piss may have been the next-best feeling ever.

I glance in the mirror. I look like absolute shit. I mean, handsome as fuck, but handsome as fuck looking like absolute shit. There's dirt and blood in my hair, all over the left side of my chest. Looks like she washed the blood off my face and around the exit wound, but the rest of me is disgusting.

And almost all of that is Paulie's blood, not mine.

I could shower it off. There's a shower *right there*. I've never wanted a shower more in my life.

But I need my sweet nurse to think I'm still passed out until I connect with Salvo, which means finding a landline somewhere around here. I have no fucking clue why Paulie—*one of our own guys*—would shoot me. And since I actually know what I'm doing with a gun, he's no longer available to explain this situation to me.

So until I know what the fuck is going on—whether he was acting alone, whether he was acting on someone's orders, and if he was, was that someone from a rival Famiglia or from within ours?—I can't go home or to the Cat.

And, until then, I need my angel to think I'm passed out so I don't have to answer any of the million questions I bet she's going to ask. That means scrubbing the blood and dirt off me will have to wait.

Except for my balls. They deserve attention now. I grab the towel hanging on the shower door. Wet it, soap it up. This soap smells fantastic. Vanilla. Good for you, balls. You get to smell like Zia Lucia's cannolis. I pull my boxer briefs down and give the boys a rubdown.

Love having squeaky-clean balls.

I rehang the towel, making sure the wet part is hidden. I'd throw it in her laundry basket so she doesn't end up washing her face with my ball towel, but she might notice it's missing, so I don't.

What's this girl's story? She obviously lives alone, with one small bed and a bathroom that couldn't be more girly.

And I think she's hot. At least the image of her imprinted in my brain is hot. Like the heavens were doubly on my side, not just sending a nurse to find me in the middle of the woods, but sending a gorgeous blonde one, with navy blue eyes and a tight body wearing sexy-ass scrubs.

And one who *didn't* call the police or drag me to the hospital. Fucking unicorn.

But just because she didn't call the police when she found me doesn't mean she won't call them once she finds out who I am. I don't give a shit about the actual police, but if the police find out where I am, anyone Paulie was working with—if he was working with someone—will find out too.

So nothing that lets her know I'm awake. At least my balls are sparkling fucking clean. Them and my wound sites. Most of the rest of me is disgusting, but I'm stuck with that for now.

Speaking of wound sites, how bad are they? I lift the gauze off my shoulder, pulling back the tape, ripping out a few chest hairs.

Che cazzo? *What the fuck?* Those are some fucked up stitches. Holy fuck. What kind of nurse is she, doing stitches like this? And suturing a gunshot wound all the way tightly closed—is she trying to kill me with an infection? I bet half her patients are dead by now.

I can't leave my wounds like this.

I look around the bathroom until I find her suture kit in the little cabinet. Lucky for me, I got shot in my right shoulder, not my left one.

I snip and then remove her shitty stitches that completely closed the wound site. Fucking mess. At least the tissue around the wound looks good. Pretty clean shot, actually. Almost no surface damage. I think I'm fucked on my back though. No way I can reach those stitches.

It takes me longer than it should, but after twenty minutes, I've got a few new—absolutely perfect—stitches that don't actually close the wound completely *since it's a gunshot wound.*

Why didn't she know this?

I don't restitch my side. Standing for this long is making me lightheaded, and the wound on my side's a laceration from getting grazed, not a puncture from actual bullet penetration, so her spiderweb of stitches should be fine. The scar will be worse than it needs to be, but I don't give a fuck about that. The Cat girls dig scars.

I apply fresh gauze on both sites and then pack all her supplies back where they were. I wrap the old sutures and used gauze in a paper towel and head into her kitchen to bury them deep in the garbage.

Being in her tiny kitchen reminds me that I'm fucking starving.

Feels like I haven't eaten in a week. I open her cabinets, looking for something she won't miss, but also something low-carb. That doesn't leave me many options though.

My hazy memory of this girl is that she had a tight, fit body. But looking through her pantry, it's pretty clear she doesn't watch what she eats. It's all processed white flour and sugar. Who needs multiple boxes of Pop-Tarts?

At least I find a jar of peanut butter, a half-stale box of Triscuits, and a refrigerator drawer full of apples. Those will have to do.

Actually, this is one of the best meals I've ever had. Nutty and salty and creamy and sweet. I didn't mean to finish off the peanut butter and crackers, but fuck it. She probably won't notice. I stuff the empty jar and box in the far back of her pantry, hiding them behind other crap.

The food and two glasses of water make me feel normal again. That and having squeaky-clean balls.

I rifle through the pile of mail on her counter next to a half-dead pothos plant. Poor little guy.

The mail is addressed to 'Paige McAfee.' Paige. Is that like 'page'? But what the fuck does the 'i' do? Or is it like 'beige' with a P?

Her address is in the heart of Bagliateri Famiglia territory. *Shit*. I hoped I was in a Galliano neighborhood, or at least a Calscione Famiglia one. But Bridgeport is deep in the worst possible place for me to find myself. Or for someone else to find me.

A bill. Another bill. Request for donation. Another bill. *People* magazine. Pay stub. From the Law Offices of Ferrera & Westgate LLP. Not from a hospital? Or at least at a doctor's office. She was definitely wearing scrubs. *Like a nurse.* And she sewed me the fuck up. *Like a nurse.*

What the hell was a secretary doing stitching me up? At least that explains the shitty stitches.

But fuck it. I didn't bleed to death, she didn't call the cops, and I fixed the stitches. I don't give a shit what she does for a living.

I have no clue when she's getting home, so I need to get back on the couch before she does.

Oh, and where the fuck is my gun?

I RUN UP THE five flights of stairs to my apartment. The building is only a few years old, but for some reason they installed the world's slowest elevators. They're fine when I'm carrying up something heavy, or something squirmy, and the slow rides are actually great for chatting with neighbors.

But most of the time, I don't have the patience for them and take the stairs. Like today. By 3:00 p.m., I could barely sit still at the conference table all us paralegals were working at to review the zillion documents for a bankruptcy I do not care one bit about. Jared kept joking that I was looking at the time so often, I must have a hot date tonight. But at least that was better than his usual comments about us sneaking off to the file room, which will never happen.

Jared was right that I was anxious to leave, but I was also checking the time a lot because I really love looking at the Bvlgari watch I'm borrowing from my couch guy. The face, the numbers, the metal band are all an ultra-luxe matte black. It's sophisticated and stylish, even though it's huge on my wrist. It's heavy, reminding me all day about him. Not that I would forget. And it makes me feel connected to my guy while I'm at work.

Today would've been the perfect time to use a personal day, but I used all my accrued personal days last month when I was rehabbing the cutest baby squirrels that needed to be fed every two hours. I'm on thin ice with my supervisor already, so I couldn't risk calling out sick.

And it definitely didn't help that Gina kept texting all day, alternating between asking what I was going to do if I got home and found my 'big rescue' dead—punctuated by strings of gravestone emojis—and then asking me what I was going to do if I got home and found him awake—punctuated by strings of eggplant and tongue emojis.

But I'm not at all worried that he died. I know I kicked ass on his stitches. That's not why I needed to rush home. It's all the other possibilities that keep swirling through my brain.

Did he wake up and leave, or at least try to? Is he mad that I didn't take him to the hospital? Like, did he really mean for me to help him myself, or was he in some delusional state, some temporary insanity from a loss of blood, and now he'll be pissed?

Will he be mad that I listened to Gina and tied him up? Or that I'm borrowing his watch? Or that I hid his gun? If the guys who were after him are able to track him down, he won't be able to defend himself.

Or is he waiting for me to get home to thank me for saving him?

My brain's been spiraling from good outcome to bad, from amazing to horrible, so I really need to get home to rip off this Band-Aid of uncertainty.

I'm panting from running up the stairs at top speed. I rush down the hall, remembering at the last second to avoid the weird hallway carpet bubble I might have caused last night when the luggage cart got caught coming around the corner.

My hand is shaking so much I can barely get the key to turn the deadbolt. I throw the door open and practically fall into the room and—

The glass of water I left him is still full.

The apple slices, now brown and dull, are untouched.

One of his long, tan, muscular legs slipped out from under the blanket, his foot now on the floor, but otherwise, he's exactly where I left him. Calm, relaxed, asleep.

Or passed out or whatever.

My shoulders relax, and I let out a long exhale. I *knew* he'd be fine. "Hi, honeys, I'm home," I whisper to my rescue critters, and now that includes him.

I drop my bag on the floor, toss my keys onto the little table by the door. I tiptoe over and place two fingers on his warm neck to check he still has a pulse, just to be sure.

I text Gina "Not dead" with a stethoscope emoji. She texts back offering to come over, but I tell her not to bother. I'm going to do my rounds then crash, maybe stream some trashy TV. After all the drama of last night and being stressed at work all day, I just want to veg out and watch other people's crazy, fancy lives.

I grab the browned apple slices off the plate and drop three of them into Tango's terrarium, then push the rest through the metal grates of Romeo's cage. "Give me a few minutes to change, guys." I practically skip to my bedroom, which is only three steps from the living room.

I wish I had another pair of scrubs to change into for my evening rounds, but since I don't, I opt for royal blue dolphin shorts with white piping and a heather gray tank. Sadly, I threw my green scrubs out this morning. I tried soaking them in the bathroom sink overnight to get the blood out, but it clearly wasn't happening. I ended up shoving them into the bag full of my guy's bloody clothes and tossed the bag into a trash can on the way to work.

Grabbing my rescue notebook off the table, I head toward my guy. This is where I write all my treatment notes and health stats for each of my patients. Thoughts about what worked and what didn't and what I should try next time around.

I turn to a new page for my guy. Hmmm. What do I call him? I didn't get his name, and he didn't have a wallet or anything on him.

It would be weird to call him 'Hotel' even though that's the military alphabet word for the letter 'H,' which is my usual naming convention. Vice Admiral Commander Dad would be so proud.

I could go with 'Mike' for 'man' or 'Golf' for 'guy,' but he doesn't look like a Mike and Golf is as dumb as Hotel. 'Alpha' is too on the nose, given he's tall, dark, and hot as fuuuugh.

Ooh. There we go. F. I label the top of the page 'Foxtrot.' Because, just looking at him, he seems like he'd be amazing at... dancing.

Perfect.

I take his pulse with my thumb on his wrist. Fifty-five, healthy boy. His watch has a separate seconds dial on the face, which is handy for timing sixty seconds. So much easier to take his pulse than Romeo's. That little rabbit comes in at over 150 beats per minute and wriggles around the whole time, so I have to keep restarting, and 150 is hard to count that fast.

And I'm not even sure I'm actually measuring Tango's pulse. If I try to feel him too much, he pulls his little legs and head in so that all I'm left with is his hard shell. Sometimes I think I'm feeling a slight throbbing on his belly, but I have no clue, so I usually just put a check mark next to pulse for him since I know it's in there beating somewhere.

Staring down at my guy, still holding his wrist, I hadn't realized how much blood and dirt was still all over him. Last night, my focus was just on stabilizing him and treating his wounds. That included cleaning around the wound sites, but Gina and I didn't bother with anywhere else.

I guess tonight I should take care of the rest of him.

Damiano

"ALL RIGHT, MY GUY," Paige's lyrical voice gets louder as she reenters the room. "Your turn."

She got home about thirty minutes ago and took my vitals, or her version of them at least. After that, she fed the entire petting zoo she keeps, cleaned their cages, then disappeared into her kitchen.

All while wearing the tiniest, snuggest shorts known to man that don't even come close to covering the longest, sexiest, legs I've seen outside of the Cat and cradling the most perfect peach of an ass.

Now she's heading my way again, so I'm back to eyes closed, which is a shame because I'm dying to check out the front view of my angel. My ears were still ringing last night, and my vision was a little blurry in her car from sweat and blood and dirt in my eyes. No way she's as hot as the glimpses I thought I caught.

"You, my dirty boy, need a bath."

I do. But *really*? Is she planning to drag me into the bathroom herself? Whip out the luggage cart of bumpy death rides again?

She doesn't even have a tub. Just the standup shower I was jonesing to step into. I don't think we'd fit in together, but we can try. I'm down for that, especially if she tries to fireman carry me in there. It'll hurt my shoulder like a bitch, but getting pressed up against her tight body seems worth it.

With barely open eyes, I catch her face in the light. *Fuck me*, I wasn't imaging it or conjuring her up in my passed-out, drugged-up mind. Shimmering eyes, thin nose, high cheekbones, and lips lips lips lips lips.

I almost always go for brunettes, the darker the better to get my Italian blood pumping. But blondie here, with those legs and that ass and those sex doll lips, could become a man's obsession. Easy.

"Shit. Fuck. I'm spilling." There's a clatter of dishes being placed on the coffee table, disappearing footsteps. "Dammit."

I peek, barely opening one eye. Two bowls of water, a fat sponge on a tray, and a folded towel. This should be interesting.

I'll be thrilled if this works. The caked-on blood and dirt are itchy as fuck, which sucks when I'm trying to play half-dead. If she does even a halfway decent job, then I can take a real shower next time she leaves the apartment.

She lifts my left hand up, lays it across my stomach, sighing. She sits on the edge of the couch, pressing against my hip. *Coconut.* She smells like sunscreen and vacations and no worries.

"Okay, YouTube gods. Do your thing."

A televised voice starts explaining how to give a sponge bath. It sounds like a nursing tutorial, very clinical. The voice is droning on and on, explaining what supplies one should gather. A sponge, a basin of water, an empty basin. Please tell me this isn't how she learned to suture, though that would explain a lot.

"Oh, come on. It can't be this complicated. Enough from you." The video stops. "We'll just try it my way and see how it goes."

I feel the wet of the sponge against my forehead a split second before I feel its warmth. A trickle runs down the side of my face, wetting my neck. She applies the slightest pressure, swiping across my forehead. Re-dipping the sponge, running it across my right cheek. Then left. Down to my neck.

She scrubs back and forth a bit in a few places. Even then, she's gentle. Timid. My angel is bold enough to give me a bath but skittish as she touches me.

And I like it. I might even love this. I never let the Cat girls hang all over me or touch me when we're not fucking around. They're constantly sitting on Rob's or Salvo's laps, giving them massages, cuddling. But they respect that I don't want that.

Right now though? With Paige's hands on me, I'm struggling to remember why.

She gently turns my head to the side to sponge my neck, dragging the sponge up to behind my ear. Her body heat warms my lips as she leans over me. Soft puffs of her sweet breath are cool against my wet skin as she exhales.

My brain starts sending dangerous signals south. My nipples tighten, my balls pull up.

I open my eyes and sneak a peek to watch her. *Her tits are right here.* Perfect tits barely contained in a tiny tank top. No bra. Big gumdrop nipples in full glory. It's not cold in here, not at all, so can't blame the temperature for the tents she's pitching.

She tips my head down, so I shut my eyes again, sorry to lose the view.

I could stick my tongue out and taste her. I'm half-hard and growing. Fuck.

With her touching me like this, I'm not sure I can do anything to stop my dick from growing. Not without 'waking up' to ask her to stop the bath, something I have less than zero interest in doing.

My eyes are closed, but the image of her nips poking through her tank top and her luscious ass in those tiny shorts is burned into my retinas. And she's still touching me, stroking the sponge across my neck now.

I'm losing control. The skin on my cock tightens, my balls draw up closer. With every sweep of her sponge, my cock gets longer, thicker.

He's alive and strong and powerful. Wants to rear up and buck like the stallion he is. But I*'m* supposed to be immobilized. Incapacitated. My dick and brain are in a tug-of-war, fighting to go in opposite directions of pulling this girl fully onto my lap and staying perfectly still.

Her hand cups the back of my neck as she holds my head in place, her warm thigh pressing against my side as she leans in. The soft cotton of her tiny shorts brushes against the fingers on my left hand. They're itching to trace the white hot line along the edge of her shorts, trace it down the sides, run along the back, teasing a trail below each round cheek. Barely grazing against her skin, back and forth.

Lying here with my eyes closed, her touching me on purpose in some places and touching me where she might not even realize it in other places, is throwing my brain into overdrive, making my cock swell more.

I need to get him under control.

Think disgusting thoughts. The time Rob accidentally stepped on that guy's eyeball after I popped it out of the socket. The way it smeared deep into the tread of his shoe. Rob was right that I shouldn't have left an eye on the floor, but he should know better than to step without looking in my workshop. Even I felt bad for the guy who watched it happen with his good eye.

Yeah, that's doing the trick. My dick's settling back down to half-mast.

Paige slowly pulls the sheet back, exposing my chest and abs. "You're a work of art, you know that, right?" She pauses as if I'm going to answer her. "Seriously. Why would anyone want to shoot at this?" She lays a warm hand on my abs and sighs. "I can't believe I'm totally perving out to a half-dead guy." She rubs the sponge in a circle around my hard and tight nip.

It's *fucking good.* So fucking good that I have to wipe the smile off my face, hoping she hasn't noticed it.

But seems her attention is focused on my chest. Another circle around my nip.

Rotting garbage. Gli Azzurri losing in the finals. Scraping that eyeball gel off the floor of my workroom after it dried. Thank fucking god for floor drains. And not just floor drains. Floor drains with built-in industrial garbage disposals. Fucking brilliant addition to my workshop.

She's moving down to wash the happy trail below my belly button. That's my weak spot. *Right there.* Right fucking *there*, Paige. You keep touching me there, angel, and no telling what happens next.

Actually, what would happen next is crystal fucking clear. I'd cup the back of your neck, guide those lips down to my chest, for starters. Let you lick that nipple you just made squeaky clean. Guide your hand down to my throbbing cock. Over my boxers at first so you can tease me a while longer. Then you can free him and grab him tight down at the base while you nuzzle your cheek against him.

Fingernails trace a line up and down *right there.* I'm going to lose my shit if she keeps going.

Slow strokes up and down my happy trail. Captivatingly close. But still way too fucking far from where I need her.

Up and down, *right fucking there.* Setting me on fire from the inside out.

The need to slide my hand into her hair, to grab hold of the back of her head. Steer her exactly where I need her. Control her. Pull her on top of me. I don't even care where she lands. On my lap, on my cock, pull her up to sit on my face. Doesn't fucking matter. My fingers ache with need to feel her, to meld into her. It's fucking torture keeping my hands still.

The only sounds in the room are her soft breaths, the dripping of water when she squeezes the sponge, and the rabbit in the corner tugging on his water bottle, clanging it against the wire cage. If he's planning to clang that all night, I'll have to do something about him.

"This is getting gross."

I open my eyes to see Paige carrying the bowl of water away. Jesus Christ, those tiny blue shorts. Teeny-tiny, hugging that ass, framing each plump cheek.

I take a second to adjust my dick and give him a hard 'down, boy' squeeze while she's out of the room, but quickly get back to how she left me. Except I leave my left hand where she was sitting, hoping that she sits right on it when she comes back. Maybe a finger accidentally slips inside her shorts.

No way we're making it through this sponge bath without her noticing my steel rod. He's still covered by the blanket, but at the rate she's going, he won't be for long.

She comes back in, holding a bowl with both hands. I want to watch her, watch what she does, look at her face. Her tits. Those thighs. I want to stare at them. But I dutifully close my eyes so she doesn't catch me.

"Let me know if the water's too hot." She giggles like she thinks it's hilarious that she's talking to an unconscious guy.

Seems she switched to a washcloth now instead of the sponge. It's even better because I can feel her fingers through it as she rubs my abs, moves lower. Every so often, she must be re-dipping it, because it's a fresh burst of hot, wet heaven.

"Dammit, everything's getting soaked." She presses a dry towel along my side, her hand against my hip.

"You owe me a new couch, by the way. And not another one from Goodwill. Pottery Barn, at least."

I'll buy you a new couch. For hiding me, I'll buy you a new apartment, angel. But not in a shitty Bagliateri Famiglia neighborhood like this one.

"So... what do I do... down *here*?" She tugs the blanket down toward my feet. "Oh... oh my."

Yeah, 'oh my.' My rock-solid dick is pressing up hard against my boxers, dying to get out.

"Well, that part of you definitely still works. Do I..."

Yes.

Whatever you're thinking, yes.

Please, yes.

Something.

Anything.

Everything you're thinking about doing, yes.

Please.

"I mean, you need to be clean *everywhere*, right?"

Right. Yes. Absolutely. Make me clean.

Please, angel.

"Maybe I should... take a peek? Medically speaking, I mean." She's silent and not touching me for a long minute. "How about this, if you don't want me to peek, say 'stop' and I won't look." She waits a full ten seconds that feels like ten minutes. "Last chance."

Her warm finger tucks under the waistband of my boxers, lifting an inch, letting a cool burst of air in.

She gasps. A pleased gasp.

Oh, angel.

"Maybe warn a girl first, huh, big guy?"

She likes my dick. She thinks it's the best dick ever. She probably wants to lick it.

I'm going to lose it. I'm going to fucking lose it.

The need to push my hips up toward her, to thrust in her direction to get her and my needy cock closer together is killing me. Thrust him up or pull her down. Either. Both.

"I mean, I should wash *him* too, right? It's medical. If there's blood or dirt on him, I should definitely wash it off." She tugs my boxers the rest of the way down, shimmying them from under me. As subtly as possible, I lift my hips so she can pull them down.

I can't help but watch her. She's entirely focused on my rod standing straight up at attention. She's so focused on him that she doesn't seem to notice me watching her.

She shifts so she's kneeling on the floor. Kneeling right next to my junk. Perfect profile view of her little torture shorts, her flimsy tank top, her tiny waist. Exactly the hot, tight body I thought I saw in the park. All of that, right within reach.

"My god, you have a nice dick. I mean... It's... I..."

Say it looks delicious. Say you've never seen such a perfect dick. Say you need it in your mouth.

"And uncut? Jesus take the wheel." She sits back on her heels for a second, lets out a long breath, then leans forward again. "Just because I can't see any dirt or mess down here doesn't mean there isn't any, right?"

She turns toward my face, and I slam my eyes closed, hoping she didn't catch me watching her.

Then, there it is.

The rough texture of her washcloth.

The heat from the water.

Wet fingers grab hold through the cotton.

One long, slow, warm stroke from base to tip. A slight swirl at the top.

Fuuuuuck me.

I groan.

Not just a little groan, but a full-on unstoppable moan.

Paige shrieks and launches herself backward, her bowl clattering to the floor. "Oh my god, I'm so sorry. Are you awake?"

Cazzo. *Fuck.*

I keep playing dead. No way she's going to buy it, but I'm going to try. My dick is starting to play dead, too, scared soft by her scream.

"Hello?" She pokes the left side of my chest. "Are you in there? Can you hear me?" She pauses, waiting for me to answer. "Was that just, like, a reflex? Or are you waking up? Hola?"

After a minute, during which I'm pretty sure she's hovering over my face, staring at me, she continues the bath, rubbing down my thighs, my shins. She gives me an exceptionally pleasant foot rub.

But no happy ending.

Then she cleans up, disappears into her room. Now I hear the shower on.

And she's in there. Alone. Naked. Probably still thinking about how perfect my dick is.

"Pronto." Salvo answers his phone on the first ring.

"Sono io." It's *me*, I whisper into Paige's iPad. It's awkward as fuck to hold this with one hand, but I can't risk using the speakerphone option. Even though Paige went to bed an hour ago, there's only a thin door between us, so I need to be quiet.

"About fucking time. Hold on." There's rustling in the background, a door clicking shut. The roaring background noise disappears. "Where the fuck are you, man?"

"Bridgeport."

He blows out a puff of air. "*That's* complicated. You got an address for me? I can be there in twenty-five, thirty minutes. I'll get in without drawing attention." Salvo knows it's risky to come into Bagliateri territory without permission from Joey Bags. We don't let them in our neighborhoods, and they don't let us in theirs.

"No, man. Not yet." I trust Salvo with everything, but I don't know why the fuck Paulie shot me. I don't know if he was acting alone or on orders from someone. "I'm better off laying low a while longer."

"Yeah? You alright? The amount of blood at the park, I was expecting to find your corpse, not your phone."

Salvo and I have a system for when I need to lay low, which happens every so often, being the enforcer for one of the most powerful Famiglie in the country.

When I don't show up somewhere I'm supposed to be—like the Cat last night—he tracks my phone and heads there. If he finds the phone stashed *on top* of my wallet, it means 'meet me at the safe house at noon the next day.' Wallet on top means 'wait for me to call you.' Phone tucked inside the wallet means 'I'm not going to make it, avenge the fuck out of me.'

He knew to wait for my call.

Salvo gives me shit that if I have the wherewithal to stash my wallet and phone in a safe place, then I could just text him instead. But then he'd know I'm in a fucked-up situation hours sooner. No question that he'd drop whatever he's doing and hightail it to me right away, probably bringing Rob along too. I respect the intention, but if I'm already deep in shit, the last thing I need is to have to protect them while they're trying to rescue me. So I don't send a text, I throw up smoke signals with my wallet/phone stack.

"I'll live. Took one in the shoulder, it went straight through. Another grazed my side. I've had worse."

"You know Paulie's dead?"

I pause to make sure there's no sound coming from Paige's room. Just the noisy as fuck rabbit still clanging away with his water bottle. "That's what happens when I shoot someone in the throat."

He huffs. "Fuck you, Dom. You just cost me a fucking grand."

"How's that?"

"Rob took one look at Paulie and said that had you written all over it. I said no fucking way. *No fucking way you shot one of our own.* But Rob called it. What the fuck, man?"

"He shot me first. In my fucking back, that piece of shit."

"Cazzo."

"He was aiming for my head, but he fucking sucks, so he ended up hitting my shoulder. Alla cazzo di cane." *Really shitty attempt.*

"Why the fuck would he shoot you?"

"No clue. He was acting super fucking cagey when I picked him up, sweating bullets, wouldn't look me in the eye. Tried to get me to stop somewhere to talk before we met up with Joey's guy. Whined like a little bitch when I wouldn't pull over."

Something about Paulie set off all sorts of alarms for me.

"When he missed his kill shot, I popped one off straight in his throat before Joey's guy lit it up. I got a couple shots off after that. I clipped Joey's guy in the leg."

"Aww, you miss your gut shot?"

Salvo knows I love a good gut shot. Some people prefer a headshot square in the T-box to ensure flaccid paralysis. That's precisely what I was trained to do in the Gruppo Operativo Incursori. You hit a specific section of a person's face—the T-box—and they drop without even flinching first.

There's a time and a place for a T-box shot, like when my GOI team was activated to deal with hostages being held at gunpoint and I needed to neutralize the gunman without so much as a twitch of his trigger finger.

But when I can play, I go for the gut. Not because it's a bigger, easier target, even though it is. But because of the look on the prick's face, watching that red circle grow on their abdomen, knowing they can't do shit about it. Intense pain with a high likelihood of death, but not necessarily a quick one. You miss out on that with a kill shot to the T-box.

So, yeah, I prefer a gut shot when the guy deserves to suffer. But Joey's guy probably didn't.

"I don't think Joey's guy was in on Paulie's move. Maybe he was. And if that's the case, his days are numbered. But Paulie didn't set up that meet. He didn't know anything about that meeting until the drive over. There's a good chance Joey's guy heard Paulie's shot and reacted. I can't fault him for that."

"Shit."

"Yeah. So..." I hate asking this. *I fucking hate asking it.* "You have any idea why Rob wanted me to meet with Paulie last night?"

"What are you asking, man?"

"Just asking what I'm asking. Rob's never asked me to take a ride-along before. Wondering why he suddenly wanted me to take Paulie on one."

Salvo's voice is slightly muffled. "Why did you tell Damiano to talk to Paulie last night?"

"That Dom on the phone? Tell him if he's not dead to get his ass back here already."

"What was the deal with Paulie?" Salvo asks him again.

"There was no deal. Paulie was nagging the fuck out of me to be put on Dom's crew. It was annoying as shit. Easiest way to get him off my dick was to make Damiano deal with him."

"That's it?"

"That's it. Why? Dom asking you about this?"

"Don't worry about it." His voice returns to full volume. "Did you hear all that? You satisfied?"

"Yup." For now. "People think I'm dead?"

"Naah. They did for a minute, but the Cat girls were freaking out and weren't going to be able to perform. I almost had to close for the night."

"Aww, they care."

"I finally said fuck it and told the girls you were fine."

"If the girls know I'm alive, everyone knows by now." The girls are great at many, many things. But keeping their mouths shut isn't one of them.

He lets out a long breath. "Paulie, huh? I didn't see that coming. I figured shit went sideways with Joey's guy. Why the fuck would Paulie turn?"

"No clue. And I have no fucking clue if he was on his own or if he was working with someone. And I don't know if he turned on *me* or on the whole Famiglia."

More fucking clanging as the rabbit grabs the end of his water bottle, pulls, then releases it. Again and again. No way I can sleep with this racket. I walk over to its cage.

"It's always fucking something, isn't it? How are you still breathing without a hospital? There was a shit ton of blood everywhere."

I reach in and pick up the rabbit. He struggles and kicks at first but calms down when I pet low behind his ears. The same way Batuffolo liked to be scratched when I was a kid.

"Most of that was Paulie's. He burst open like a fucking water balloon. I didn't bleed much. He used a shitty little .22, that stupid fuck. Joey's guy had a 9mm. But I pulled Paulie on top of me when Joey's guy started shooting. He bled all the fuck over me."

"Sounds like he was more useful dead than alive." Salvo pauses for a minute, then gets all serious. "So where are you, man? And don't tell me Bridgeport again without giving me an address. Who do you even know in Bridgeport?"

I'll give him some details, but not enough for him to come get me. "This girl in the park found me. She brought me home and patched me up. I'm at her place."

He laughs out loud. "Only fucking you would pick up some girl while you're bleeding out."

"Come on, if it was you getting shot at, two of the Cat girls would have thrown themselves in front of the bullets to keep you from getting hit."

"They do take good care of me."

I can hear the smile in his voice.

"Or more like, they would have thrown each other in front of the bullets."

"What can I say? I have a magic cock."

"Anyway, I thought this girl was a nurse, but now I think she's like, a secretary or something."

"A secretary patched you up?"

"Seems like it."

"The fucking balls on her. What was she going to do if you died on her kitchen table?"

I wasn't worried about that. I'd already stopped the bleeding. I would have gone to the hospital if this were life-threatening. I don't have a death wish. "I haven't figured her out yet."

"She hot?"

"She is."

"You hit that yet?"

"Naah. I'm stuck here for a few days, I think."

"Perfect excuse to forget all about your no-sleepover rule."

"No can do, man. This girl, though... She's temptation personified. Fucking stunning. But rules are rules for a reason."

"Rules about not fucking hot girls are stupid rules. And wait a minute. Are you telling me you finally found a girl that could gaze into your baby greens and not drop to her knees at 'ciao, bella'?"

"There has been no eye-gazing."

"What? How's that possible? The Look—that's your move. Your eyes fucked up or something?"

In the background I hear, "His eyes better not be fucked up, Salvo. Tell him his eyes better not be fucked and to get his ass back here already."

"My eyes are fine. I only got to look at her for a minute when she first found me at the park. I've either been actually passed out or pretending I'm passed out since she found me. When she's in the room, I keep my eyes closed. She thinks I'm in a coma or some shit."

"Come on. How long is she going to buy that?"

"No clue. But she seems to dig taking care of me." And I'm into it too. "I'm going to ride it out as long as I can. I don't want her asking me any questions. I don't think she's connected, but I'm about as deep in Bagliateri territory as it gets. Don't know if she knows people or if she gets scared, kicks me out onto the street. Pretty sure she's past calling the police, but I can't be positive."

"And she's buying your sleepy-time act?"

"Seems so. I'm telling you, man, I can't figure this girl out."

"How so?"

"First off, she's in the woods all alone at night. Then, she's got all these fucked up animals in her apartment, a rabbit missing its lucky foot, a deformed turtle. And tons of medical supplies, but she works in an office. She wasn't freaked out by all the blood and she brought me back to her place like she was on a mission. Crazy as this sounds, I think she might be, like, my guardian angel or something?"

"I don't know, man. Sounds like she might be the exact opposite of that. She sounds like she's a fucking witch."

"What? No."

"Hear me out. The chick is alone in the woods, probably dancing in circles and chanting some voodoo shit. She sacrificed that poor rabbit's foot. She's probably going to cut off your dick and grind it up into some witchy dick powder. I have no fucking clue."

"Stop. She's not a witch."

"I'm picking you up, man. No fucking way I'm leaving you there. Give me the address or I'll trace this phone number."

"Relax with that superstitious bullshit."

"How do you know she's not a witch?"

"Because she's not a fucking witch."

"Uh-huh."

"I need to get some sleep." I grab a carrot from Paige's fridge and hold it for the rabbit.

"Seriously man, grattarsi le palle." *Scratch your balls (for good luck).* "You're going to need it."

"I'll call you tomorrow, asshole."

I delete the call from the call log, then put Paige's iPad back where it was. Since I saw her enter her passcode when she was loading the sponge bath video, I'll be able to use that whenever she's not around.

I lie back down on the couch with the rabbit almost asleep on my chest. Paige didn't retie my wrist after the sponge bath. Not sure if she forgot, or if she changed her mind about needing it. Either way, I'm definitely not redoing it on my own.

I close my eyes. Salvo is crazy with all that Old World superstitious bullshit. Paige is totally normal. There's an explanation for all that other shit.

I'm sure of it.

I quickly rub the cornicello hanging on a chain around my neck just in case.

Damiano

PAIGE LEFT FOR WORK around 8:30 this morning. I waited an hour to see if she'd come back. When she didn't, I hit the shower. The sponge bath she gave me was heaven, and I want her to do again. And again. But she actually did a pretty shitty job of getting me clean.

That may have been the best shower of my life, not including showers I've taken with any of the Cat girls. No question, those were better. But this one was great in its own way, washing off the caked-on blood, then jerking off to Paige in those tiny shorts with her big nipples peeking through her tank top, using her coconut-scented conditioner as lube.

I'd love to shave too, but she would definitely notice that. I keep a neat five o'clock shadow trim, which is a bitch to maintain, but the Cat girls love it. But now, after an extra thirty-six hours, it's getting unruly.

There's pounding on the apartment door. Who the hell is that?

I wrap a towel around my waist and grab my Glock from where I slid it under the couch. I've got ten rounds left.

I don't want to shoot someone in Paige's apartment. It'll be loud. It'll be messy. It'll be really fucking hard to dispose of a body while I'm hiding out, and there's a high likelihood a neighbor will call the cops.

More banging.

No way it's any of Joey's guys coming for me. If they knew I was hiding out in their territory, they wouldn't knock.

Her door doesn't have a peephole, so I can't see who it is. "Yeah?" I use my nice voice, not looking to start any beef, though the banging didn't exactly come across as a neighbor looking to borrow a cup of sugar.

"Let me the fuck in, asshole."

Of fucking course.

I open the door.

Salvo strolls in, looks me up and down. "Maybe I should come back when you're decent?"

"When am I ever decent?"

We one-arm hug. It's good to see him.

"I was expecting you to look like shit, man. Not like a Calvin Klein ad." Salvo motions to the towel around my waist as he steps around me and into the apartment.

"Told you my shoulder wasn't that bad. I'd be back on the job already if I knew why that fucker shot me."

Salvo sits at the little dining table, dropping a duffel bag with a thud. "Rob's pissed as fuck that you think he had something to do with this."

"I don't think that." I did. For a hot minute. But lying on the couch with nothing to think about all night except the million different scenarios of what the fuck is going on, not a single one involving him made any sense. He had all the opportunity in the world, but no motive.

No motive unless you count the fact that I text his nineteen-year-old sister sometimes, which in his mind would absolutely justify taking me out, but he would come straight at me over that. He wouldn't send an unreliable shot like Paulie and if he wanted to get rid of me for any other reason, he'd just tell me to fuck off and put me on a plane back to Rome.

"It was weird fucking timing, so I had to ask. But I don't think that at all."

"You need to tell him that."

I shrug. "Tell him that if I thought he was trying to kill me, I would have killed him first, and since I didn't, he should know that I know he wasn't involved."

"I'm not telling him that."

"Fine. Tell him I know that if he wanted me dead, he'd just punch straight through my skull." We start most days off in the boxing ring Rob installed when he converted an entire floor of an old factory into his loft.

"You're missing the whole fucking point. He treats you like a brother, and not in the Famiglia 'we're all brothers' loyalty oath way. You're in his inner fucking circle, man, and it's a tiny fucking circle. You, me, his dad—that's it. He'd do any fucking thing for you. So you even *thinking* he'd get Paulie to take you out—thinking that even for a second?" Salvo shakes his head at me. "You broke his fucking heart, man."

"You said he was pissed, not that he was hurt."

"He's pissed you hurt his feelings."

I let out a long breath, rub the back of my neck. I'm completely in the wrong on this one. Rob has treated me like a brother from the moment we met. Him and Salvo are the reason I moved here from Rome. They even asked me to move into the loft with them, but I need far more alone time than that would've allowed.

So I fucked up on this one.

"I get it. I'll talk to him. You got clothes in there for me?" I motion toward the bag Salvo brought in. "Let me get dressed so we can go to the Cat. I'll go straight to him and deal with this."

"Naah, bro. You're stuck here for a while."

"He's that pissed that I can't come home?"

"No, *you asshole*. He's that worried someone inside might actually have been working with Paulie. He wants you to keep laying low, assuming you're safe here. He wants to see if anyone starts pestering us to find out where you are or slips up and mentions that Paulie shot you. The story everyone's heard is that Joey's guy opened fire on both of you. None of our men should know any different. So he wants to see if anyone slips up."

I nod. It's solid thinking.

"Plus, that keeps you away from the Cat girls until he says you can come back, which I'm pretty sure is his way of saying 'fuck you, Dom.'"

I smile. That probably is the best way to punish me.

"Here." He kicks the duffel bag over to me. "Clothes, burner phone, your protein shake shit—the Damiano Zucco essentials kit."

Salvo knows me well.

"And Bianca's in there. I can't believe you ditched her."

"The only lady allowed in my bed overnight." I rummage through the bag until I find her. She's irreplaceable. "I had no idea where I was going to end up, or if Joey's guy was coming back with reinforcements. I knew she'd be safe with you."

Bianca is my Extrema Ratio S.E.R.E. 1 dagger. Specially-issued by the GOI. Only *actual* elite special forces can get the S.E.R.E. 1. There's a modified civilian version, the S.E.R.E. 2, anyone can buy if they have an extra $700 laying around to spend on a knife with a shit ton of built-in safeties.

"I have no clue if you're joking about bringing your knife into bed with you."

I wink at him. Let him wonder.

But I'm not joking. Bianca sleeps under my pillow, my hand wrapped around her smooth grip.

I pull a canister of protein shake, a shaker thermos, and a box of almond milk out of the duffel. "You want one?"

Salvo shakes his head. He's in great shape, but he's not intense about maintaining a tight protein-to-carb ratio like Rob and I are.

"How'd my place look?"

"Fine. No one had been there. Alarm was still on. Nothing out of place. I watered all your plants while I was there."

I stop making the shake for a minute, look him in the eye, and nod. My plants are everything to me. I even picked my apartment for its massive floor-to-ceiling windows with eastern exposure so they can thrive.

"So how'd you track me down? Renatta?"

He nods. "Simple number chase. She was annoyed as fuck that I bothered her for something so basic."

Renatta is Salvo's sister and our tech guru. The girl is terrifyingly good at finding out shit.

"She do a background check on Paige?"

"Yeah. Nothing crazy popped up. She's from San Diego but moved around a ton as a kid."

She looks like a California girl, or at least what I think a California girl looks like. Blonde, tan, bikini body, happy.

"Her dad was a Navy pilot. Now has some command post back in San Diego. Her brother's Navy, too. Stationed here at Great Lakes."

"Was the dad flying helicopters or jets?"

"No clue. Does it matter?"

I shrug my shoulders like it doesn't, but it might. Most Navy helicopter pilots fly rescue missions or supply runs. But the *jet* pilots are fighters. Deter the enemy with brutal force if necessary. Entirely different mentality. My mentality.

"She moved here four years ago. Oh, and get this—she's been trying to get a wildlife rescue permit but keeps failing the test."

Huh. "You need a permit to rescue roadkill?"

"Apparently." Salvo gets up and starts looking around Paige's apartment, checking out her knick-knacks and photos.

"You come up with anything on Paulie?"

"Nothing helpful. Sounds like he started acting squir-rely sometime last week, but not crazy enough to raise any eyebrows. His apartment looked normal, his bank account looked normal."

And the question I don't want to ask. "Any word from Joey Bags?"

Salvo nods. "He reached out last night, pissed as fuck that *you* opened fire. He's claiming it was unprovoked, and he wants you to answer for it."

"I barely clipped the guy."

Salvo shrugs. "Not according to Joey. He's claiming the one guy was DOA with a bullet in his leg and another in his back and that a second guy may never walk again. Says you hit his spine."

"*What*? No. That's total bullshit." I take a drink of my shake, wipe my lip. "There was only one Bagliateri soldier. There was Paulie—who I shot in the throat, not the back—and the guy I clipped in the leg. And my shot was clean to his outer thigh. No one's dying from that. The guy shouldn't even have a limp."

I should know, I was shot in the exact same spot on a GOI mission.

"Joey's telling a different story. And the guy he's saying has a bullet in his spine? Davide Ferrante."

Jesus.

I put down my shake. I stare at Salvo, waiting for him to tell me he's joking.

Fuuuuck.

I take a few steps, then spin around and come back. I open my mouth to say something, but I'm at a loss. *Fuck.*

Shit got fucking real.

"Massimo's brother?" I don't know Davide. I could probably pick him out of a lineup, but that's about it.

But I know Mas.

I've known Mas a long fucking time. And he happens to be the enforcer for the Bagliateri Famiglia. The same 'hurt people real bad' role that I have, but with our rival Famiglia.

"No fucking way that was my shot, Salvo. No fucking way." I'm back to pacing. "Davide wasn't even there. And I'd never shoot someone in the back. And I did not shoot Davide."

Cazzo.

Salvo shrugs, as he picks up a framed picture of Paige and another girl and smiles.

"Fucking Joey. What does Rob think?"

"It's above Rob. Joey's calling for a sit-down with Roberto."

That stops me in my tracks. I sit down at the table.

Rob runs almost all the Galliano Famiglia day-to-day operations, but his dad, Roberto, is the official head of our syndicate. "Joey and Roberto haven't had a sit-down in almost a decade." I was still in Rome back then, working for Rob's uncle Giacomo. Right after that meeting was when things started going to hell in Chicago. That's when Giacomo started having me bounce back and forth between the two cities.

"Might be another decade. Roberto told Joey 'va fa Naboli.'" *Go to hell.* "Told him that he's not sitting down with him over a couple of soldiers."

"I want to kill Paulie all over again. Shoot him in the gut this time. Watch him suffer." The kid got off too easy with a quick death.

"You and me both, especially now that Mas is fired the fuck up over his brother."

"I got to get out of here." I've got to go talk to Massimo, tell him what actually happened. I reach for the duffel for clothes, but Salvo kicks it away.

"Nope. You're staying put. Rob's orders. Rob's direct, very clear, do-not-look-for-a-loophole orders."

But I need to go deal with this. "Salv, I—"

He shakes his head. "Joey's up to something, and if he had anything to do with Paulie, it means Joey wants you dead. Word is, Massimo wants a piece of you now too. And we still don't know if anyone else on our side is involved. Rob says for you to keep laying low, so you're gonna keep laying low." He stares at me hard.

"But if Joey's trying to start a war—"

"Nope. You're staying put, man."

"Salvo."

"Doesn't fucking matter what I say. Rob said to stay put, so you're staying put."

Cooped up here while all hell is about to break loose and I can't do a fucking thing to stop it or to make sure Rob and Salvo are safe is going to be absolute torture. But Rob is my boss.

"How'd you get here?" No way Salvo drove into Baglia-teri territory in his big-ass Mercedes Sprinter van.

"Uber. Figured no one would be looking into the back-seat of a shitty old Civic."

Damiano

A towel-dried Paige comes into the room. She got home from work an hour ago, did her make-believe doctor rounds, then took a shower after the rabbit pissed all over her.

Now she's in another pair of tiny shorts. Buttercup yellow this time, with a dark-blue T-shirt that says 'Navy' in faded gold letters.

She picks up her turtle from its cage and plops herself down on the floor, leaning back against the couch I'm on. Her wet hair presses cool against my side. I glance around the room and realize the couch is the only place to sit besides the two mismatched chairs at her tiny dining table.

She lets the turtle walk under and around her legs. It takes a few steps, then stops, another few steps. "Go on, get your steps in, T."

Paige sets her iPad up against some books so it's standing up in front of her. "All right, Toms, what trouble are you up to tonight?" she asks the screen as she starts a show.

For fuck's sake. I'd give Salvo's left nut to never watch reality TV. A few of the Cat girls constantly talk about different shows they're obsessed with. It would be rude to cut them off just so they can blow me, so I smile and nod and watch how pretty they are when they're excited about something. Then I let them blow me.

Paige's phone lights up on the coffee table. From this angle, I can read it right over her shoulder.

Spencer

Hey

She glances over at me, then turns back to her phone.

Paige

Hi

Up for company?

And there's the boyfriend. Figures. No *way* this girl doesn't have guys all over her.

But, then again, the Paige giving me a sponge bath? *That* Paige didn't seem like she had a man. So maybe not a boyfriend. Plus I don't know many boyfriends that would let their girl have a complete stranger sleep on her couch.

Tonight won't work. Sry!

Come on

She taps her lip a few times before responding, hesitating. She nods to herself, then types.

How about tmrw? I could come to your place

You know my roommate is weird about company. Your place.

She huffs.

Doesn't invite her to his place? Definitely not the boyfriend. Kind of surprised, I'd think most guys would give their firstborn to call this girl theirs.

> My apartment is out

> Y?

She looks over at me again. It's dark enough in here with the lights off that I don't think she can tell I'm watching her. She stares off into space for a few seconds before she responds.

> I'm rehabbing a cute little fox and he needs it quiet

A fox, huh? I can live with that. And I can live with cute—I can be absolutely adorable at times. But 'little'? Maybe she needs to take another peek into my boxers.

> We can be quiet. You're already quiet. I can be quiet too.

> Can't we be quiet at your place?

> Babe

"Give me a break," she mutters, then puts her phone down, face down. She restarts the show on her iPad.

After a few minutes pass, she picks it up again to find his response waiting.

> Come on, I'm 2 blocks away. Invite me up. Your fox won't even know I'm there

> We could meet for dinner somewhere?

She stares at the screen, waiting for an answer. There aren't even bubbles. I don't know this guy, but I know exactly what his answer will be.

Five minutes later, her phone lights up again.

> IDK it's getting late.

"Whatever." Paige tosses the phone down and picks her turtle up, stands. "I'm telling you, Tango," she carries him back to his tank, "guys are so frickin' confusing."

What are you confused about, angel? Your boy wants to fuck you—can't say I blame him—and he's either got a live-in girlfriend or he's afraid you won't leave after he nuts, so he doesn't want you at his place. It's crystal fucking clear, angel. Open your eyes and you'll see it too.

I actually feel bad for the guy having to work so hard to get some. But I do completely agree with him on not bringing girls back to his place. I've never brought one to mine.

Paige mopes into her kitchen, then comes back with an overpoured glass of wine. She restarts her show.

As mindless as the show is, I'll admit that the girls are smoking hot and the bitchy blonde one is fucking hilarious. She's also absolutely terrifying—and I think that as someone who tortures and kills people for a living.

Fifteen minutes later, Paige gets up and pours herself a refill. She plops back onto the floor hard, hitting the couch and bouncing my hand onto her shoulder. "Oh, hello, you." Her cool fingers wrap around my hand. She turns it over, traces a circle in my palm with her thumb, barely touching. "Would *you* invite me to your place?" She lightly scrapes her nails up and down all my fingers at the same time. "Take me out to dinner? Introduce me to your friends?"

She twines her thin fingers with my thick ones and squeezes, like we're holding hands.

I should squeeze her hand back—seems like she could use that right now—but I'm not going to blow my cover.

"You'd take me out on an actual date, wouldn't you?"

I haven't been on an actual date in a decade. Back then, I was still living in Rome, right before I left for the Navy. Violetta, with the big brown eyes and the pouty bottom lip and the short skirt that fluttered in the breeze.

She offered to wait for me until my enlistment was over, wrote to me every few days. But when I was recruited into GOI, I broke it off. Being unattached was a requirement for enrollment in special forces. We had to commit to putting country first. Wives, girlfriends, the possibility of having a kid, those were all distractions and vulnerabilities.

I haven't even thought about dating since then. I bang it out most days with a Cat girl or two. But dating? Relationships?

Paige places my hand flat over her collar bone, like I'm holding her. Like she's mine to hold. She goes back to watching another episode of her show with my arm draped across her.

The show is playing, but all my attention is focused on her skin against my fingers. Smooth and soft. Her pulse racing against the tip of my finger. Her long blonde hair is in a big floppy bun on the top of her head, leaving an ear, her delicate jawline, her thin neck exposed.

Paige is the complete opposite of the Cat girls. She's easily as hot as any of them, hotter than most of them. But she's perfectly at ease with no makeup, messy hair. She spends her time trying to help broken animals. Was willing to help a complete stranger without asking anything in return.

The Cat girls aren't exactly asking for anything in exchange for fucking around, but they all know that after Salvo, I rank next highest. Rob makes his appreciation crystal fucking clear when the Cat girls keep his senior guys satisfied and completely uninterested in getting tied down. And the girls do a mighty fine job of it.

Paige shifts her position, and my hand slides down, resting on the top of her tit over her shirt.

No *bra.*

My pinky is resting on her stiff nipple. Her firm gumdrop nipple.

She isn't moving my hand away. She might even be leaning into it?

Don't squeeze.

Don't caress.

Don't pinch.

Don't do it, man. She's tipsy as fuck, but not drunk enough to believe you're squeezing her tit while passed out.

Yeah, she's *definitely* leaning into my hand, my hand that would perfectly cup this glorious tit if I flexed. Jesus fuck, what's she trying to do to me?

This is definitely all-natural. Natural and perfect. Making my cock throb.

I need some fucking relief. I very slowly move my right hand from next to me on the couch to my dick to give it a slow, firm squeeze. He's dripping, and it's just enough lube for a few much-needed strokes, except that it simultaneously causes stabs of pain in my right shoulder.

Fuck you, shoulder, you don't matter right now.

Paige reaches forward a little and picks up her iPad. I can't help but throw in a little tit squeeze as she does, hoping her movement hides mine. *So fucking firm.*

She leans back into place, my hand snugly tucked into her shirt.

This is complete torture. Her tit's in one hand, my cock's in the other, and I can't move either without her knowing I'm awake. I should add some version of this to my 'enhanced interrogation' routine to get motherfuckers to talk, 'cause honestly, I'd tell her all my secrets right now for her to rub her tits all over my cock, let me jizz all over her.

She must be done watching her show because she's typing a new website address.

Oh, for fuck's sake, angel. She's putting on porn.

She types 'stranger on my couch' into the porn site's search bar, but that results in a bunch of 'stepsister anal' hits. I mean, we can watch those. I don't watch much porn, given that the Cat girls are like live-action porn I get to touch, but some of the thumbnails on her screen look good.

Some look really fucking good. That third one—that third one down looks unbelievably good. Pick that third one. Or, maybe, bookmark it for when you're at work tomorrow and I'm here all day long with nothing to do but think about this perfect tit that's still in my hand.

Paige must not like the options though. She enters a new search. 'Sexy patient.'

I have to give my dick another squeeze. Pretty sure this girl's about to play with herself *right here* next to me, with my *hand* on her *tit*, watching porn, and not just any porn, but porn that sounds a hell of a lot like she'll be thinking about me while she does it.

Maybe my hand can slip down lower, slip into those tiny shorts. Then she can grind against it, riding it till she explodes.

'Sexy patient' loads a screen full of girls in tiny panties with male doctors about to give them a hot beef injection. Paige changes her search to 'sexy *male* patient.'

She's trying to kill me. That's it. This girl brought me here to save me, but really, she's trying to kill me.

Kill me or work her voodoo magic on me, voodoo magic that's messing with my head, making me think that maybe I can 'wake up' a little, fool around with her some, then 'pass back out' after I blow my load without her getting too suspicious.

Like sleepwalking, but fucking instead. Maybe she's tipsy enough to believe that's a thing?

I mean, I don't know for sure that it's *not* a thing, so maybe I can pull it off. And she's buying the coma act, so maybe it's worth a try.

She scrolls halfway down the page. "Bingo." She clicks on a thumbnail of a guy with dark hair lying in a hospital bed, his arm in a sling, a blonde nurse standing next to him, holding a clipboard. The girl's wearing a nurse cap and a white thong and nothing else. *For fuck's sake*, that could be us.

Paige moves my hand off of her. Places it back onto the couch.

No.

She stands up with a drunken wobble.

No.

She picks up her glass of wine.

Don't go, angel.

"Nighty-night, my loves." She blows kisses to the animal cages, then drops a warm, lingering kiss on my cheek.

Her magnificent ass and those phenomenal tiny shorts disappear into her room. With wine and porn.

And the drawer full of vibrators I found when I was looking for my gun.

Fuu-uu-uuuck.

Paige

I SPLURGED AND BOUGHT two brand-new sets of scrubs during my lunch break today. One set is baby blue, and the other is a pale purple that will look amazing against my light hair.

Then, on my walk home from work, I noticed this sad little mostly dead fern that someone put out with their trash two buildings down from mine. A spot on my counter is about to open up since the poor little pothos I tried to rescue is beyond all hope, so I have just the spot for this fellow.

I walk up the five floors to my apartment with a little extra pep in my step.

"Hi, honeys, I'm home." I don't bother to whisper, since my guy seems to sleep through however much noise I make. I go change into my new scrubs, the blue ones, and leave my hair down because I happen to be having a fantastic hair day.

I grab the clipboard I snagged from my office's supply room this afternoon and start my usual rounds. Romeo first because he tugs on his water bottle nonstop, banging it against the wire cage until he gets a snack. Then Tango. Both are doing great.

Even the plants in my apartment—also all rescues—are looking good. Actually, a few of them look perkier than usual. Go me!

I go to the kitchen sink to wash my hands since I was touching the turtle. Huh? The little pothos I thought was done for and was planning to throw away has a new bright-green leaf about to unfurl. "You go, greenie!" I give him a high-five with my pointer finger.

Now onto changing all of my guy's bandages. I fill a tray with bandage supplies and head to the couch. "You're up next, my guy."

I pull the sheet covering him aside and just enjoy the view for a long minute. His abs are ridiculous. Like literally chiseled onto his body. I sit on the edge of the couch, his warm body pressing against my thigh. I slip on latex gloves and carefully remove the bandage on his side. "This looks good."

I make notes on my clipboard. 'Wound (left flank): Nice and clean, a healthy shade of pink around the edges, no foul smells.'

Even the bandage looks clean, so I guess there hasn't been any bleeding or weird discharges. I wash the area with hydrogen peroxide on cotton balls, slather on a thick layer of bacitracin ointment, and apply a new bandage.

Now for his shoulder. The tape on his chest lifts right off. Goddamn, I did a good job on these stitches. "You, my guy, are welcome." Gina said the stitches looked 'all sorts of fucked up' when I put them in, but they've settled into place nicely, perfectly spaced and even. My very best yet.

I am so going to rock the rehabilitator license test next month!

I roll my guy onto his side, toward me, pulling him practically onto my lap, so I can look at the back of his shoulder. His big body is like a weighted blanket, warm breath on my knee. Scrubs may be highly professional, but they are paper thin.

Okay, so the stitches on his back don't look anywhere near as good as the ones in front. Maybe because he's been lying on them, sort of compressing them? Maybe I should turn him over every few hours or prop a throw pillow under him? I've never had to worry about 'coma care' with any of my critters before, so this part is all guesswork.

And it's not like he'll ever see his own back anyway.

I clean and re-bandage the area, then toss my latex gloves onto my tray. I run my fingers along his back to feel for bed sores or anything like that, but all I feel is his smooth skin and firm muscles.

I honestly can't stop myself. His back is so smooth and firm and warm, I rub up and down, following the deep dent along his spine. I use my nails on the upstroke and the pads of my fingers on the downstroke. I could do this for hours.

Seems like he likes it too, his body completely relaxing onto me.

My phone chimes with a text, but I can't reach it with his weight on my lap. I enjoy the pressure on my lap for a few more minutes, then lean him back onto the couch. His left arm still draped across me, heavy and warm. His hand practically cupping my ass. It's almost like he's copping a feel, but pretty sure that's just wishful thinking on my part.

"What's your deal? Are you ever going to wake up for me?" I run my fingers across his eyelids, along his cheekbones. "When you do, are you going to stick around or just get up and leave?" I stare at his gorgeous face, wishing I could see those bright green eyes again. "I hope you stay awhile. I'd like to meet you for real. I don't even know your name."

My phone chimes again. I can reach it now.

Spencer

> How's my foxy girl?

Alright, that's kind of cute. I'll give him credit for that one.

Paige

> I'm having a great day! You?

> Depends on whether you invite me over or not

I sigh. *Wow, Paige, tell me about your great day. I'd love to hear about it. What? Your animals, plants, and your random guy are all doing great? You're awesome, babe! Now tell me more about you.*

> Sorry. Still can't have company

> Don't you miss me?

Do I?

I bite my lip while I think. I'm not sure Spencer has crossed my mind at all since his last text. Most days, I'm wondering if he'll text and want to see me that night. I'll check my phone a few times, hoping there's a message. But today, I completely forgot all about him.

So, no. No, I don't. Not at all, actually.

In fact, sitting here, with my couch guy's warm arm around me, this is all I need.

Well, this and cleaning out Tango's enclosure, since that starts to reek if I don't do it at least every third day.

Damiano

MUFFLED SINGING COMES FROM the corner of the room, interrupted by an occasional squeal from Paige. I've got to take a peek at what this girl is getting herself into now.

Hmph, cleaning out the turtle's cage. Not nearly as interesting as I was hoping. Then again, with Paige's snug scrubs framing her perfect ass, there will be no complaints from me.

Paige's phone vibrates on the desk next to her. She reaches down to answer it.

"I have an idea," some girl announces on speakerphone, her voice vaguely familiar.

Paige bundles up a handful of newspaper from the bottom of the terrarium, her shirt rising as she lifts her arms over the top of the enclosure. "I don't know, G. I never like your ideas."

"You'll like this one. It's going to make your guy wake up."

"Is it smelling salts?"

"What? Oh, maybe. I don't know what those are. But that's not what I'm talking about. I was thinking—and let me finish before you say 'no.'"

"No."

"Shush. That's not how conversations work. So... if touching his dick got him to groan, you should touch it more."

Hey now.

"*Gina!*" Paige whisper-shouts back. "I never should have told you about that. I already feel guilty about it."

"Get over that. Real doctors and nurses touch their patients' dicks all the time. It's part of good bedside manner. Now hear me out."

Paige should absolutely hear Gina out on this one.

"The guy hasn't moved an inch in... how many days?"

"Four. Well, three, plus the night he got here."

"The guy hasn't moved an inch in three-and-a-half days. He hasn't woken up. Don't even get me started on how he hasn't eaten or drank anything or needed to use the bathroom and doesn't seem to be suffering because of any of that. Setting those *biological miracles* aside, the one time the guy actually showed some signs of life was when you touched his dick."

"So?"

"So touch it again."

She looks over her shoulder at me. "I don't think that's how comas work."

"I don't think *any of this* is how comas work. But it does seem to be exactly how *your guy's* coma works. So next time he gets a woody, touch it for real. Go all in—lick it, suck it. Suck it so hard he wakes up and shouts for his momma."

I like Gina. She's very smart, very thoughtful. She's very practical. A clever girl who gives excellent advice that should absolutely be followed to the letter.

"Not only is that not medically realistic, it's also, like, completely inappropriate. I don't have his consent."

Oh, angel, you do. You have my consent. You have all my consent.

"You're looking at it the wrong way, P. Think of it this way—if it wakes him up, he'll forever be grateful you cured his 'coma' or whatever this is. And if it doesn't wake him up, he won't even know about it. It's win-win."

Paige empties the turtle's food dish into the trash bag by her feet. "That's like a guy molesting some girl he roofied."

"No. It's not like that at all. First, you didn't drug him. I mean, yeah, you did. But that was after he was shot and you aren't the one who shot him and those pills should have worn off by now. This is different. You're saving his life, so he owes you one for that. Also, you didn't call the cops on him, so he owes you for that too."

Paige goes into her little kitchen, runs the sink. "And what *he* owes *me* is to let *me* blow *him*?"

"Precisely. And then, when he wakes up, he should go down on you for an hour. At least an hour."

Come on. Who is this magical friend?

Paige comes back in, drying her hands on her shirt.

"Be serious, G. There will be no unsolicited blow jobs, but your advice is appreciated as always. Can we please change the topic? How did your interview go? Was today's the last one, or is there one more?"

Oh, interesting. Gina is interviewing for a new... I don't give a fuck. They should hang up and Paige should decide I'm really dirty again and should give me another sponge bath—which I fucking loved, completely separate from the fact that she might blow me this next time.

And she should wash my balls this time. Carefully lift and cradle each plum, run the sponge around it. A warm, soapy wash, followed by a slightly cooler rinse, followed by her lips nuzzling against each one separately, then both at the same time. Lightly blowing until they're dry. Then move on to my rod, lapping at the tip like a lollipop.

Do all that for me, angel, and I promise to wake up.

Fuck, I'm solid wood. Pretty sure the blanket is hiding it, but I can't exactly check with Paige in the room. *Down, boy.* At least I can give him a much-needed squeeze with my right hand since it's already under the blanket.

It's not enough, but it takes the edge off.

"Okay. Plan B, then," Gina says.

Paige starts cleaning out the rabbit cage, the rabbit nipping at her wrist when she gets near it. "Am I going to regret asking what Plan B is?"

"I think you regret most of our conversations."

"You know that's not true. You're my ying." Paige sighs. "Tell me about Plan B."

"Use him for hookup practice."

Paige looks over her shoulder at me, then lowers her voice to a whisper. "I don't need hookup practice and I already said I'm not going to molest him."

"I don't mean *like that*. I mean, use that mouth of yours a different way. Practice telling him exactly what you want. Practice demanding that your needs get met first, before the guy's."

"Come on, G."

"Don't 'come on, G' me. Wouldn't it be nice to tell Spencer, or whoever's next up, exactly how you want to be touched? Exactly where and for exactly how long?"

"The guy should just know that stuff."

"Sure, and welcome to the land of women not reaching orgasm until after the guy rolls over and goes to sleep. Oh, wait. You're already the mayor of No O Town."

"But I don't want to be the mayor. Can't I just be, like, a normal citizen?"

"No. And the only way to abdicate your throne is to spill your guts to sleeping beauty over there. Be completely open and honest with him because if you can't be honest with the complete stranger napping on your couch, who can you be honest with?"

"I'm honest with you."

"Yeah, but neither of us swing that way, so unless you want me to start pulling aside whoever you're hooking up with and telling him what you want for you, you're going to have to practice telling that guy. Or... that can actually be Plan C. If you're not going to tell guys how you want it, I'll tell them for you."

"That is honestly the scariest plan out of all three."

"I know! We absolutely should go with that one. Text me Spencer's number. I'm going to make him rock your world with a whole slew of things you don't even know exist. Maybe plan to take a personal day off work the day after because you'll need the recovery time."

"Or how about I give Plan B some thought and we put a pin in Plan C for some other time?"

"You mean never?"

"Yes. I mean exactly never. I'll mark that on my calendar. Do you want to come over for pizza and to stare at Couch Guy's chest with me some more?"

"That's all you tonight. Home game. I'm on my way to the stadium now."

"Okay. Yell loud."

"Always do. And you—try telling your guy one thing you'd like and see how that feels. Just one. It doesn't even need to be a big one."

"Okay, guy. The rug is making my butt itch. You've got to make some room."

Paige has been sitting on the floor, leaning against the couch, since she hung up from her call with Gina. She's been watching *Grey's Anatomy* and taking notes in a little book. But now she's standing, and I'm back to eyes closed.

She reaches behind my neck and lifts me to a half-sit. She squeezes herself into the corner of the couch, then lowers me back down onto her lap.

I guess we're sharing the couch now.

Her lap is an excellent pillow. Warm and firmer than the mushy pillow she'd put under my head days ago. No matter how I fold it or crunch it, it's too soft and fluffy. But Paige's lap is perfect.

Her finger lightly traces my eyebrows, along my nose. She pets my four-day beard. "You were sporting a perfectly groomed five-o'clock shadow when you got here. Maybe I should try shaving you?"

Please don't. Please don't come anywhere near my face with a razor or scissors. Not with anything sharp. Not after I've seen your ability to give stitches. *That* will absolutely make me 'wake up.'

"What are you like anyway?" She runs her fingers through my hair, all the way to the back of my head, her nails scratching my scalp. Feels fantastic. "Are you a jerk? Or are you secretly sweet? Are you the life of the party? Hmmm. I bet you're a quiet one. Always watching. Sometimes it feels like you're watching me."

More scratching my scalp. I lean into it without meaning to.

She sighs loud and long. "So, my guy, here are some things I'd like you to do to me."

This should be good. Really good. Sexy as fuck when a girl makes bedroom demands.

"I would like it if you, or, uh, a guy would... I mean, I'd want you to want to... to, like..." She huffs out loud, still petting me. "To, want to... at least sometimes to..."

There are so many things that could fill in these blanks. Come on, angel, name one. Any one. My answer will be yes. To anything.

Except to kissing.

Or to cuddling after the fact.

Or to spending the night.

Other than those things, yes to anything.

She inhales deeply then lets it out slowly. "I'd like it if you... uh, nope. Not going to happen. Sorry, Gina. If he can't read my mind and know exactly what I want, he isn't the guy for me."

So glad my boss has her quarterly management update to-day. She won't notice me taking an extra-long lunch hour. Her meeting gives me just enough time to run home, change, then get back to my desk for five-and-a-half more mind-numbing hours of document review.

With my 'special guest' at home, I skipped laundry night, so I had to wear a push-up bra I bought for nights out, not for long days sitting at a desk. The thing is killing me. It's a 32B, a band *and* a cup size smaller than my actual size that I bought on super sale. But the scalloped lace on the top edge of the cups is gorgeous and has a delicate fringe that peeks out slightly with some of my going-out tops. Looks sexy as hell.

It's great for a few hours of drunken clubbing, but absolute hell for a full day sitting at my desk. It's like there's a pretty python squeezing every breath out of me, digging into my sides. Plus, Jared wouldn't stop staring at my boobs all morning, which was slowing down our team's doc review rate.

The thing is so awful that I don't even take the stairs like usual, opting for the slowavator instead. I need to get this thing off and probably need to throw it away too. Or donate it.

Or maybe these cups can make comfy little beds for my next squirrel or baby bunny? If I rubber band the underwire part around a plastic takeout soup container, the bra cup could be like a little hammock.

I think that will work great actually. I should design things for real.

Pretty sure I have a clean sports bra in my drawer. At this point, even uniboob is better than suffocation. Or I'll grab the least dirty one from my laundry basket.

I go over my in-and-out-quick plan as I walk down the hallway, stepping over the zug under the rug. Run in, change bras, grab the last pack of strawberry Pop-Tarts to eat on my trek back to the office, and get back before Marci's meeting is over.

As I open the door, it occurs to me that if my sports bra is right where I think it is, I might even have time to—

Couch guy is sitting at the table.

Awake.

"Oh my god. You're up." I drop my keys and bag on the floor and stumble toward him.

Holy shit, I did it. I actually saved him. "You're alive."

And he stayed. He waited for me.

He's sitting at the table, holding a chicken wing up to his mouth, about to take a bite.

Wait. *What?*

He stands up, chicken wing in one hand, Romeo nestled in the crook of his other arm, sound asleep.

Why is Romeo so calm? And where did the takeout come from?

I move toward him. "No, sit. Save your energy. Don't make yourself dizzy. Sit. When did you wake up? How are you feel—"

"Dom," comes *another man's voice. From my bedroom.* "I'm not going to wipe my ass with takeout napkins every time I take a shit here. I promise you, she's not going to notice missing toilet paper. Next time, I—" The guy stops talking when he steps into the room and sees me.

"Who are *you?*" I look back and forth between the two of them.

"Cazzo." Bathroom guy looks over to couch guy. "Come vuoi giocarci?"

"What's going on?" I take a step back toward my front door.

'Dom' tosses the chicken wing into one of the takeout food containers.

I look at his very healthy-looking body. He's wearing a sweat jacket, unzipped, no shirt underneath, and joggers that fit him perfectly. Those aren't Tom's old clothes that I had left on the end table in case he woke up while I was at work.

This guy did not just wake up. No way.

"What is happening?" I whisper. I thought he was broken. *I thought I was fixing him.*

Dom's face is serious. Lips tight. He is not excited to see me.

"How long have you been awake?" I barely hear my own voice. I take a deep breath, fold my arms. "How long have you been lying to me?" I should call the police.

Dom looks at the other guy. Bathroom guy's eyes shift to the table, mine follow.

The gun I hid that first night is on the table next to the food containers.

I have got to get out of here.

"Come sit down with me, Paige. Let's talk." His voice is strong, his accent heavy. Nothing like the raspy sounds he could barely make that first night.

And he knows my name.

I take another step backward toward the door.

"Come sit down. *Please.*"

I shake my head and take another step toward the door.

"I insist."

"I need to go." I turn toward the door.

Chk-chk.

My feet freeze in place, but the rest of me slowly turns toward bathroom guy.

All I see is the end of a gun. The rest of the room is blurry, but the square black end of a gun *aimed at me* is in perfect focus.

"No, we insist. Sit." He motions toward my table.

I close my eyes. This can't be happening.

"Put it down, Salvo." Dom sounds calm, maybe even annoyed.

"She can't fucking leave, man."

"She's not going anywhere. Put the gun down. Paige, take a seat."

Dom steps between Salvo and me.

I take another step back toward the door, stumbling over my purse. I have to get out of here.

"For fuck's sake, Paige, stop running away and come talk to me."

"I need to go. I need to get out of here." I take another step back. My apartment has never been this big before. How have I not reached the door yet?

"You really don't give a shit about your own safety, do you? He pointed a gun at your head, and you're still trying to leave?"

I shrug my shoulders and take another step back. I reach behind me for the doorknob.

I'll go to Gina's and—

Salvo steps toward Dom. "I said, you can't leave." He presses the gun into Romeo's fluffy back, the rabbit still nestled in Dom's arm. "Take a seat."

Dom pushes Salvo's arm away. "The fuck, man?"

Romeo lets out a big toothy yawn, clearly not caring about anything that's happening. But I have to protect him.

I rush over and grab my rabbit off Dom's arm. "What kind of monster are you?" I pull Romeo in close, shielding him with my body even though he's clawing to get away from me.

Salvo moves across the room and blocks the door out of my apartment.

Now I'm trapped in here with them.

"Who are you people?"

"That's Salvo. *He's leaving*. Now. I'm Damiano. Damiano Zucco. Put the rabbit away and sit with me. We need to talk."

Damiano and Salvo argued in what I realize might *not* actually have been Spanish, then Salvo left. I put Romeo back in his cage while Damiano put his gun away somewhere.

Now it's just the two of us, sitting at my table. It's never looked as tiny as it does with him at it.

I let out a long breath. Now that the other guy is gone, I can relax. Damiano won't hurt me. I'm absolutely sure of that.

In fact, he's just staring at me. A few seconds staring at my mouth, my cheeks, my eyes. Like he's memorizing my face with those hypnotizing green eyes.

My phone has been vibrating almost nonstop from inside my bag by the door. I point over my shoulder with my thumb. "That's either my boss wanting to fire me for not coming back or my friend, Gina. If it's Gina and I don't answer, she'll eventually show up."

Damiano nods. He gets up—with no struggle at all, not even a wince of pain—and grabs my bag. He lays my phone on the table and answers it on speakerphone.

"I know who he is," Gina says, followed by a loud slurp on a straw. Most likely her iced pumpkin spice latte afternoon pick-me-up.

"Yeah?" This information would have been more helpful *before* I got home.

"Yup. He's the enforcer for the Galliano crime family, Damiano Zucco. *Told you* he was Italian, not Mexican. I knew it. I totally knew it."

"Okay."

"Do you know what this means?"

"That you were right and I was wrong?"

"No. I mean, yes. But I'll gloat about that later. I'm being serious right now, Paige. Have you heard of the Galliano Famiglia?"

"No. Should I have?"

"I mean, you? Maybe not. You didn't grow up here. But for those of us who did? Yeah. Definitely. That name is a big fucking deal. Everyone born and raised here knows about the four families that pretty much run the city. When I was a kid, there were five. I don't know why, but now there are only four."

She takes another loud slurp. "They're the mob, Paige. Like Al Capone. Or Donnie Brasco, or what was the movie with the horse head, the one with James Caan when he was hot as fuck? Or the Ray Liotta one when he was a gangster and he was hot as fuck? Is that the same movie, or was that a different one? I don't remember. But somehow, all the mob guys are hot as fuck, your guy included."

Damiano dips his head a little, smiles. His stupid, gorgeous, bearded smile. And his glittery green eyes that I keep trying to look away from but don't know how to.

Don't forget he's been lying to you, probably for days. Maybe this whole time.

It'll be easier to be mad at him if I'm not looking at him. No doubt that face lets him get away with anything. I turn toward the one window this room has.

Why are my plants on the windowsill?

I look around. All my plants have been moved. I lean forward to look into the kitchen. The little pothos is missing from his spot on the counter.

They're *all* on the windowsill or on a stack of books next to the window.

"You still there, P? Did Marci walk by? Hello?"

"I'm here."

She whispers this next part, "I'm pretty sure he kills people, Paige. *That's* why he had a gun. Not for self-defense. And *that's* why he didn't want the police or the hospital. He wasn't worried someone would come finish him off, he was worried he'd get arrested."

He doesn't look offended or upset by anything Gina is saying.

"Don't go home after work today, okay? Come to my place so we can figure out what to do."

"Maybe."

Damiano reaches for a notebook from the small stack of them on the table. He scribbles "how does she know this?" in tight, perfect cursive. I was saving that notebook. I don't know what for—I hadn't figured out what was special enough to write in it yet. But now that he's written on a page, the whole book is ruined.

He taps his scribbled note with the pen.

"How did you figure out who he is?"

"I was thinking about it more and more—that all signs pointed to him being part of the Famiglias, except the Mexican flag tattoo part. So I decided to kill two birds with one stone. I needed to get my nails done anyway, so I went to Lucinda's Cresta since that's where all the mafia wives and girlfriends get their hair done."

"Why do you even know that?"

"Everyone from here knows that."

Damiano nods.

I close my eyes for a second. I'm such an idiot.

"So these two girls our age walk in, already fully dolled up walking *into* the salon, and I'm like, jackpot. I was trying to figure out how to ask them if they knew anything about some guy getting all shot up in the park when they start yapping away about him on their own. The first one was saying her boyfriend was going to earn some huge prize for finding Damiano and bringing him to their boss and then he was finally going to buy her the ring she wants. Actually sounded like a really tacky ring if you ask me, but that's not my point."

Damiano pulls a phone from the pocket of his hoodie—*since when does he have a phone?*—and texts something to someone. My body slumps low in my chair. Am I actually this gullible? I thought I was doing the right thing. I thought I was helping a stranger in need.

"Then the other one said that there was no way the first one's boyfriend could take Damiano out and that he's crazy if he's going to go up against the Galliano enforcer. Then something about Damiano's wanted for shooting a couple of their guys *in the park*—that's how I knew I was right—so why would her boyfriend think he has a chance against him and that he'll probably end up dead trying."

Damiano's barely reacting to any of the things Gina's saying, like it's all no big deal to be accused of those things.

"Then the first one asked why the two of them don't just find some dentists to marry because life would be easier. Then they had this whole conversation about how, since a dentist gets some medical training, maybe one would actually know what to do with a girl's clit and, you know what, Paige? I think they were onto something there, because remember that—"

"Gina, did you talk to them at all? Did they know you were listening?" No way she kept her mouth shut.

There's a pause.

"I mean, I totally joined in on the clit conversation, because remember that X-ray tech I was seeing a while back? He could—"

"Gina."

"What? Oh, come on, who doesn't love a good clit-lashing? Oh wait, Tom wasn't a giver. And don't even get me started on Spencer. You really need to start demanding some reciprocity, Paige. Woman the fuck up already. Did you practice saying what you want with your house-guest?"

Damiano tilts his head slightly, smiles at me. *Oh my god. He's heard everything, this whole time.* Maybe he can use his gun to put me out of my misery.

I close my eyes. "I have to go, G."

"Okay. Yeah. Call me when you're done with work. And come straight to my place, okay? Don't go home until we figure this out."

"Love you." I press the end button on my phone. I stare at Damiano for a long minute, my arms crossed. "I suppose you're going to tell me she has it all wrong?"

He shakes his head. "Most of that was right. Or close." His obviously *Italian* accent is so strong now that I feel like an idiot for missing it in the car. "But there's more to it. Let's start over." He reaches his hand out to shake mine.

I mean, I guess we are just meeting.

I reluctantly take his hand. It's big and warm. And was on my boob, and I totally perved out over it. *And I touched his dick. While I thought he was in a coma, I touched his dick. But he was awake for that.*

"Pleasure to meet you, Paige." He isn't letting go. He's staring at my mouth. Is he thinking about his hand on my boob too? Or my hand on him?

"Hmm," is all I manage. I pull my hand back. "If you're so Italian, why is your tattoo the Mexican flag?"

He shakes his head. "This?" He points to the flag on his chest. "This is the ensign for Italy's Navy. Il Tricolore plus a crown and coat of arms. Mexico's flag has an eagle in the center, no?"

Maybe he's right. Now that I think about it, I think I remember Mexico's with a bird on it.

"Why are people trying to kill you?"

"I don't know."

I don't have patience for being lied to anymore. I really don't. I stand up. "Okay, well, it was nice knowing you. You should leave now." I walk over to the window and grab my little fern and put it back on the coffee table. Then I go get the pothos and return it to its little spot in the kitchen.

Damiano sits silently, watching me.

I move two more plants back to their normal spots, then look over my shoulder at him. "Oh, you're still here?"

"I don't know why people want to kill me *this time*, Paige. Someone from another Famiglia is claiming that I killed one of their guys and shot another in the back. I promise you that didn't happen."

"Right, because a guy who carries a gun and breaks into someone's car completely covered in blood would never shoot anyone."

"Not in the back. I've never shot anyone in the back."

I just stare at him, blinking my eyes intentionally.

"I aim for the throat if I need someone to die immediately and aim for the thigh if I just want them to fuck off. The night you found me, angel, I took one throat shot and one leg shot. Both hit exactly on target."

He's got to be joking. No way he'd just casually admit to shooting people. He's too calm about it. He actually seems more concerned about whether or not I believe him than he is about confessing to murder.

"The guy I shot in the leg, he crawled to his car and hightailed it the fuck out of there, I assume to get medical attention. Exactly the point of the leg shot."

I did see an SUV speeding away, but that doesn't mean he's telling the truth. "And the other guy? Doesn't sound like he crawled away."

Damiano shrugs his shoulders. "He shot me first. *In the back*, you might have noticed." He points to his shoulder. "I shot him in self-defense."

I grab another plant from the window and take it back to its correct spot. "So you kill people? For a living? That's, like, your actual job?" I'm trying to act as casual about this as he is.

"That's not how I would describe it. I keep order, keep things running smoothly. I keep the people I care about safe." His eyes follow me as I go back and forth from windowsill to shelf, windowsill to table, putting my little greenies back where they belong. "Fewer people die when I do my job."

"Yeah, sure sounds like it." I pick up two plants, then stop. I look him dead in the eyes. "When did you wake up?"

He hesitates. "Paige." He walks over, stopping right in front of me. He's got at least six inches on me. I have to crane my neck up to see his face. He looks from one eye to the other, searching.

His lips part like he's going to answer, but then he doesn't. Instead, he takes the plants out of my hands and walks them back over to the window. "Your plants aren't getting enough natural light. These need full eastern exposure."

He goes into the kitchen and grabs the pothos, too. Then the fern from the coffee table.

Every plant that I just put away, he's putting back by the one window this room has.

What the hell?

I step in front of him. "Don't touch those. They're mine. And they're finally doing really great. They're—"

I stop.

I look over at the window, then back at the shelf on the far side of the room where most of them normally live. Where they're definitely not getting direct sun. "Have you been taking care of my plants? While I thought you were lying there half-dead?"

While I thought I was taking care of you, you were taking care of my plants?

He doesn't say anything. He puts the bonsai tree on its usual spot on the shelf, even though it's obvious he wants to move it back to the window.

"You moved them to the window each morning, didn't you? Then back to their normal spots before I got home?"

He doesn't deny it. He just looks at me like he's sorry I suck so bad at life.

I slump down onto the couch, dropping my head into my hands. Defeated. "Were you even in a coma at all?" I peek up at him.

The look on his face—*pure pity*—answers my question.

I wasn't helping him. I wasn't even helping my little plants. "You didn't need me."

Damiano moves in front of me. Lowers down onto his knees. He reaches up and tucks my hair back behind my ear. "Of course I needed you, Paige." With his stupid, perfect accent, it comes out like 'beige' but with a 'P.' A part of me loves it.

"Uh-huh."

His thumbs rub the outsides of my thighs. "You got me out of the park."

I swallow hard, fighting back tears. "So you needed my car."

He smiles. "You hid me."

"You needed my apartment."

He shakes his head slightly. "You stitched me up."

I stare at him a long minute. "Did I though?" *My* stitches never look as evenly spaced and perfectly sized as the ones on his shoulder do. Mine always look shitty, like the ones on his back. "How did you even learn to do stitches like that?"

"Six years in the GOI."

I shrug my shoulders. No clue what that means.

"Special forces in Italy's Navy. Gruppo Operativo Incursori. Like the U.S. Navy SEALs, only better dressed," he says with a wink. "Medical training is a part of the program." His eyes drop down to my lady parts for a long second. "Six months of medical training."

Oh my god, he's thinking about what Gina said.

And now so am I.

Damiano lets out a long breath. "I needed you, Paige." He slides his hands up onto my thighs, parts them slightly. His grip on my thigh tightens. He licks his full lips. "I still need you."

Even with him kneeling in front of me, wedged between my knees, I try to squeeze my thighs together to stop that tingly feeling.

"You did such a good job taking care of me. Let me take care of you now." He leans forward and kisses the inside of my right thigh, just above my knee. He looks up at me, his bright green eyes twinkling with mischief. "Let me show you exactly how grateful I am."

Damiano

I FINALLY HAVE MY hands on this sexy as fuck angel. Now I can touch her however the fuck I want.

Days of her touching me, taunting me. Always stopping short. Slowly killing me. And now she walked in the door, looking like the perfect fucking snack, her mouth dropping into the perfect O.

She's here. I'm here. I'm up. I mean, I am literally up with my rod pressing against my waistband. I'm eye level with stunning nipples busting the fuck out of her shirt. And I'm finally touching her.

She's pissed as fuck at me, as she should be, but she's not telling me to fuck off. She's not pushing me away.

My phone vibrates in my pocket with an incoming text that I am definitely ignoring.

I slide my hands up her thighs, back to her ass. Pull her forward, forcing her thighs open so I fit between them.

I've exercised complete restraint all week. Restraint when she pranced around in tiny shorts and no bra. Restraint when she put my hand on her perfect tit. Restraint when she tugged on my dick. Restraint when she was in the next room, touching herself, thinking about me.

Restraint's over now. I am going to touch the fuck out of this girl. Consume her.

She's watching, waiting. Looking hungry as fuck, practically panting. Such a good girl all week, she deserves this.

I bite her thigh through her pants, tugging on the fabric with my teeth. I reach up to unbutton them, watching her as I pull down the zipper. Her eyes are half closed, she's biting her bottom lip.

She lifts her ass slightly as I tug on her pants. 'Atta girl. Exactly the silent permission I need.

I pull her pants all the way down. Squeezing her ankle as I kiss the inside of her thigh again, finally my lips on her skin. I lick my way up toward a sliver of cotton candy pink panties peeking out from between tan thighs. Bellissima.

"Open wide for me, angel."

She takes a breath in, nods her head, slowly spreads her legs only another inch or two wider.

"All the way." I lean forward and breathe her in. "Fuck. I can smell how turned on you are." Fucking delicious, lighting me up. I suck on the taut skin inside her thigh.

She watches me like she's in a trance.

I push her panties to the side, exposing a tuft of hair so blonde it's almost white. I spread her legs as far as they'll go, exposing the prettiest, slickest, pinkest pussy I've ever seen.

"Look at you, angel. All this is for me?" I wait for her to answer, slowly grazing her thigh with my scruffy cheek.

"Damiano."

"Yeah, angel?" Like I don't know what she wants.

"Please, Damiano."

I'm tempted to make her beg for real, but we've both been waiting *days* for this.

I pull her ass toward me so she's practically hanging off the edge of the couch. I lean in with my tongue wide and flat. One long lick from as low as I can reach, swirling to a stop around her pretty little clit. I suck the tiny bud into my mouth and nurse on it like a starving baby.

Paige's hands grab the back of my head.

"Go ahead, angel. Steer me to where you want me."

"No, you're good. Right where you are... It's good... really good."

I tug on her clit, rub my finger along her slit.

She's pushing herself toward me to get what she needs, sliding onto my finger while I suckle. So fucking tight.

She pulls my head against her, mashing my face into her sweet, sloppy mess. She's grinding up and down on my face, chasing her orgasm. *Don't stop.*

I'm moaning so loud, slurping so hard, that I barely notice my phone vibrating with an incoming call. This is a brand-new phone, new number. Only Salvo and probably Rob have it.

But Paige is close to combusting, I can tell. The backs of her thighs tense up, her toes are pointing hard, she's holding her breath. She's dying for it. Another few seconds and she'll explode on my tongue.

My phone starts vibrating *again*. Neither one of them would call unless it was important and calling twice means the sky is falling.

I sit back on my heels and look at my angel. Her legs spread, her pussy glistening. The little tuft of hair matted to her skin by her slick or my spit or probably both.

She opens her eyes to find mine when she realizes I've stopped.

"Don't move." I pull out my phone and see Salvo's name.

"When did you get a phone?" Her voice is raspy and needy and sexy as fuck. She won't like the answer, so I don't give her one.

"Pronto," I say into the phone, my eyes locked on Paige's. I lick my lips that are drenched with her. I stare at her shiny cunt, smooth and wet and spread open waiting for me. Fuck, I want to get back in there and gorge on her.

"Word is Joey Bags knows where you are and his guys are heading your way. I'm coming back to get you." A car honks in the background.

"Don't." It's too dangerous for him to come here, get me, and get out if Joey's guys are already on their way here.

"I'm already en route."

The heel of my hand is pressing on Paige's hip to keep her from getting up. I rub my thumb over her swollen clit. She's sitting up slightly, watching my hand on her. She can't take her eyes off where I'm touching her. I can't take my eyes off her face.

"Turn around and go home. I'll get us out of here."

Paige looks at me, surprised.

"Us? You bringing the girl?" Salvo sounds surprised, too.

"Se sanno dove sono, sanno di lei." *If they know where I am, they know about her.* "How'd they figure out where I am?"

"No fucking clue. One of the Cat girls heard from a friend that a bunch of them hopped in their trucks and started heading your way."

I really don't want to leave right now. "You have an ETA for them?" As much as I want to finish Paige off, making sure she's safe comes first.

I stand up and give my rod a hard squeeze near the tip to get him to calm down. Playtime's over, big guy. Back in your pen.

Paige sits herself up and closes her legs. She punches the couch next to her, with a huff. The girl is all worked up. She was so damn close. So fucking adorable, all pouty because she didn't hit the mark.

"No ETA," Salvo tells me. "Just that they're on the move, so get going."

I end the call. This is shit timing.

"Angel?"

She looks a little confused by me calling her that, but blinks it away. "I could hear all that. You should go. But I'm not going with you."

"Yeah, you are." I adjust my junk again, pushing him down in my joggers. I reach my hand out to pull her up.

She doesn't take my hand.

"I'm not going with you."

"You are."

She shakes her head.

I look up at the ceiling and count to five. "Are you always this stubborn?"

"No. I'm not. I'm actually not stubborn at all. I'm really accommodating most of the time. Too accommodating, *obviously*. But look where that keeps getting me." She stands to pull her pants back into place, fastens them. Then she drops back onto the couch and stomps her foot down. The poor girl was seconds away from exploding in my mouth, and now she's frustrated as hell.

Don't worry, angel. We'll climb that mountain again.

I walk over to her closet and take out the pet carrier and an empty pink tote bag I noticed when I was looking for where she hid my gun. The box of tampons was actually a great idea. I'd gone through the entire apartment twice before I looked in there.

"What are you doing with that bag?"

"I'm packing for you."

"Don't. Put that back."

I head over to her animals. I put the turtle in the carrier, then pick up the rabbit, stroking between its ears a few times before I put it in too. "Do you have a ditch bag?"

"A what?"

"A bag of your absolutely essential shit for when you have to leave in a hurry."

She stares at me like I have two heads. "Of course I *don't* have a ditch bag. I'm a normal person. Normal people don't have to escape their apartments in a hurry because a bunch of gangsters are coming after them."

We don't have time for this. "Grab your absolute essentials. You've got two minutes." I load a few of her plants into the bag, the ones that are higher maintenance. The succulents she overwaters can stay here to dry out, and so can the bonsai, but the rest can't go more than a couple of days without attention, and I don't know when it will be safe to come back here.

I look over. She hasn't moved. She's still on the couch watching me.

Fuck it. I'll buy her anything she needs. That idea actually feels oddly fucking right. "Either start walking or I'm going to throw you over my shoulder, which will probably pull out some of my stitches, and I'll probably bleed all over your carpet, but that's fine by me."

She shakes her head.

I take two steps toward her.

"Okay, okay." She gets up. "Don't pull your stitches. I'm not going to stitch you up again."

That's a relief—both that she's coming without a fight and that she'll never put stitches in me again, but I'm pretty sure she meant it as a punishment.

I hand her the pet carrier and grab her keys off the floor from where she dropped them when she walked in. "Let's go." I've got the duffel of plants and—oh, I dash into her bathroom to grab her birth control pills and toss them into the bag.

I mean, she might forgive me for all this, so...

I zip up and pull on the hood of my sweat jacket, stuff my Glock into my waistband since I don't have a holster on, then grab her hand. It's so tiny in mine.

I drag her, her animals, and her plants out the door. I know taking the elevator is risky, but so are the stairs, and I don't want our cargo jostled more than necessary. The doors open, and the elevator is empty, so we step in. Now that I'm not dragging Paige and have a free hand, I pull my Glock from my waistband as subtly as I can. Paige isn't looking at me, isn't talking to me. But at least she's cooperating and not running away or yelling for help.

The elevator doors open to her building's garage. "Where are you parked?" Before she answers, I see the same brown and white Blazer I crawled into a few days ago halfway down the row of parked cars. "Let's go. You drive." I put the plants and pet carrier in the backseat, stretching the seatbelt around the carrier to buckle it.

She hasn't moved to get in.

"Paige, we have to go now. Once we're out of here, if you want me to put you on a plane to Hawaii, I will. You don't have to stay with me. But we need to move."

She reaches for the door handle slowly, tentatively. Like she's not sure if she should come with me or run the other way. I open the driver's door and nudge her in. I jog around to the passenger side, still holding the keys since I'm not entirely sure she won't try to drive away without me at this point.

I climb in, then recline the passenger seat all the way back. I'm hoping Joey's guys don't know what Paige or her car looks like, so if they don't see me, they may let her drive by. "You know how to get to Lincoln Park?"

She nods. "Straight up Halstead."

"Good." I hand her the keys. "Drive normal, but fast. Don't make any unnecessary stops."

She looks at me, her lower lip quivering. It's settling in that she might be in actual danger. "I can't do this."

I put my hand—the hand that isn't holding my gun—on her thigh. "First of all, call me Dom. And second, of course you can."

She shakes her head.

"You rescued me from the park, you stitched me up, you cleaned me up. You made me feel like a fucking king just by rubbing my back. I'm pretty sure you can do anything, angel."

She looks at me, full of hope behind wet eyes.

"But all you need to do right now is drive."

Tires screech somewhere in the garage. No clue if that's Joey's guys coming for us or one of Paige's neighbors simply coming home.

I need to get her moving and I know exactly what will convince her. I squeeze her thigh, "plus, who else is going save me?"

Her lips part. She wants so bad to believe I need her.

"And the kids." I motion to the animals in the back seat. "We need you to save us."

Paige swallows hard, her blue eyes glistening. She finally nods, then starts the engine. She shifts into gear like a badass and throws it into reverse.

"We just passed 18th Street."

Paige has given me an update every few blocks. It's not necessary, I know exactly where we are, but updating me seems to be keeping her mind off of what we're running from.

Running isn't my style. Not at all. Alone, I'd stay and fight and win. But keeping her safe right now is more important than protecting my ego.

She shifts into third.

"You're doing so good, baby."

"The Suburban's still following us." Paige's eyes dart up to the rearview mirror. "And now there's a second one."

Joey Bags' guys all drive tinted-out black Suburbans. I asked Paige to let me know if she noticed any on our tail, and she noticed one a few blocks back. Apparently, there's a second one now.

Paige couldn't have a more noticeable car with its two-tone brown-and-white body panels. Definitely the only car of that description in the entire city. If they're following us, there's no point in me ducking down anymore, so I put my seat up.

I look around. There are actually *three* Suburbans on our tail and it's another five or six minutes until we cross into Galliano territory. "Don't worry about them. You've got this." I discreetly rack the slide on my Glock to load a bullet into the chamber, fake coughing to cover the metal click.

Paige yanks the wheel hard to the right, jerking us hard into the next lane. I smash against the passenger door, crushing my injured shoulder, dropping my gun. Fucking hurts.

I reach down and grab my Glock off the floor and turn, ready to lean out the window and shoot whoever's crept up on us.

But they're all still two or three car lengths away.

The fuck? "Why did you change lanes like that?"

"Why do you have your gun out?" She's staring at it.

"Because we're in a car chase. Why did you change lanes?"

"Because we're in a car chase. I don't know, it just felt like I should. Evasive maneuvers." She jerks us back into the left lane, then swerves, making giant S-turns across two lanes. "Serpentine! Serpentine!"

"Cazzo! Stop swerving! You're going to roll this death trap."

She steadies back into a single lane, then looks in the rearview mirror. She glances at me for a second. "But... I feel like... like maybe I should do it again? To lose the guys chasing us."

"No, you should *not* do it again." I put my hand on the wheel, holding it steady—and straight. "We don't need to lose them, we only need to get to Chicago Ave. Just go straight. Nice and easy." I look over my shoulder into the pet carrier. The rabbit is huddled in the corner. The turtle is hiding in his shell. Don't blame him.

Paige nods, but I can't tell if she's agreeing with me or just acknowledging that she heard me.

I dial Salvo, but I don't put him on speakerphone. "We're coming in hot."

"I'm tracking you. You're almost here. I'll head in to give you cover."

"Stay put." This fucking guy putting his fucking neck on the line. And I bet he's got Rob in the same car *and* that it's Salvo's very noticeable Sprinter van instead of one of the twenty Land Rovers we have, making for an extra high value, extra obvious target. "We're too close. There isn't time for you to get to us before we get to you."

Salvo huffs. "Fine. Once you make it to La Clark, you're good. We're all here. You got a dozen of us lining the avenue. No way the Douchebags," Salvo's nickname for Joey Bags' guys, "will follow."

Paige starts yelling. "He's going to hit us! Oh my god, he's going to ram us!"

One of the Suburbans has caught up to us. "Go faster. We're almost—"

Paige's car jolts forward a little as the Suburban bumps us.

Paige throws her truck into fifth, skipping fourth gear like the little badass stunt driver she is. "Shoot him, Dom. Shoot him. Oh my god. Shoot him! He hit Jo-Jo."

Opening fire in the middle of the day from a moving car is dangerous, and if Joey's guys fire back, Paige might get hit. We're close enough to La Clark that I don't need to risk that. "One more block. You've got this."

"Shoot him!"

I smile at my vicious little angel. Pretty sure she couldn't actually handle me landing my shot, *which* I *would*. But I'm not complaining about this side of her.

"Are you laughing at me? They're trying to run me off the road, and you're laughing at me?"

"No, baby. I'm not laughing at you." I try to hide my smile, but I can't. And I can't fucking wait to get her back to my place. "You're doing so good. We're almost there. You want to serpentine some more?"

"Maybe?" She glances at me with a smile, then turns back to the road. "Oh my god, Dom! There's more of them! Up ahead. They're everywhere!" She downshifts. "I'll turn onto—"

"No, no, go straight. Those are my guys. That's the cavalry. Keep going straight." A dozen Land Rovers very conveniently have the intersection blocked so even though it's a red light in our direction, we're clear to blow right through. Fucking love Salvo. "Run the light. Don't worry. We're good."

As we cross into our territory, horns start honking in celebration. Paige jumps in her seat, but I give her thigh a squeeze. "You did it, angel. You saved me again." I look in the side mirror as several of our Rovers move to block the road completely. No way Joey's guys could get through that.

She stops in the middle of the road, turns toward me. Her golden hair sticking to her face, her eyes full of life. "I did it? I did it, right?" Huge fucking smile on her face. "Holy shit, I did it."

Sexy as fuck watching her shift her way through that mess. I was lying when I told her I'd put her on a plane to Hawaii if she wants. She's coming home with me. "I think you just earned yourself another reward, angel. One with no interruptions. Make a left onto Sheffield."

THE ELEVATOR FROM DAMIANO'S garage to his apartment is pretty spacious, but he's standing close to me with his hand on my lower back. His touch might be the only thing stopping me from shaking—from the adrenaline, from excitement, from kicking ass in *an actual car chase*.

But also from confusion, from fear. What would those guys have done if they'd caught up with us?

What would Damiano have done?

"You good, angel?"

"I think so?" I'm actually not sure. I take a deep breath and have to remind myself to let it out.

The elevator doors open.

"Just make yourself at home. We can continue our conversation from before after you've settled in. Yeah?"

I nod again, even though I'm not entirely sure whether 'continue our conversation' means the conversation we were having about him faking his coma and being in the mafia and me being an absolute idiot, or the 'conversation' his mouth was having with my va-jay-jay.

I seriously hope it's the second one because that was *so close* to an actual orgasm caused by an actual other person, and also because I'm not sure where I stand on that first conversation. This entire situation is unreal, and I sort of feel like the mafia stuff only happens in the movies and not in real life and maybe it's just like an allegory and hyperbole or something.

On the other hand, he has a gun, Salvo has a gun, we were just in an actual car chase *with guns*. But back onto the first hand, nothing about him seems dangerous to me. He should seem dangerous. The guns, the gunshot wounds, him admitting that he actually shoots people. But, back to the second hand again, he was so helpless and needy on my couch, and so magnificent shirtless with Romeo nestled so sweetly on his arm.

I don't know what I'm supposed to be thinking right now.

The door to Damiano's apartment beeps unlocked after he enters a ridiculously long passcode on the keypad. "After you." His hand on my lower back nudges me inside.

I didn't have time to think about what Damiano's apartment would look like, but if I had, there's no way I would have pictured it looking anything like this.

Or *feeling* like this. Like I'm in an enchanted garden, but indoors. There might actually be elves and fairies here. Holy shit. "What is this place?"

There are plants everywhere. Some huge ones in built-in planters by the windows. Some normal-size ones, on stands and on the floor. The place is overflowing with lush, flourishing plants in a sea of deep greens. One entire wall is windows, and there are skylights along one side.

And it smells earthy. Not like dirt, but like I'm in the middle of a magical forest, far, far away from a city. Fresh air. The freshest air. It's more like California than Chicago for sure. I bet that at night, with the lights off and just the moon shining in, I'd think I'm outside in the middle of nowhere.

I turn toward Damiano. He's different in here already. Relaxed. There's no tension in his shoulders, his forehead is smooth, his smile easy. I'm relaxed too. Or distracted, at least.

Damiano leans down and opens the pet carrier. Romeo hops out and skitters under a couch. He carries Tango over to a large built-in planter filled with snake plants. The planter is bigger than Tango's terrarium at home, and the sides of it look high enough that he can't climb out. The little guy hasn't stepped on dirt in months. He's going to love being in there.

Damiano unpacks the duffel of my plants, lining them up on a worktable that has a sink and some large bins under it, a shelf filled with empty pots.

I walk around his jungle, peeking at him through large, thick leaves. "Are you a botanist or something?" This is the last hobby I would have guessed for a so-called mafia killing machine.

Oh my god, isn't bone fertilizer a thing? Does he use body parts to feed his plants? Is that why his look amazing and mine all wither away?

He looks over his shoulder at me, lets out a long breath. "The plants were all my mamma's. I took them when she went into hospice." He reaches for the leaf on a nearby orchid, gently squeezes it between his fingers. "Near the end, she wasn't worried about dying. Just about her plants, what would happen to them." He takes a long breath, lets it out slow. "I promised to take care of them forever. She passed two days later." He does the sign of the cross, kisses his fingers, and holds them up to the sky for a second.

I have to look away. "She had a really green thumb."

"No, actually," he quietly laughs. "She didn't. She loved plants, always had room for one more. But she overwatered some, gave full sun to shade plants, shade to ones that needed more light. She didn't know what the fuck she was doing most of the time. But she loved taking care of them while they lasted."

My black-thumbed soulmate. I can never get the formula quite right for how much to water, when to re-pot. "They look amazing." I duck under the huge leaf of a banana plant. These plants are seriously thriving. I lean in and sniff a pretty flowering one that's on a stand by itself. "And they smell even better."

"That one's a vanilla orchid. Each flower lasts only one day. Then another one sprouts a while later. You have to be patient with that one."

Damiano unzips his sweat jacket, tosses it on a chair. Shirtless, he's some sort of chiseled god of fauna. He dumps one of my spider plants out of its bright yellow pot onto his workspace. "See this?" He points to the tight ball of roots. "This one's been needing a bigger pot for a while. The roots were suffocating, all packed in there like this." Without being particularly careful, he pries the root ball apart. "Could even split this into two plants if you want."

I'm sort of listening to what he's saying and sort of getting lost in the rippling muscles on his back. The deep indentation along his spine. How tall he is and how much broader his shoulders are than his waist. I had days of enjoying the front of him while he was on the couch. This is my first chance to really soak in the view of him standing and from behind.

He grabs a terracotta pot from the shelf, scoops in some gravel, then some soil from the bins built into the table, then puts my little plant in. He's still talking, something about proper drainage and aeration, fertilizer.

I'm nodding my head like I'm paying attention, but I'm not. I'm entirely focused on how low his sweatpants are sitting. How one little tug and they'd be down around his ankles. How—

I touched his dick.

While I thought he was in a coma, I touched his dick. Then told Gina all about it.

And I put his hand on my boob.

He was probably wide awake for all of that.

Should I apologize? I definitely need to apologize.

I cover my face with my hands. I am absolutely mortified.

Damiano walks my newly potted plant over to his wall of windows. "I've been wanting to do that this whole time. I'll get to the rest of them later. That one couldn't wait." He goes into his open kitchen and rinses his hands. "You hungry or want a drink?"

I shake my head, which is still buried in my hands. I probably should be hungry by now, but I'm too overwhelmed to feel it. Plus my brain is still hyped up from SUVs chasing us and my body's still all tense from in my apartment when Dom made me almost combust.

And my bra is *still* suffocating me. I forgot all about it with *the actual car chase I was in*, but now we're here and Damiano is acting like everything is perfectly fine and perfectly normal, so fine and normal that he's... gardening.

Somehow, the man looks completely comfortable, completely casual, leaning against the edge of the table. Like he wasn't shot a few days ago. Like he didn't shoot a bunch of guys. Like *he wasn't in an actual car chase.* Just standing there shirtless, with the thin fabric of his pants showing the outline of his big dick that I touched while I thought he was passed out. I almost can't look at him.

Except I can't take my eyes away from him either. His dark happy trail is like a neon sign, drawing me in and pointing straight to where I'm trying *but failing* to look away from.

Part of me wants to step into his arms and have him hold me, and other parts of me want to run into another room, locking the door behind me.

Damiano makes a clicking sound with his mouth, drawing my attention up from his abs. But apparently, the clicking wasn't for me. *Romeo* races to him, skidding to a stop at his feet. Holy shit, that three-legged rabbit can move fast. I've never seen him move like that.

Damiano scoops him up, holds him against his bare chest with one hand, petting him with the other. Romeo's back legs flop down on either side of Damiano's arm, like that's his designated nap spot. Like the two of them have this all worked out.

Do rabbits purr? I swear I hear Romeo purring.

And give me a fricking break. First off, screw you, Romeo. That rabbit has never come to me once. It's why Tango gets to roam around on the floor in the evenings but Romeo doesn't. When I tried to let him, he just hid under the couch, and it was impossible to get him out. Last time, I had to nudge him out with the Swiffer handle.

And second, now Damiano looks even hotter. Holding a stupid fluffy bunny in his big arms, wicked smile on his face. Rippling abs still beckoning. Come on, cruel world, give us mere mortals a break.

And now my nips are getting all hard and achy. I huff out loud and cross my arms. I know we need to talk about everything that happened and that's still happening—like, is my apartment being ransacked right now?—but I have got to take this bra off before I pass out.

"Do you have a shirt I can change into?" Being braless in the fitted blouse I wore to work, to the job I'm probably fired from, is going to put the girls on total display.

Damiano tilts his head to the side slightly, staring at my boobs. I'm sure he can see the girls standing at full attention since I'm either blessed or cursed—depending on the situation—with big nipples that are almost impossible to hide. "No, I don't think I do."

I let out a heavy breath. "Are you serious? In this *entire* apartment, you don't have a single shirt I can borrow?"

"Borrow? No." He walks over to a corner filled with plants and puts Romeo down on the floor. "Trade?" He nods his head, looking me up and down, biting the side of his lip.

Given that he ruined my green scrubs with all his blood and dragged me away from my apartment, I kind of feel like he owes me some new clothes, but I don't want to make a whole thing about it if he won't even lend me a shirt. "Sure. Let's trade shirts. Not sure this one will fit you, but whatever floats your boat."

"That's my shirt now?" He motions with his chin.

"Uh, after you give me one of yours."

Damiano disappears into what I assume is his bedroom and comes back with a perfectly folded white tee shirt. He places it on the table on the far side of the room.

I walk over to grab it, but he steps in front of me. We're toe to toe.

One of his big hands lands on my hip and squeezes, sending tingles up my spine. "I'm going to need my new shirt first." His other hand tugs at my collar. "Right now, angel."

"Yeah, I'll go change." I try to step away, but his grip tightens. Electricity jolts to my core.

Dom throws me a chin lift. "Be a good girl and give it to me right here."

I know he's making a move and doesn't actually want my shirt, but I also know this is a bad idea. He lied to me. He used me. He doesn't really need me. He might kill people.

But there's also the parts that make this a really, really good idea. Like his lips and his hands and his hypnotizing accent and his abs and that happy trail I want to tug at with my lips. And the thick bulge pressing against my belly. And how *close* he got me before.

And the way he calls me 'angel,' like I really did rescue him.

All those parts make this a fantastic idea. "I want to give you this shirt."

"Yeah?" His hand slides up my waist, one of his thumbs rubbing even higher. My achy nipples are practically pulsing. "You shaking from the car chase?"

"No."

"Then why?"

"I think," I swallow hard, "because of you?"

The left side of his mouth rises in a half-smile. Dom leans in, buries his nose in my hair. He inhales deeply, then he pulls back and looks deep in my eyes. "Are you afraid of me?"

"Should I be?" I bite my lip.

"Naah, angel. Being here with me," he brushes my hair out of my eyes, tucks it behind my ear, "is the safest place on the planet."

"Okay."

He laughs. "Okay? Okay what?"

I shrug. "I didn't know what to say to what you said. So I just said 'okay.'"

"When you're with me, say whatever's on your mind."

"Okay."

"Okay?" Dom laughs. "What's on your mind right now?"

"Right now?" I look up at his eyes, down to his wet lips. "Main thing on my mind right now is taking my bra off."

He groans low and deep. "That's on my mind too, baby." Damiano nuzzles his face into my hair, nipping at my neck, inhaling. Pulling me fully against him.

"I'm being serious. It's making it hard to breathe."

"Hmm? I can take a look. All that medical training. Let's put that to good use." He bites my neck.

I think he's suggesting going down on me again. Either that, or he really wants to check on my breathing, but I'm pretty sure it's my clit.

"The shirt's mine, yes?"

I nod. Barely. The talking part of my brain has completely disengaged, too distracted by how I'm about to get to touch his insane body *while he's awake and touching me back*. Too distracted by his hands and his mouth on me. Too distracted by the actual possibility that a guy might make me explode without me doing the handiwork. Too distracted by—

Dom pulls *a huge frickin' knife* from his pocket.

Holy shit. I try to pull away. "Why do you have a machete?"

"Relax," Damiano's grip on my hip tightens, he nuzzles against my temple. "It's just a knife. I told you you're safe with me, angel. Always. My new shirt, however, is in grave danger."

Damiano slides the tip of the knife under one of the buttons on my blouse. A swift flick of his wrist and the button flies across the room, pinging against the tile floor.

Romeo scurries after it like a dog chasing a ball.

I tip my head back. Damiano dives right in and bites my neck again. He's not being shy. He's not being gentle. "You taste like fucking heaven."

He leans back, looking down at the knife, a half-smile on his face. "Have I mentioned how much I hate my new shirt?"

Another button pings against the floor, cool air tickling my belly.

He's going so damn slow I'm going to lose my mind. His rough fingers ghost my tummy, barely touching. Completely teasing, lighting tiny fires inside me. Maybe he really does torture people for a living because this is killing me.

I can't take it anymore. My insides are all twisted and tingly and needy. "I hate this shirt, too." I grab the plackets with both hands and rip the shirt the rest of the damn way open.

Dom sucks in a quick breath, slowly smiles. He slides my shirt back, off my shoulders, letting out a long, slow breath. "But I love this bra. For fuck's sake, angel. Look at you. Capolavoro." The back of his finger rubs up and down my tummy.

He may like the look of this tiny push-up bra, but I need it off. With or without his help, it's got to go. I reach for his hand—the one holding his scary frickin' knife—and hook it under the fabric between the girls. The fabric is already pulled taut because this damn thing is too small. A slight yank on his wrist slices right through, the cups springing apart in opposite directions.

"Fucking hell, Paige." He sounds desperate as he tosses his knife onto the couch with a dull thud. He cups underneath each of the girls then stares at them. "Potrei guardarti tutto il giorno."

I'm panting and can barely get the words out, "What does that mean?"

His eyes meet mine for a second before they go back to my tits. "That I could look at you all day."

"Oh." I like that. But maybe there's been enough looking? Maybe it's time for more touching? I reach up and trace the lines of Damiano's flag tattoo with one finger.

Dom moves one hand, resting it between the girls. He strums his fingers. Slowly.

His other hand reaches down and traces the tiny dolphin tattoo on my hip bone, barely touching me again. He slides his hand onto my hip, gripping tight and pulling my lower half against his, pulling me against his thick bulge.

Sparks sizzle and spiral inside me like fireworks that want to explode out of my nipples. I push my hips against him.

Damiano licks his lips. I've never kissed a guy with this much scruff before. I lean in toward his lips.

But he cups my cheeks, then pushes his hands into my hair, grabbing hold, pulling my head at an angle, exposing my neck. "Banchetterò con ogni centimetro di te."

"Tell me."

"I'm going to feast on every inch of you."

"Yeah. That's a good idea."

He sucks on my neck. One hand tangles into my hair, holding my head while the other lightly traces up and down my side.

I wrap my arms around his neck, one stroking his velvety hair. Dom leans down and sucks my nipple into his mouth, circling it with his tongue. Biting.

I moan surprisingly loud. I never moan. I cover my mouth with one of my hands.

Dom comes back up to my face, gripping both sides, pushing my hand away. He looks deep into my eyes, his nostrils flaring as he exhales. "You're going to let me hear everything, yes? Promise me."

I nod.

"No, angel. Say it so I can hear it."

"I promise."

Damiano picks me up and throws me over his good shoulder. One hand holds my calf and the other squeezes my ass. He struts into the bedroom like carrying me is no big deal.

It is definitely a big deal.

He flops me onto his huge bed, managing to pull off my pants and panties in one smooth motion, then crawls halfway up the bed, stopping when his head is tit-level. Big, warm hands cup my boobs, his thumbs rubbing over my hard nips. "These nipples."

I arch my back, pushing the girls closer to him as I wrap my legs around Dom's thigh.

"I could spend forever right here, angel." Dom sucks one nipple into his mouth, then blows on it. Again on the other side. He goes back and forth, sucking and licking and blowing cool air that's setting me on fire.

I reach down and push the girls together, hoping he takes the hint.

He hums his approval, then laps at both nips at the same time. Biting, sucking, blowing. My eyes roll to the back of my head.

Dom reaches up toward the top of the bed and grabs a pillow, stuffs it under his head like he's planning to camp out at my tits for a while. My ex would spend *maybe* ten seconds at my tits, like it was something to check off on the to-do list before getting himself off. But Dom isn't showing any signs of moving on, which is good because he's setting me on fire *down there*.

His hands and mouth are on the girls, but I swear something is building up deeper inside me. I'm squirming, but not pulling away. I'm panting, but definitely not asking him to stop or slow down. I want his fingers back down on my clit, but I don't want them to stop what they're doing.

I dry hump his thigh for the friction, pumping my hips against him, chasing it.

Dom laughs quietly. "Such a greedy girl. You need more?"

I nod. It's the highest form of communication I can manage while he's sucking one nipple and twirling the other and speaking in that voice with that accent.

Dom scrapes his fingers down my tummy, his short nails searing a path, while the other hand keeps tuning my nipple to perfection. He teases along my thigh, squeezes my ass. His fingers get closer and closer to where I need them but stop short and change direction.

My head is thrashing back and forth, I'm gripping the sheets like I might fall out of the bed, and I may even be panting like a dog, but I do not care. I am seconds away from exploding *from someone else touching me.*

"I swear if you stop this time to answer your phone or to do absolutely anything else right now, I will literally kill you."

Dom pulls away from my nip with a *pop.* "Oh, you're the killer now?"

I pull his head back to my nipple. "Yes. You stop and you're a dead man."

He finally moves his fingers to my clit, lightly rubs a circle with his thumb, slides two fingers inside me.

And just like that, my whole body stiffens like a board while my insides spasm and quiver. I moan loud enough to wake the dead.

"Fuck, angel. I can feel you coming. Feel you squeezing me."

After a few seconds, I relax into the mattress, like a pile of mush. "Wow."

Dom slides his pants down, tosses them across the room. "The next time you come, I want this pretty pussy choking my cock. Think you have another one in you?"

"Honestly?" I pause to catch my breath. "I didn't know I had *that one* in me. So if you think you can find another one where you found *that* first one? By all means, Christopher Columbus, go for it."

He smiles and strokes up and down his thick shaft.

"Or wait, Columbus was Spanish. Who's an Italian explorer?"

Dom reaches for my hand, places it on his dick, and guides it up and down his shaft. "Cristoforo Colombo was Italiano."

"No, he was Spanish."

"No." Dom pulls me by my hips so his naked body is spooning my naked body. His rock-hard, steaming-hot dick presses against my back.

"Uh... pretty sure he was."

He tugs on my earlobe with his teeth. "No, angel."

"Just tell me another Italian explorer's name to use instead."

Dom slides his dick between my legs, starts rubbing against my kitty from behind, his warm breath huffing on my neck. "Another Italian explorer? Marco Polo."

"No, a real person."

"What?"

"That's not an actual person."

Dom's rubbing the tip of his cock against me faster and faster. The wet slapping sounds would be vulgar if it didn't feel so good.

"Marco Polo was an actual person."

"No, I don't think so."

"Marco Polo was the—"

"Maybe save the history lesson later and give me something else right now?" I reach behind me and grab his ass, pulling him closer.

"Oh, angel. Demolirò la tua graziosa fica e poi la bacerò meglio ancora e ancora."

I look over my shoulder at him, questioning, waiting for the translation.

He smiles, a perfectly wicked smile.

"You're not going to tell me that one, are you?"

He shakes his head. "No, I'm going to show you." He lines his fat head up with me.

Dom wraps his arms around me, one diagonally across my chest, the other around my arms. He kisses the back of my neck as he thrusts into me all the way on the first go. Every inch of him grinds into me. Pleasure swirls around inside me, and he hasn't even started moving yet. It's like every nerve ending in my body has abandoned its normal post and is zooming through me to get to my little kitty.

"Fuck, angel. You feel incredible."

He pulls halfway out then thrusts back in. Even with his big dick, I'm so wet for him that it's all good. It's all very good. Dom's warm breath puffs into my ear with each thrust, one hand pinches my nipple.

He picks up speed and reaches around to my clit. I'm sensitive there right now, but given what he's already made my body do, I'm just going to lie back and enjoy the ride. Let him do whatever he wants because holy hell, I'm moaning and groaning and I might have even screamed out his name at one point.

"That's it, angel. Let me hear you." Dom pulls my hips back and pushes my shoulders forward to adjust our angle. "Look at how good you take me."

I look over my shoulder at him. He's staring down at where we connect. His mouth is dropped open, his upper lip snarled. His face and neck are flushed red. He's an absolute masterpiece.

He sucks his thumb into his mouth, wetting it. He glances up and catches me watching him. A half-smile appears on his face. He holds eye contact as he reaches his wet thumb down and slides it into my ass.

I close my eyes as pleasure and weirdness twist through me. I am literally drooling on his pillow.

Dom's thrusts are getting erratic. Deep, shallow, deep again. And his breathing is picking up. He's getting close.

"I'm going to come so hard for you, angel. Così fucking forte." He rubs my clit in tiny circles again. "But not until you go again first. Come for me like a good girl."

With his thumb probing in the opposite rhythm of his cock, turning me inside out, and his other hand on my clit tugging me toward the finish line, plus his breathy whispers in my ear—yeah, I can do that. "I think I can c—" *Oh oh oh oh oh.*

All the air huffs out of my lungs as my orgasm slams into me, ricocheting through my insides. Every part of me stiffens and shakes at the same time.

Dom grabs my hips with both hands, holding me in place while he drives into me. Indecipherable sounds grunt out as he rams his way to the finish. It's a jumble of English and Italian, and I have no clue what any of it means.

His body goes stiff with one final groan. Then he squeezes my hips once, flops onto his back. The cool air tingles against my sweaty back now that he's not pressing against it. His breathing starts to even out.

Do I cuddle against him now? Are we, like, together and so now we cuddle?

Or do I ask if there's a guestroom I should go sleep in tonight?

Or I could go to the bathroom and hide there for a little while.

"Paige?"

I'll never get sick of hearing my name with his heavy accent. I get giddy when he calls me angel, but when he says Paige like that...

"You still with me?" His hand lands on my ass and squeezes.

"Barely. I think you launched me into another dimension for a few minutes there."

"Come back to my dimension." He pulls me toward him. He starts stroking my hair exactly the way he was petting Romeo. "Give me five minutes. Then I can go looking for number three if you're up for it."

"As tempting as that sounds, I need a nap then food."

"Probably a shower, too."

Oh my god, do I smell? I pull away.

"Get back here. You smell like me. You smell perfect."

Paige

DAMIANO AND I ARE standing at his sink, both facing the mirror. I love how much taller he is than me, how he looks now that he shaved and I can see his whole face.

"Do you have an extra toothbrush?"

He opens a drawer and looks inside, shuts it. Checks another drawer. "No. Use mine. We'll go get you whatever you need in the morning." He reaches around me for his toothbrush, his warm arm wrapping around me. He squeezes toothpaste from a metal tube, some Italian brand I've never heard of, then hands it to me.

"I can't use your toothbrush."

"Why not?" He shrugs his shoulders in the mirror.

"I don't know. Germs?"

"Angel." Damiano puts his hands right above my hip and pulls me back against him. He nuzzles into my hair. "I was inside you. Many different parts of me were in many different parts of you. You can use my toothbrush." He moves my hair over my left shoulder and kisses my neck. The man is obsessed with my neck.

"Not all the parts of you were in all the parts of me." I nudge him with my shoulder.

He freezes, looks at me in the mirror, his mouth open. "Is back here an option already?" He reaches down and squeezes my ass cheek. "Fuck, angel. I figured it was too soon. But if you're into it, we can—"

I roll my eyes. "I didn't mean that your *monster dick* hadn't been up my *butt*, you perv. I meant that your *tongue* hadn't been in my *mouth*. You haven't kissed me."

He's struck silent. He's still looking at me in the mirror, but his sly smile is gone, his brow furrowed.

Did he not realize we hadn't kissed? Or did he think I'd be okay with that?

"I..." He stands up straight. "I don't... We can't..."

He's adorably confused right now.

I'll give him a minute to figure this out. I pick up his toothbrush and use it. Is this *lavender*-flavored toothpaste? Bizarre, but oh-so-delicious.

I spit into the sink as neatly as I can. My ass rubs against him when I bend over. He's still trying to figure out what to say. Mister In-Control is so befuddled right now, I kind of love it.

Either that or he's super distracted by the thought of some ass play.

"Would you look at that? The big bad mafia killing machine is speechless." I turn to face him. "Rabbit got your tongue?"

He's searching my eyes. What is he looking for? "Paige, I don't kiss. I—"

"Shh." I put my finger on his lips. I'm not open for excuses today, not after he just turned my life completely upside down. "Here's how this part is going to go. Put your hands back on my hips."

He opens his mouth like he's going to object, but I tilt my head, giving him a stern look, or at least my best attempt at one.

His big hands slowly wrap around my waist. I melt into his touch.

"See, big guy? That's not so bad. You follow all my directions, and *you* might even earn a reward."

His head falls back, his eyes close. Something like a groan comes from deep in his throat. "Is it anal?"

"Oh my god, stop." I laugh as I wrap my arms around his neck, run my nails through his velvety short hair.

He leans into my hand, like when you scratch a dog's ear just right.

"Now, I'm going to kiss you, and you're going to kiss me back."

"Angel, I don't—"

"Damiano." I shake my head, then lean forward. Our lips are as close to touching as they can be without actually touching. We're breathing each other's air.

I place one light peck on his lips. He doesn't freak out or push me away. I grab his bottom lip with my teeth, tugging at it lightly before letting go.

He squeezes my hips hard, his fingers digging in.

I reach down for his left hand, slide it up from my hip to my boob, lacing my fingers onto his and making them squeeze my hard nip. "There, one little peck, and you already earned yourself second base."

Dom stares at me. He's struggling with what to do here.

I lean in and kiss him again. More than a peck this time. He lets me kiss him for a full minute, but still isn't kissing me back. He's definitely undecided about this, but he didn't pull away.

I pull back, bite my lip. "Good boy."

He stares at me a few seconds, then looks away. "Did you just 'good boy' me?"

I nod.

"Huh."

"Did you like it?"

Dom runs his thumb across my lips, pushing firmly in the middle. He tugs it toward him, then lets go. He nods slowly. "Fuck it. Get over here." He yanks me up against him and dives into my mouth.

His lips are on mine. His tongue searches for mine. It's all grunts and heavy breaths and fingers gripping my ass.

I could live right here forever.

Dom's hand slides down past my ass, hitches my right leg up against him. I wrap my other leg around him too. His hard dick presses directly against my clit like this.

He turns us and walks us toward his bed, carrying me like I don't weigh a thing.

"You ready for your reward?"

He shakes his head. "Nope. More of this."

Damiano

NAVY ELITE FORCES TRAINED me to be a light sleeper. It can be the difference between someone sneaking up on you or you slicing their throat first.

So even though it's two in the morning, of course I hear Paige's bare feet padding across the hardwood floor to come find me on the living room couch.

"How come you're up?" I ask.

She startles, covering her tits with one arm. My angel came to find me in only her tiny panties. Fantasy girl. "I rolled over, and you were gone."

I have a strict no-sleepover policy, as in, I've never slept over at a girl's place or fallen asleep with a girl in one of the spare bedrooms in Rob's loft. I've never even had a girl in my apartment before today.

No sleepovers, no cuddling after. Until a few hours ago, no kissing. Affection while we're banging, sure. I've been known to worship a woman for hours. But not after. The Cat girls all seem to understand this without me ever having to explain my boundaries.

But Paige isn't a Cat girl and I can't tell her any of that, especially since the no-sleepover policy extends to her too. But I also can't ask her to leave since her apartment isn't safe, and that's entirely on me.

So I left her in my bed to come crash on the couch.

For her own good.

If I let her get too close to me, she becomes a target for anyone out there looking to get at me. Back in GOI, the quickest way to get someone to talk wasn't to hurt *them*, it was hurting a loved one. Just the threat of hurting a loved one was usually enough. Shitty as fuck, but effective as hell.

And the Bagliateris' enforcer, Massimo, trains his guys the exact same way. Non mostrare pietà. *Show no mercy.*

I've dragged Paige deep enough into this mess by asking for her help that first night in the park. I've put a bullseye on her already, but it would be ten times bigger if the Bagliateris thought I cared about her. So I need to keep my distance. I owe her that much.

But I can't tell her any of that. Especially after she barged through my no-kissing barrier. Which I fucking loved. I loved how she tasted and I loved how she demanded I give her exactly what she wanted. I loved how soaking wet it made her.

She sits on the edge of the couch, waiting for my answer. Soft light from the kitchen glows behind her like a halo.

"My shoulder hurt in the bed. Thought I'd try the couch."

"Your shoulder wasn't bothering you all day."

I shrug. I can't tell if she's trying to call my bluff. "Maybe it was all that exertion?" I motion toward the bedroom.

She smiles at me, then looks away all shy. She liked all that exertion.

"I can give you a massage. Turn." She tugs at the blanket and pushes my legs aside before I can answer. She rubs her hands together to warm them up, her gorgeous naked tits jiggling side to side. I mean, no way I'm saying no to having her hands on me.

And I'm pretty sure she's offering me a massage because making *me* feel good makes *her* feel good, which right now makes me feel like shit about leaving the bed in the first place. But a topless goddess offering to rub me all over is not something I possess the strength or will to decline.

I sit up and turn so she's behind me. It's not a position I love. I prefer to have my back to the wall, no one behind me. Even more so since Paulie fucking shot me. But I quickly ease into perfect comfort with Paige there, her familiar hands on me.

"This looks really good." She taps next to the wound on the back of my shoulder.

After dinner, I walked her through how to remove the stitches on my back and had her apply a clear Tegaderm dressing. Same on my side. Much more comfortable than the bulky gauze bandages. Plus, the clear dressing means we can keep an eye out for infection without having to change the dressing.

She digs a knuckle into my deltoid.

Oh, fuck yeah. I grunt.

She giggles. "Did you grow up in Italy?"

I nod. "Roma."

"Is that Rome?"

"Sì."

"What brought you here?"

"My mamma grew up in Chicago, but then she fell for my dad on one of his trips here. She followed him back to Rome, then they had me. We came here every summer to visit my nonna. I loved it here."

She digs her elbow in. "Lay flat, then tell me more."

We shift positions so I'm on my stomach and she's straddling my hips. Her warm thighs press against my sides, my growing hard-on pressing into the couch cushions.

"Nonna died when I was fourteen. Mamma didn't want to come back to the States after that. But I kept coming anyway. My boss, Rob, his mom took me in those summers. I lived in their house, ate her cooking. She grew up in Italy, so it felt like home away from home."

Paige presses her thumbs into my left shoulder just right.

"Then I'd go back to Rome for the school year. By then, I was training under my dad. He had the same job I have now, but in Italy working for Rob's uncle."

"Is enforcer what you wanted to be when you were little?"

"Always."

"Living the dream. Wait. If your mom was living in Italy when she passed, how did you get all her plants here?"

"Rob chartered a private jet. That's not as big of a deal as it sounds though. Whenever there's a big group of us coming or going, he charters one."

"Was there a big group for that trip?"

"No. Just Rob and Salvo and me."

"My boss—if I still have one, I've probably been fired for not going back to work after lunch—is not chartering me any planes. She barely approves my Uber reimbursements when I work late."

"Rob and Salvo flew out to pay respects, but I think they mostly flew out to make sure I'd come back to the States with them and not stay in Rome."

"Did you want to stay?" Paige runs her fingernails up and down my back. I may never want to get up, not if it means moving away from her magical hands.

I'd shrug my shoulders but can't the way I'm lying. "Rob's uncle is the capo dei capi—that's the boss of all the bosses of all the Famiglie around the world. He wanted me to stay in Rome and work for him."

"But you didn't."

"I thought about it. But things in Rome had been calm for years, and things here were a complete mess back then. The families were fighting a shit ton. Famiglia business was spilling into the streets, and civilians were getting hurt. Rob's dad—and therefore Rob—needed more muscle on their side. I'd just finished my second tour with the GOI. It was good timing for a change of scenery. So I got on the plane."

"I'm a Navy brat. Have I told you that? My dad's an Airedale and my brother's a frogman."

It's cute that she's using military slang. "Yes, I knew you were a brat. Lift up a second?" I turn over under her so now she's straddling my stomach. Much better view this way.

Those fucking nipples. Mozzafiato. *Breathtaking.*

I grab her hands and lay them on my chest. "Keep rubbing. Are they still enlisted?"

She starts kneading my shoulders, which means she's leaning down over me with the tips of her long hair ghosting across my chest.

"They're both lifers. My dad oversees SFTI training back home in San Diego, and Brian does tactical instruction here at Great Lakes. He's why I moved to Chicago."

"Are you two close?"

She nods. "We moved around a lot as kids because of my dad. That meant changing friends all the time. We ended up pretty close because of it, even though he's four years older. He's my rock."

"Do you like Chicago?" I run the back of my finger up from her hip, along her side, tracing around her gorgeous tit, then back down. I circle the dolphin tattoo right above her panty line.

"I like it enough. But I miss the beach, and I don't like the cold. I hate that part actually. No matter how many layers I put on, it's never enough."

"Same for me. Winters in Rome are like late Spring here. I only saw snow twice there in my entire life, and it lasted less than a day both times." Rob and Salvo still give me shit for wearing a puffy coat, gloves, hat, and a scarf on cold days, but fuck them. I hate being cold.

"Twice still has San Diego beat. But I do love the snow here. Just not the cold part."

I move my hands down to her thighs, slightly grind her against me. Pretty sure she can feel my stiffie poking at her back.

"If your *shoulder's* feeling better, we should go to bed?"

"For sleep?"

She shrugs. "We may have some unfinished business."

I squeeze both her ass cheeks and grind her down onto me at the same time. Then I slide one hand into her panties from behind, loving how warm it is in there. Everything about this girl is heat and warmth. "Back here?"

"Oh, you think you've earned that?"

I nod. I do, I really do.

"Yeah? You think just being a tall, dark, and handsome rabbit whisperer," her voice hitches as I rub, "is all it takes to get an all-access pass?"

I mean, that's usually how it works. But I'm always up for a challenge. "You want to make me work for it? Decide if I'm worthy?"

She nods, a wicked gleam in her eye.

I grab her hips, loving the annoyed look she shoots me when my hand leaves her panties. She's light as a feather as I lift her up a few inches.

"Dom, what are you—" Her voice trails off as it becomes crystal fucking clear what I'm doing when I pull her forward then lower her onto my face. "Yeah. Good idea. This, uh... Yeah, okay."

You want convincing, sweet girl? Let's let my tongue do the job.

Damiano

"DID WE REALLY HAVE to come all the way out here for this?"

"I told you—this is the only store in Chicago that sells proper rabbit supplies. Edible hay is hard to get in the city, but the guy that owns this shop orders it special for me."

We're sitting in my Rover parked outside the pet store Paige insisted we come to. She was about to go by herself, and take the L no less, but no fucking way I'm letting her head into Falco Famiglia territory—or anywhere outside of Galliano territory—alone until this shit is worked out and I know she's safe.

I was paranoid as fuck just taking her to the Lululemon in Lake View to buy some clothes, and that's as deep into our territory as it gets. Paige didn't seem to notice me looking over my shoulder the whole time we were there. She was too busy flipping the fuck out over me paying $150 per pair of leggings and $80 each for T-shirts.

But the Christmas-morning look on her face when she carried her two shopping bags out—bags she clutched to her chest like they were a newborn baby when I offered to carry them for her—made them worth every penny.

And dropping $900 on new clothes for her was the least I could do. Plus, I liked taking her shopping and buying her shit. I liked putting that smile on her face.

But now she's torturing me in ass-hugging camo-print leggings and a pink baby tee that shows an inch of her tan tummy. Her silky blonde hair's in two long braids. She's fucking perfection. I didn't want her to leave my bedroom, let alone leave the apartment.

Yet here we are, deep in Falco territory. The Gallianos aren't at war with the Falcos, but they're more aligned with the Bagliateris than with us, so I want to get the fuck out of here as soon as we can.

"We need to be in and out in five minutes. Yes?"

"I'll be quick."

I look down at my wrist to check the time, but realize Paige is still wearing my watch. I haven't asked for it back. I like seeing it on her wrist, seeing her smile whenever she looks down at it.

Given how much she freaked out over the cost of her leggings, I wonder what she'd do if she knew that watch set me back $18K.

"I mean it, Paige. I don't like being in this part of the city." And I especially hate driving into another Famiglia's territory in my Range Rover. On the rare occasions I leave our territory, I usually take my Ducati. My motorcycle stands out just as much as a Galliano-signature hunter green Range Rover, but the maneuverability in traffic can't be beat. Plus it's easier to shoot someone from a bike than from inside a tin box.

We cross the street and enter the pet store. It smells like stale animal piss. Caged birds squawk, drowning out the buzz of some radio talk show. The linoleum tiles are cracked and dirty, the acoustic ceiling tiles are water-stained and yellow. This place is a shithole.

Paige practically skips to an aisle near the back. "Hey, Roger!" she says to the clerk without stopping to talk to him.

"Oh, hey, Paige... Uh... How's it going?" He stands up and leans forward over the counter to watch her ass as she passes. "You need my help with anything today?"

I clear my throat *loudly* to get his attention. "Focus on helping me. What do I need to housetrain a rabbit?"

He looks me up and down, then sits back down onto his stool. He picks up the copy of the *Tribune* he was reading. "Housetrain a rabbit? Just keep it in a cage. Change the lining every few days. It'll be fine."

"Naah, man. I want to let it hop around my place most of the time, don't want to keep a wild creature in a cage."

He shrugs. "You could try a cat litter box. Third aisle."

This kid isn't nearly as interested in helping me as he was in helping Paige. "Thanks."

I head to aisle three. I make eye contact with Paige over the top of the aisle and throw her a wink.

She winks back and tries to hide a smile. Halfway down the aisle, I see her wink at a hamster. God, she's fucking adorable. And waking up with her this morning—waking up finding myself wrapped around her like a fucking python with my arms and legs all pulling her in tight—it woke something up inside of me. Something that feels whole, that feels so fucking good.

I head over to the counter to put the litter box down. Out the front window, I spot two guys eyeing my SUV. One's on his phone, the other's looking around. Definitely Famiglia men, but not my Famiglia.

Adrenaline starts to surge through me, giving me that tingly energy I get when I'm on deck, when I'm about to throw down. When I'm about to conquer.

Seems like they know it's my truck but don't know which store I'm in. That buys me a few minutes.

My senses sharpen, my blood pumps faster, my pulse throbs. My balls pull up tight, into fighter mode. My body reminds me I'm fucking invincible and have one singular focus: obliterate all threats.

These shitheads are within fifty meters of Paige, but I guarantee they're not getting any closer.

I jog-walk back to her. She's still only picked out two things. I step right behind her, pulling her back into me, her ass in these worth-every-penny leggings rubbing against me.

She sighs, then hugs my arms without dropping her items. "I know you said to hurry. I'm trying to. I am."

"Change of plans, angel. Take all the time you need." I kiss her neck. She tastes like my shampoo, but a Paige-flavored version. "I'm going to make a phone call outside. You stay in the store so I don't lose you, yes?"

"Yes, boss. But be quick, I hear we're in a hurry."

One more nibble on her neck, moving her sexy-as-fuck braid out of the way. I walk toward the front of the store, adjusting my dick that just woke up to say hi to our girl.

"Hey, man." I lean on the counter and speak quietly to the clerk. "Paige's very recent ex is outside. The dickhead won't leave her alone. I'm going to go have a little *talk* with him. You think you can keep her in the store while I'm gone? If she heads toward the door, tell her she forgot something and send her to the back to look for it, yes?"

"Yeah, man. I'll keep Paige busy." He nods his head slowly like a fucking creep.

My fists tighten with the urge to rupture his windpipe. *He's just a college kid with a crush.* She didn't pay any attention to him when we got here, and there's an actual threat outside. *Let it go, man. Let it go.* Deal with the actual problem outside first.

I leave the store. I took note of the alley one storefront away when we arrived. That'll be a decent place to dance with these fuckers. I pull the hood of my jacket on, then wolf-whistle to get their attention as I tuck into the alley.

By the time they cross the street, I'm a few feet into the alley, leaning against the wall. Even at midday, the tall buildings on either side cast shadows, leaving it dark in here.

"You call for backup?" I ask, giving away my location.

Their heads jerk in my direction. "We don't need back-up, asshole," the shorter one tells me, spitting on the ground.

The taller one points a 9mm at me.

I have my Glock, but the thing is loud as fuck. Not ideal for 11:00 a.m. with a decent amount of foot traffic in the area. Bianca, though, she's a quiet girl. Barely whispers on the thrust in, the softest gurgle on the way out.

I push off the wall. "You're here to kill me?"

He nods.

"Then you're going to need backup. Go ahead, give them a call. I'll wait."

They look at each other, giving me the opening to lunge at the one with his gun out. One clean punch to his throat with my fist wrapped around Bianca's handle, making it a punch with the equivalent of brass knuckles on.

He's done.

The second one takes a step backward, turns to run. *Pussy.*

I grab a handful of his hair, jam Bianca's blade up against his throat. "How long until your backup arrives?"

"We didn't... call for... any."

"Fuck you. Of course you did. How long till they're here?"

I can feel him swallow hard. He's either stubborn or stalling. I don't have time for either. The last thing I need is Paige to come looking for me and see me kill someone.

Scratch that. The absolute last thing I need is for their backup to arrive and head into the pet store while I'm in this alley waiting for this prick to piss his pants.

I step my body back away from him, holding him at arm's length as I plunge Bianca into his neck. I push him away from me as I pull her out so that none of his blood sprays me.

He hits the ground twitching.

I wipe Bianca off on the first guy's shirt, also checking that he wasn't just passed out.

I pull the guy's wallet from his pocket. Address on his driver's license is only three blocks from here. *Fuck*, I was hoping these were Bagliateri guys that somehow wandered into Falco territory, but so much for that. Rob's going to be pissed as fuck I took out two Falco guys, but they started it.

I grab the guy's phone, then take a quick video of his face with my phone. I'll email the video to Renatta with a note asking her to drop that into the 3D modeling software she created for me so I can get into guys' phones even after their faces are no longer available. Most facial recognition software stops recognizing people pretty quick after they find themselves in my workshop. And they never just tell me their codes the easy way. Renatta took all of twenty minutes to create the perfect software solution for me.

And thank god phones switched over to face recognition. Salvo thought it was hilarious this one time to switch around all the fingers and phones I had paired together, and it took me an hour to get them all matched up again.

Normally, I'd do some amount of clean up even in an alley, at least spend time checking for cameras and shit, but not with Paige all alone in the store. I throw two middle fingers up in the air in case there are any cameras, then head back inside.

"You got a sink?" I ask the pet store clerk. There isn't much blood on my hands, but I'm not touching Paige until I've scrubbed them.

"Bathroom's in the back. Turn left at the fish tanks."

I pass Paige, still picking items out.

Her arms are completely full, and she's trying to grab something else. "There you are." She throws me a huge smile framed by her messy braids, the light streaming in the window behind her making her glow.

I freeze mid-step. The glimmer in her eyes knocks me on my ass. It leaves me speechless, powerless. This girl is my kryptonite. It takes me a long second to make sounds come out. "You get everything you need?"

"Almost. Just one more thing. Can you grab some of this?" She pushes her armful of stuff toward me.

"Yeah. Give me a sec." I hold up my non-bloody right hand, "I picked up one of the hamsters and it took a piss on me. I'll be right back. Then we need to go."

She bites her lip and nods, but I'm pretty sure she's going to keep shopping until she's done shopping no matter how much I rush her.

I'm back forty-five seconds later and, as expected, she hasn't moved toward the register.

Which is actually good because I look toward the front of the store and see what I assume are the backup guys the first two called crossing the street. Heading right for the pet store.

"Did you see the fish tanks in the back?" I ask Paige. "I've always thought about getting some fish. Go see if you like any of them."

"*You* want a fish? You don't seem like the fish type."

"No?" I put my hands on her waist, gripping her warm skin and nudging her toward the back as I squeeze past her to get to the front of the store. "Not like a goldfish, but maybe one of the fighting ones?"

"*Ooooh.* You mean the ones that are really pretty but like to be completely alone and are vicious as hell when another one gets too close? That actually sounds about right for you."

"Angel, you call me 'pretty' and 'vicious' in the same sentence, and I may take you here and now." I tug on her braid with one hand, slide my other hand up her side, rubbing the outside of her perfect right tit knowing that with her hands full of pet supplies she can't do much to stop me.

She leans into my hand slightly and giggles. "I'll go pick a betta for you. You take some of this up to the register."

She dumps all her crap into my arms, then I watch her pert ass as she walks away. Is that in play, or is it off limits? She was teasing me with it last night, but didn't actually say yes or no. Please let it be in play. We can work our way up to it. I can be a patient man.

Paige turns into the dark hallway near the bathroom. It's illuminated only by the lights from the fish tanks. With her out of sight, I adjust my dick, shake my head to refocus, then move to the front of store.

I drop all her supplies on the counter and lean in toward the clerk. "Keep Paige by the fish tanks until I come get her." I pull my money clip from my pocket and toss it to him.

"Huh?"

"Go to her *now* and keep her back there. And keep your mouth fucking closed."

He watches me pull Bianca from my belt clip, then knocks over his stool as he scrambles toward the back of the store.

I tuck behind a rack near the front door. The birds screech and squawk even louder with me here, but nothing I can do about that.

The tiny bell over the door jingles as it opens and again as the door closes.

It's the last sound the first guy hears, unless his brain had time to register the sound of Bianca puncturing his jugular and blood spurting out.

"Give me a minute," I whisper to the second guy as I drag the first guy's jerking body down an aisle so Paige won't see him.

"I'm not *waiting* for you to be ready for me to hit you."

"Professional courtesy, man. Come on." I dump the first guy in the corner, step over him and move toward the second guy.

"Fuck you, Damiano." He pulls a billy club from his jacket, snapping his wrist out and down so it telescopes out. Those things hurt like hell. I really don't want to be hit with that. A solid whack from one can break a bone, easy.

"You hit me with *that*, I'll kill you so fucking slow your teeth will have time to rot. Let's go bare hands."

"Fuck you. I am definitely hitting you with this."

So be it. The aisles in here are pretty narrow. He won't have much room to swing, won't get much momentum. Another advantage of my beautiful Bianca—she's the in-and-out type, not the big swinging type.

"Hey, Dom?" Paige yells from the back of the store. "What color do you want? You get to pick. They have, like, every color."

I turn to answer. "Gree—"

My head snaps back from this asshole striking me in the jaw.

Fuuuuck.

Fuck. When was the last time I got blindsided by someone standing right in front of my fucking face?

Never. The answer is fucking never.

I shake my head to reset. Then I glare at the motherfucker while I answer Paige. "Green, white, or red. Those are always my color choices, in that order." Good old il Tricolore.

"They have red. But this blue one is really cute," she shouts.

"Whatever you pick will be perfect."

"*Whatever you pick will be perfect,*" the guy mocks in a girly voice. "No one told me the Galliano enforcer was a big fat pussy."

"Yeah? How's it going to feel to get fucked by a big fat pussy?"

The prick swings his club at me again but doesn't get much power behind it. I let him connect, knowing the momentum will turn his body somewhat to the left. The move exposes a direct path to his aorta, but those bleed like a bitch, spewing all the fuck over the place. Easy target, but at this close distance, I'd take a bath.

Instead, I slash the back of his hand, making him drop the club. I spin him around. Pull up tight against his neck with my forearm to choke him out. The guy fights me, knocking a ton of shit off the shelves, but my grip is solid and this isn't my first rodeo. After twenty seconds of exerting himself while I crush his windpipe, he's done.

If I were alone, I'd leave him passed out and be long gone by the time he comes to. But he came at me with Paige nearby and he was pretty much a dick, so I snap his neck. That's almost impossible to manage on someone who's fighting back, but this guy's passed out, so it's easy.

I drag him to the same aisle as his buddy and kick all the shit he knocked off the shelves into a corner. I send a quick text to one of the guys on my crew about needing a clean up, then turn to head back to Paige.

And just in time too, as Paige and the clerk come walking up to the register. She's carrying a blue fish in a baggie in a little bowl.

The store takes Apple Pay, which is good since I tossed the clerk my wad of cash earlier and no way I'd let Paige pay for anything while we're together. The cat litter box does a pretty good job of holding whatever Paige picked out, so I'm carrying that in one arm and a small bale of hay in the other. Paige is carrying my new betta that she's already named Bravo.

I'm sensing a theme with her pets' names, and I'm fucking into it.

We're almost out of the store, I'm almost about to let out the breath I'm holding in, when Paige freezes in her tracks. "Oh my god. What are they doing there?" She's pointing with my fish to the two guys slumped in a pile at the end of the first aisle.

"Who?" I play dumb.

"Those guys."

"Weren't they here when we got here? Homeless guys taking a nap, maybe?"

"What? No."

"Weren't those guys already there, Roger?" I stare at him so fucking hard his balls are probably shriveling up.

"Uh... Yeah. We're letting homeless guys sleep in here now. Gives them somewhere warm and keeps the animals company."

"Oh, Roger, that's really sweet," Paige whispers as if she doesn't want to wake the 'sleeping' guys.

Roger beams at Paige's praise.

"It's not *that* sweet. Let's go."

Over the past week, Romeo and Tango have fully settled in at Damiano's place. Romeo's made himself completely at home, like this is his forest. And last night, as I watched Tango burrow into the dirt in the big planter, I realized he's ready to be released.

Now, I'm sitting on Damiano's silky carpet, giving Tango his evening kale-and-apple snack. Romeo was here a few minutes ago but abandoned his dish of carrot sticks to follow Damiano into the bedroom. That rabbit is obsessed.

Black combat boots appear next to me. Damiano reaches down and strokes my hair. My eyes slowly peruse upward. Black cargo pants snug on his thick, muscular thighs. A black T-shirt snug across his chest, hugging his tight abs. A brown leather holster vest looping his muscular arms, his huge knife clipped to his belt. Hot damn, this man wears clothes like an action movie star. I can't blame Romeo for following him around on all fours. I have to fight the urge to do the exact same thing myself.

"Are you going somewhere?"

"I've got to go to work, angel."

"No suit?"

"Not tonight." He walks over to a cabinet, uses his thumbprint to unlock it. He pulls out two guns, sliding each into a separate holster pocket. "I'm going to figure out who's setting me up."

"How are you going to do that?"

Dom looks at me for a long minute without answering, then turns away. "I'm going to ask some people what they know." He closes and relocks the cabinet.

"And they're just going to tell you?"

"I have excellent people skills."

I smile. "Do you though?"

He smiles down at me.

I stand up, then hand him Tango. "Give me two minutes."

"Two minutes for what?"

"To change. Can you put Tango in the planter?" Romeo is doing excellent with his housebreaking, but it's not even an option with Tango, so into the planter he must go.

I head into Dom's bedroom closet. He cleared out a few drawers and some hanger space for all the clothes he bought me. I hate how much he spent, but I'm completely in love with the stuff.

Black clothes defy my California sunshine daydream roots. But navy should be close enough. I pull on leggings and a shirt Dom bought me. The shirt is fitted and has a boat neckline and three-quarter sleeves, and I swear I feel like Jackie O. Or Holly Golightly.

Maybe I need big sunglasses to top this off?

I look over my shoulder.

Damiano's leaning against the bedroom door jam, watching me get dressed. Smiling. "Where do you think you're going?"

I lean into the mirror to put on clear lip gloss. In the reflection, I catch him staring at my ass. "I'm going with you."

His eyes flick up to mine. "No, you're not." Then go back to my ass.

"Of course I am. I actually do have good people skills. People will tell me what you need to know." I go to pass him to get my shoes from the foyer, but Dom's thick arms wrap around me, pulling me against his big, warm body. He smells fantastic, wearing the Drakkar I saw on the shelf in his closet.

"You can't come, Paige."

"You have no idea how good I am at convincing people to do stuff. Gina calls it my superpower. You need people to talk, they'll talk to me." I reach up and stroke the velvety back of his head.

"Superpower, huh?"

I press into him, loving how his body feels against mine. "Just you wait until I use it on you."

"Angel, I'll already give you anything you want."

"See? It's working. And right now, what I want is to come with you."

"It's too dangerous."

"Remember how good I was driving here?"

"You were fantastic, but the answer is still no." He kisses my neck. "How about I go work for a few hours, and when I get back, you let me work my superpowers on you?" His hand slides under my shirt, up my tummy. He pushes my bra up and out of the way to cup the girls, brushing his thumbs across my nips.

"Are you just trying to distract me?"

He twists my nip like a radio dial. "Is it working?"

"Yeah, but—"

"Give me a few hours. Drink some wine, take a bath, be in nothing but my bathrobe when I get back, yeah?"

I can't quite form words at the moment, with him squeezing my nip and his big hard stallion pressing against me, surrounding me with his warm breath and nibbles on my neck. I sort of nod.

"You make it hard to leave, angel."

The second I hear the elevator ping down the hallway, I grab the keys to Jolene and a knife from the entire drawer full of folding knives, throwing knives, butterfly knives, and hunting knives Damiano has in his kitchen. I tiptoe out the door behind him.

I'm going to take the stairs down to the garage and wait until he pulls out, then I'll hang back half a block behind him, like the Suburbans did when they were following us the other day. And then when we get to wherever he's going, he'll have to accept my help.

He has no idea how good I can be at interrogating someone. People love talking to me. Complete strangers on the bus tell me their life stories. The other day, an eighty-year-old lady was telling me that she got chlamydia from a retired history teacher named Walter who was sleeping with half the ladies in their retirement community.

The stairwell door requires a hard push to get it open. I put enough shoulder into it that it swings open, and I spill into the stairwell, my hair falling into my face. I push it back with a giggle.

"You lost, little girl?"

Jesus fucking Christ. I jump a mile high, and my heart literally stops beating.

I cover my face with both hands but quickly realize that's the wrong reaction to being surprised in a random stairwell. I play it off by pulling my hair up into a ponytail, using the elastic that lives on my wrist.

Damiano is leaning against the stairwell wall, arms crossed against his wide chest. Watching me.

"Oh. Hi. What are you doing here?"

"What am I doing here? What are *you* doing here?"

"Uh... oh, taking a walk. Getting some fresh air? You know."

"You need a weapon for that?" He motions to the outline of a knife in the long pocket of my leggings. Of course he noticed that.

I nod. "Totally."

He pushes off the wall and steps toward me. "You weren't planning on following me, were you?"

"Me? Follow you?"

He nods.

"Uh, no. Wait, are *you* following *me*?" I fold my arms to mimic his stance. "Really, Damiano. I'd expect more from you."

"Angel. Are you being naughty?"

"No."

He steps toward me. Dressed in all black, Damiano's menacing as fuck. But the way he licks his lips, he's sexy as hell.

"Are you sure?"

"Yes?" I bite on the tip of my finger.

He cups my chin, tilts my face up toward him. It's an exciting mix of tender and assertive. "Naughty girls get tied up and spanked."

"Oh." Umm... I've never been tied up or spanked before. "Are you being serious?"

"Am I being serious about tying you to my bed so you can't follow me out on a mission? Abso-fucking-lutely. That's happening, Paige." He brushes his thumb across my bottom lip, tugging it. "Am I being serious about spanking you for being a brat? That one's up to you."

I might like getting spanked, so I'm thinking maybe? "Naughty girls get spanked?"

He nods, licks his bottom lip, his deep green eyes sparkling. He totally wants this. I do, too.

"Okay, fine. I *was* following you to work. I *completely disobeyed* your *crystal-clear* instructions." And here's the kicker to drive Damiano fully over the edge, "and I was going to put myself *in grave danger*."

Dom's nostrils flare as he inhales a deep breath. "Oh, angel. I'm going to have to teach you a very important lesson, one you'll remember every time you sit down for a week." Dom throws me over his shoulder and yanks open the stairwell door, marching us back into his apartment.

I guess his work can wait.

"Don't I need a safe word?"

"No." Damiano's straddling me. He's still fully dressed in his all-black combat outfit, his T-shirt stretched tight across his chest, showing the peaks of his tight nipples. He stripped off my clothes as soon as he flopped me onto the bed.

He lifts my right arm above my head, wraps a rope around my wrist and snugs the knot tight. He loops it around the center of his headboard, then pulls the slack out.

"But you're tying me up."

"I am." Dom picks up my left arm, kisses the inside of my wrist, then ties the other end of the rope just as snug as the first.

"So shouldn't I have a safe word?" I tug against the ropes, testing out how restrained I am. My arms can move side to side, but I can't pull them down.

"You don't need one."

"Maybe I do? Just in case?"

Dom slides his hand down the underside of my arm, slightly more pressure than a tickle. He reaches down and tugs on my right nipple, twisting it slowly, not letting go. He's in no hurry here. "Do you *want* a safe word, Paige?"

I nod. I do. I really do.

"What do you want it to be?"

I try to hide my smile. "You're the boss. You choose."

"Fine. Apricot." He grabs onto my other nipple, twisting both of them slowly, looking down at the girls from above me.

"Apricot?"

"Apricot. But you're not going to use it. You're going to take everything I give you." He checks the ropes, making sure my wrists are snug.

My body is on edge, like a live wire. I'm on the verge of giggling, not because this is funny, but because I have no clue how to control myself right now.

"Say, 'yes, Damiano, I'll be a good girl and take everything you give me.'"

"Yes, Damiano." I pause, fighting back a giggle. "I'll be a good girl and take—" I bury my face in my arm to hide my nervous laughing. I can't help it.

"Oh, this is funny to you?" Dom raises an eyebrow, questioning me. "Alright." He climbs off me to kneel by my side. With one hand, he grabs my hip and flips me over, forcing me face down on the mattress. He traces down my spine with his finger, rubs a circle on my bare ass cheek.

Now I'm giggling uncontrollably. "I'm sorry, I'll st—"

Thwack!

Oh god. I pull away from him instinctively.

Holy hell, that hurt.

"This still funny?"

"No." My ass stings where his hand connected. The area around it tingles.

But I think I liked it. I think I liked it a lot. I tentatively push my ass up toward him for another.

Dom inhales. "Now, about your behavior. Promise you won't try to follow me to work again."

"You should take me with you. I can be help—"

Thwack! Thwack!

"Dom!"

He grabs high on my thigh and pulls my right leg wide toward him, spreading my legs apart. He slides his fingers down to my kitty, cupping me and giving it two light taps. "Say it."

I try to push into his hand. I need more.

"Say it, Paige."

"Hear me out, I—"

Thwack! Thwack!

He smacked my kitty. Twice. And hard. *What the hell?*

"Okay, okay. I won't follow you again. I promise."

"Good girl." He slips his hand lower and rubs my throbbing clit, I press into it. "Whose job is it to keep you safe?" His deep voice is calm. How is he so calm?

"We can keep each other—"

Thwack! Thwack!

"Dom!" I pull my legs closed.

He lets out a sigh. "Not sure which I like spanking more, angel—your ass with my cherry handprint glowing red or your warm, wet figa. Keep being bratty so I can find out."

"Dom," I whine. I'm so ridiculously needy right now, and with my hands tied, I can't do anything about it.

He rubs a circle on my burning hot ass, then slides down and rubs a circle on my kitty. "Whose job is it to keep you safe?"

I hesitate because I truly believe we can keep each other safe.

Thwack!

Okay, I'm caving. My ass is on prickly fire. "You. You. It's your job to keep me safe."

"Good girl." He rubs my little kitty. "Now, whose job is it to keep me warm?"

I smile into the pillow. "Mine."

He squeezes my thigh, his fingers digging in. "And whose job is it to spread these luscious thighs wide open for me?" Dom nudges my legs further apart. "Wider, angel. Come on, as far as they go."

I stretch as far as possible.

"Good girl. Don't move." He climbs off the bed and leaves the room.

"Wait. Where are you going?"

I pull against the ropes. There's no way he'd leave me here tied up and dying for some relief while he goes off to work. Yes, it would stop me from following him, but no way he'd leave me like this for hours.

I'm about to shout my safe word. I'm—

"Relax, angel." I turn my head to see him leaning against the doorway, staring between my spread-eagle legs. He's holding a glass of water, swirling it. The clinking ice cubes are the only sound in the room. "No way I could leave like *this*," he reaches down and squeezes the tip of his erection bulging in his pants, "with you lying there like *that*."

I let out a breath of relief now that he's back. I lick my lips as he walks toward me with his pants outlining his huge bulge. He places the glass on the bedside table, then unzips his pants.

He climbs onto the bed, kneeling next to my head. "Stick out your tongue." He guides his giant dick to me, rubbing it around my lips like lip gloss.

Dom hasn't let me suck his dick yet. Every time I've moved in that direction, he's grabbed my hips and pulled me onto his face instead.

I take a deep breath, inhaling him. I love his smell. Musky and a little sweet, like we're in a warm, tropical cave. I stick out my tongue and lick him.

I lean forward as much as I can to take more of him, but he pulls back.

"Uh-uh. Naughty girls don't get to suck big, fat cocks." He pulls further away. "Stick out your tongue and leave it out."

I whine. I actually whine, but do as he says.

"Lick, but do not take it in your mouth."

I lap at him, at every angle I can manage. I shimmy forward so I can get up onto my forearms in a lazy plank. I could take him deeper from this angle. I'm thinking about it. I look up at him—he's staring at my mouth, watching.

I've never been all that into giving blow jobs. Just one of those things you do for a minute or two and wait until it's over. But this dick? I want it so bad. I want his hands wrapped around my head, pulling me deep onto him. I want to make his eyes roll into the back of his head, to give him all the pleasure he gives me every day.

I suckle at the tip, then open wide, hoping he accepts the invitation.

I lean slightly forward, my eyes locked on his. Seems like he's not going to stop me. I—

Thwack! Thwack! He reaches lower to my pussy. *Thwack!*

I'm so turned on, I start rubbing myself against his bed. I need the friction. Lying prone like this with my hands tied up, it's hard to get pressure where I need it. I buck my hips up to give him a hint. "Please, Damiano. *Please.*"

"Poor baby, are you being needy?" He pushes down on my lower back, holding me still and stopping me from trying to get the friction I'm dying for.

"Yes." My voice hitches. "*Please*, Dom."

"Should have thought about that before putting yourself in danger. Naughty girls don't get to come."

What?

No.

No, no, no, no. "But, Dom, I—"

He's teasing his fingers near my slit. "They get spanked." *Thwack!* "But they don't get to come."

I groan as I try to pull against the ropes.

"What about good girls?"

He hums with approval as he reaches over and fishes an ice cube out of his glass. "Good girls get stuffed full of cock until they can't take it anymore." He swirls the ice cube on my burning hot ass, which feels fantastic, an icy cool stream of water dripping down, tickling my thirsty kitty. "Good girls get all the good things."

"I promise to be good. I swear, Dom. I really, really need to be good for you."

"Maybe you're lying?"

I probably am. And I still might follow him after. But right now, all that matters is that he gives me what I need before I lose my mind. "Please. I promise not to follow you. I promise to listen when you tell me to stay here. I promise to do whatever you say."

He shifts to a push-up position with his entire body over mine, the heat of his chest scorching my back. He lowers himself so half his weight is on me, the other half on his forearms that are pinned on either side of my head. He leans down close to my ear, sweet breath sending chills down my spine.

"Promise me for real, Paige. Promise me you'll let me keep you safe." He nibbles my ear.

The fat head of his dick nudges against my sloppy wet lips. I'm completely engulfed in him, surrounded by his hard, delicious body.

I try to shimmy backward for more contact, but I'm locked in place. "I promise. For real. You can keep me sa—"

Dom slides in hard and deep. His cargo pants are barely pulled down, the stiff cotton and cool metal belt buckle rough against my sore ass. His forearms frame my forearms as he rocks into me. Each thrust forces a breath of air out of me, making me pant out loud.

Dom's grunts get louder as he goes harder.

"I need you, baby. I need you so bad." He's whispering in my ear. "I need you safe and I need you to take everything I give you." He thrusts in even deeper. Deeper than he's ever been. He reaches one arm under me, rubbing my clit between two fingers.

The backs of my thighs tense up, my toes point, every part of me clenches tight.

"Fuck, baby." Damiano grinds a slow circle deep inside me. "I can feel you pulsing around me."

My whole world shatters. I moan his name, long and loud, as my insides explode brighter and hotter and flashing whiter than ever before.

"Fucking hell, angel. Here... I... *go*..."

Dom holds me close as we both catch our breath. Then he crawls down my body, leaving a trail of kisses down my back. He nips my sore ass cheek hard before climbing off, but I'm too orgasm-drunk to complain.

I roll onto my back, watching him. Waiting for him to untie me.

He pulls his pants back up and tucks himself in, re-buckles his belt. He pulls his shirt up and off, tosses it into his laundry basket, and grabs a new one from the closet.

Redressed, he squats next to the bed, reaching under it.

"What are you doing?"

"Getting you set up."

"Set up for what?" I sit back on my elbows now.

"See this?" He holds up one of his knives.

I nod. I can't remember if this one has a name. It's nowhere near as scary as Bianca, so it probably doesn't.

"This is for you." He places the knife in my hand.

"Okay. What am I supposed to do with that?"

"Cut the rope. Untie yourself."

"You do it. Just use Bianca."

"Naah, baby. This buys me a three-minute head start. That's how long it should take you to cut through that rope. By then, I'll be long gone, so no point in trying to follow me."

"Just untie me. I said I wouldn't follow you."

"You did. But did you mean it?"

I look away. It's entirely possible that I did not.

"Do not leave me tied up if you're leaving."

"Three minutes. That's all it'll take you. You've got this." He leans down and kisses my forehead while he twists my right nipple.

Then he walks out of the room.

"Dom?" I hear the front door open and close. "Apricot, Damiano. Apricot!"

Damiano

SALVO LOOKS UP FROM his phone. "Why are you late?"

I shoot him a don't-ask look. He doesn't need to know that dealing with Paige cost me thirty-five immensely enjoyable minutes.

Plus, the guy I'm carrying in a firefighter hold is heavy as shit, and my shoulder is still fucked up. I drop him onto a chair bolted to the floor, then zip-cuff his wrists to the post behind the chair. I walk over to the mirror on the wall to make sure I didn't reopen any stitches, but they look fine.

"You're never late. Something go wrong?"

I shoot Salvo another look, which he'd notice if he ever looked up from his phone. "Can I get started here or do you need some foreplay first?"

"Let's do this." Salvo's ready to throw down whenever fists start flying, but he barely tolerates the interrogation portion of my job. I don't care if he joins me in my workshop or not, but Rob tells him to be here in case I need backup.

I turn to the two guys tied to chairs. One's been stewing in his own piss since I dragged him here earlier this afternoon, before going home to have dinner with Paige. The one I just carried in is starting to regain consciousness. Good.

I pull up a three-legged wooden stool and sit facing them. "Gentlemen, Gallianos don't usually have beef with Falcos. But seems like we do now. I don't want that. Salvo doesn't want that. I promise you, you don't want that. So, one-time deal in the spirit of keeping the peace. You have sixty seconds to tell me why Paulie shot me. Who put him up to it and why? You do that, and we can go back to having no beef. You first." I look at the guy who's been here all day.

"I—"

I hold up a finger to cut him off. "Hold on a second." I walk over to a table and pick up the plastic chicken-shaped egg timer Rob's little sister let me take from her kitchen. When the time runs down, it clucks and squawks and rattles back and forth like it's laying an egg. I set it for one minute, its ticks echoing against the tile walls.

I sit back down and nod to him to continue.

"I already told Salvo, I have no clue what the fuck I'm doing here. I don't know anything about anything. I promise, man. I swear."

I look over at Salvo, concern all over my face. "Oh, shit. Fuck, man. Did we grab the wrong guy?"

He looks relieved. "Yes. Yes. You did."

"Shit, I'm sorry about that."

"Yeah, it's all good. Just let me go now."

"Here's the problem though. Help me sort this part out first, then maybe we can get you out of here. One of the shitheads that came at me last week"—came at me with Paige nearby—"*you* were the last person he called. So right when he was walking toward me in the alley, right when he was thinking *he* was going to take *me* out, he called you."

The guy's face drops. I'd say it went pale, but it's been pale as fuck since I threw him in the back of Salvo's van.

"No, man. It's not what you think."

"It's never what I think. You have any idea how often the person sitting in your chair tells me I've got it wrong?" I wait for him to answer. I look over my shoulder. "You've got ten seconds left on that timer. Why did Paulie try to kill me?"

He swallows hard. Closes his eyes.

Cluck-cluck-cluck-ba-gok. Cluck-cluck-cluck-ba-GOK. BA-GOKKKKK!

He jumps in his chair, squeezes his eyes shut.

"Nothing?"

"Damiano, man, I don't know anything. I swear."

"Okay." I get up and walk over to the shelf. I pick up three pairs of noise-cancelling headsets. I put a pair on and toss a pair to Salvo. I offer a pair to the guy in chair number two. He says something, but I can't make it out with my headphones already on. "What?"

He says something again. I pull one earmuff loose so I can hear him.

"My hands are fucking tied, man."

I smile. "Oh shit, yeah. Allow me." I put the headphones over his ears for him.

I pull my Glock from my holster. No point in dragging this out. I aim between Guest #1's eyes and pull the trigger, firing straight into his T-box. Brains paint the wall behind him.

I remove my headset. Guest #2 is screaming his head off, trying to pull out of his chair. He's yelling loud enough that I'm tempted to put the headset back on.

"What the fuck, man?" Salvo jumps up from his lounger. I can barely hear him over the guy's screaming. "You got fucking brain juice on my Jordans." He points at his high-tops. "These are limited edition, you fucker."

I remove Guest #2's headphones so he can hear me. "Think you can stop screaming?"

He nods.

I turn to Salvo. "Why would you wear anything nice in my workshop?"

"I didn't know I was coming here. You grabbed me from the Cat, remember?"

I'm not going to argue with him over this. I went to the Cat to grab *the keys to his van* and he decided to join me. His choice, not mine.

"Top drawer." I motion with my head to the cabinet to his right. He'll find the little cloth booties I stock for him and Rob and their poorly planned wardrobes. "Put those on." Then I mutter under my breath, "pussy." There's a reason I wear black here. Things get messy as fuck.

I return to my seat and to Guest #2. "Sorry you had to see that, man. But in all fairness, I did give him a full minute to come clean. He chose the path of deceit. That,"

I point to the head stump that's dripping in slow, thick globs, "was his choice."

What my newly-deceased guest didn't know was that, in addition to the phone call log, I read the shit ton of texts between the two of them about looking for me '*and my bitch*' and the texts from when he stumbled across my Rover at the pet shop, then about bringing me in kicking and screaming or tits up and the headless horseman over here suggesting that tits up would leave less chance I'd break free en route.

He was right about that. He'd at least need to knock me out. GOI trained us on a dozen ways to get ourselves untied, including dislocating my own shoulder if need be, which is pretty much the only realistic way to get out of handcuffs or zip-cuffs.

But the texts didn't say 'en route' to where. Or to who. Were they just going for the money Joey Bags put on my head after the night at the park, or is their boss, Riccardo Falco, involved with Paulie somehow and responsible for the night at the park?

Hopefully, my remaining guest can clear this up so I can go home to my pissed off angel. See what make-up sex is all about. "Now you, my friend, get the same offer. Sixty seconds to tell me—"

"Lily. Talk to Lily. She knows everything." He's talking so fast, spittle is flying everywhere. "I don't know any details. I really fucking don't, man. I swear on my dick and balls. But Lily can tell you every fucking thing."

My kind of interrogation. Quick and to the point.

"Lily who?"

"No clue. And 'Lily' probably isn't even her real name. She dances at the Tropicana. She was dating Paulie. Gave two weeks' notice to quit, but then flipped her fucking lid when she found out he was dead. She begged Riccardo for her job back."

"He take her back?"

He nods. "But he's making her pay the price for giving notice. He's working her three times harder than the other girls, making her give freebies to all the made guys."

"You know where she lives?"

He shakes his head. "I'd tell you if I knew. I swear."

"Okay."

The guy looks around. Looks at Salvo. "Okay? What the fuck does 'okay' mean? You said 'okay' to Ray, then blew his face off. I told you everything I know."

"'Okay' means, 'okay, you can leave.'" I move around behind him to cut the zip-cuffs.

"What? No." He pulls away from me.

"What do you mean, 'no'? I told you if you told me what I needed to know, you could leave. You did, so you can."

"No. Fuck that. Don't untie me, man. You said if I told you what I knew, you wouldn't kill me. So don't kill me. But you can't just let me go. A dozen guys saw you grab me. I walk out of here, and they'll know I told you shit."

"You did tell me shit."

"You gotta fuck me up, Dom. At least a little. Come on. That's only fair."

"Fine." I haul back and punch him, whipping his head back.

The kid groans out in pain.

"We good here?" I don't want to be out all night.

"No, man. You gotta, like, *hurt me*, hurt me. Like, all that squailibrato, demente, il pazzo shit you're known for." *Deranged, demented, lunatic.* "Per favore, Damiano. Te ne sarò debitore." *Please, Damiano. I'll owe you one.*

"Fine."

I'M STANDING IN THE shadows in the Tropicana's parking lot, waiting for Lily to finish her shift.

Even before this whole Paulie mess started, I couldn't exactly walk into the Can without it causing problems. The Falco Famiglia is aligned with the Bagliateris and their Riccardo Falco is engaged to Joey Bags' youngest daughter. When she turns eighteen, the two Famiglie will join. Unless she runs away first, which is my bet, given that Falco is twenty years older than her, openly fucks all his strippers, and has no qualms about smacking women around.

The Can closed thirty minutes ago, and dancers have been trickling out, heading to their cars or Ubers. Blows my mind that there isn't a single security guard out here to make sure the girls leave safely. We'd fire any one of the Cat girls on the spot for walking out without a security escort.

I chatted with one of the first girls that came out. She said Lily would be one of the last to come out because she's recently been leaving with one of the bartenders that has to close up.

Another twenty minutes later, the side door opens again, and a bleached blonde comes out with a tall skinny guy. They head to the last car parked in the lot.

"Hey, buddy, can I talk to Lily for two minutes?" I step out of the shadows into the dim glow of the neon signs.

He looks up at me, then looks back at Lily. "Fuck off, she's taken."

"She's all yours, man. I just want to talk to her."

"Take a hike, asshole."

I could be home, in my bed with Paige. My leg nestled between her warm thighs, my head snuggled between her firm tits, my arms wrapped around her smooth body.

Instead I'm standing outside a shit-ass tittie bar, freezing my balls off.

I peel two hundreds off my money clip. "Give me two minutes to talk to her. Just talk." I hold the cash out to him, hoping he takes the easy way on this one.

Lily snatches the cash out of my hand before the guy can decide what to do. "Wait in the car, Phil."

"Do you even know who this asshole is?" His tone and his confidence make it clear he doesn't.

"Yeah, baby, I know who he is. So take my advice and get in the car on your own before he slices you in half and stuffs you in sideways."

That puts a smile on my face. I like when my reputation precedes me. Less clean up.

Phil stares at me a long minute, gives Lily a long kiss—showing me who she belongs to—then walks to the car, grumbling.

Lily and I both watch him climb in the car and close the door.

She takes a step toward me, puts her hand on my belt and tries to tug me toward her.

This fucking chick.

"Looks like you forgot about Paulie pretty fast."

She leans in. "I wouldn't forget you."

"No, probably not. But I'm not here for that." I take her hand off me.

"Pity."

"Why did Paulie shoot me?"

"Hmmm. Not sure I know anything about that."

I pull my money clip back out. "Anything going to help you remember?" I peel three hundreds off, then remember what's waiting for me at home. I toss her the whole wad. That's almost three large. "Talk."

She stuffs the clip into her purse, then tucks her purse behind her like she's afraid I'm going to try to grab it back. "I say a word Riccardo doesn't like and I'm fucked."

"You don't say those words and you're fucked. Your boy too." I tip my chin toward the car.

She looks in his direction as if she's trying to decide if protecting him is worth anything. "How about you get me a job at the Cat's Meow, and then I don't have to worry about Riccardo. I'll tell you everything."

No way Salvo will give a Can girl a shot at the Cat. He picks girls he'd be into fucking if they're into it, and he won't go near anyone who's fucked Riccardo. It's a non-starter. I could lie and tell her I'll try, but I'm not going to.

"I heard you quit this place. Paulie come into some money or what?"

She looks away from me.

"Talk, Jeanine."

Her eyes dart to mine.

"Yeah, I know your address too. Grammy's probably all tucked in nice and cozy in bed already. So tell me about Paulie so I can get the fuck out of here."

"How about—"

"How about you've got ten seconds until I show your boy Phil what a pissed-off enforcer looks like."

She shrugs off my threat. Un-fucking-believable.

"*And* I take back the cash?"

She glares at me. "Fine." She crosses her arms. "Paulie was sick of Rob blowing him off all the time. You and Salvatore too. He felt like no one was giving him a chance to prove his value."

Based on his shitty aim, I'd say his value was dick.

"Riccardo noticed him hanging around here, asked me if he was a Galliano. Called him into his office a few times, but I never went in. That's all I know." She steps away like we're done here.

I'm a foot taller and twice as wide. I step in front of her. "Bullshit." No way she quit her job without knowing what the fuck was up. "Right now, I'm giving you the benefit of the doubt that you didn't play a role in that fucker shooting me. But if I'm still standing here in two minutes, my generosity expires, and I'm going to assume you were involved. I might even assume Grammy was involved too."

She searches my eyes, then looks over her shoulder toward the Can's backdoor. She lowers her voice. "Fine. They offered to make him."

The fuck? Make a low level piece of shit from another family? "Falco offered that?"

She nods.

"Okay, but what does that have to do with me? Falco can make whoever he wants to make."

"Falco doesn't do anything for anybody without them paying for it, and he sets the price." Her voice is a mix of anger and resentment.

"And I was the price?"

She shrugs.

"Why would Falco want me dead?"

"Not my circus, not my monkeys. Can I go now?"

"Any Bagliateris hanging around Falco or Paulie in the last few weeks?" I'm not ready to believe Joey isn't behind this.

She's starting to shiver out here in the cold, wraps her arms around herself. "Joey and Vinnie come in once or twice a week. Always have since I've worked here. Them and Riccardo grab a couple of girls and disappear into Riccardo's private room."

"What do they talk about?"

"Not much talk happening. Can I go now?"

Damiano

AFTER EATING TAKEOUT THE last few nights, Paige insisted on cooking for us tonight. I didn't take her for much of a chef based on all the processed food in her apartment, but of course I told her to make whatever she wanted. As long as she cooked naked.

She was afraid something hot might splash on her, so we compromised on her wearing one of my shirts, but no bra or panties. So here she is, in a crisp white button-down, collar popped, sleeves rolled up, hair in some type of floppy bun on top of her head, and legs for days.

The shirt's long enough that it's covering her sweet little pussy, but the tease of knowing it's bare and just out of sight is almost even better.

After I picked Paige's outfit, she picked mine—gray sweatpants, no shirt, and a Cubs baseball cap, on backward. I keep having to look away from her because these sweatpants don't hide my hard-on and won't hide a wet spot if my dick starts leaking in anticipation, which he threatens to do every time Paige reaches high for something on a shelf or bends over to pick up something she's dropped.

Each time she glances over at me, she looks down at my junk like she can't help it. So much so that I stepped away and did a hundred crossover sit-ups to make sure my abs are on fire. Paige stopped dead in the middle of whatever she was telling me when I came back in, then couldn't remember whatever she was saying.

I could get used to this. I could get used to everything about this. Not the part where she's cooking an all-carb dinner, but all the rest.

"This is going to be so good." Paige stirs the pan on the stove.

I'm into these random boosts of confidence Paige gets. The kitchen is a fucking mess and she definitely burning the garlic, but she's absolutely sure she's got this.

I squeeze in behind her at the stove and look over her shoulder. Whatever's in the pan does not look right. "You willing to bet on that?"

"I didn't picture you as a gambler."

"No?"

"You're too much of a control freak to leave things to chance."

"I can't control everything. I can't control you." I move to lean against the counter, still close to her but out of her way.

She looks at me suspiciously as she adds salt to the pan, paying zero attention to how much. She looks down at the pan, then up at me, biting her fat bottom lip. "What kind of bet do you have in mind?"

Whatever she's making looks awful. She added a jar of *store-bought* sauce to *uncooked* pasta, not bothering to boil it first. But she looks really happy cooking for me, swaying her hips to the music she's playing.

I plan to eat every bite of whatever she puts on my plate, no matter how awful it is. I'm that whipped by this girl. "I *bet* this is going to taste fan-fucking-tastic."

"And I bet—wait, you're betting that I get this *right*?" She stops stirring and looks up at me.

"Of course, angel. You can do anything." Probably not cooking, though. And definitely not giving stitches. Or actual sponge baths.

"Uh... okay." She smiles and looks away bashfully, returns to stirring her dish. "And if you win?"

"*When* I win... you ride my face for an hour."

She looks up at me for a long minute. "And if you lose?" Her voice cracks. She doesn't want me to lose.

I step close behind her. Press up against her. "This." I slide my hands under the tail of her shirt, cupping her bare ass. "This right here."

She stops stirring. "Damiano."

"I'll make it so good for you. I promise, baby." I kiss her shoulder then take a few steps away before the urge to slide right into her takes over. "And anyway, dinner's going to be amazing. I can tell."

She surveys the mess she's made, her lips twisted, her eyebrows tense. "I think it will be good. I'm following a recipe. The parts of it I remember. I saw a TikTok of someone making this. It looked easy enough." She looks up at me, unsure of herself.

"It smells good." It smells like something is burning. I look around and see one of the potholders is too close to the flame and is smoldering. I move it away without her noticing.

She lifts a spoon to her mouth, takes a taste. Scrunches her nose a little.

"Take the bet, Paige."

"I mean, it's sort of win-win. Right?"

Fuck yeah. Fuck yeah, it is. Heads, she sits on my face. Tails, I get her ass. That is abso-fucking-lutely win-win, and her thinking that too has my dick instantly at full attention.

"Oh my god, Dom, you have to stop looking at me like that."

"Like what?"

"Like we're not going to make it to dinner. Can you go set the table or something? I need to focus on the last few steps. I can't focus with you here."

I grab plates, silverware, and glasses and head to the table. I'm not sure an actual meal has ever been served at this table before. It's great for laying out weapons and ammo before a job and cleaning them after, but a meal?

I could put us at opposite ends of the rectangle like we're royalty, or across the short side like normal. But I don't like Paige being that far away from me, so I set two spots side-by-side at the table big enough for ten.

She walks over with a bowl of pasta burnt to the point of being charred and black in some spots. "Bon appetit."

I shake my head. "*Buon* appetito."

"Buon appetito." She smiles.

"Sit here," I pat my lap.

"But I don't have panties on."

I pull her down onto me. "Oh, is that right?" I can feel her heat through my pants. Does she really think I forgot that part? That part's branded into my brain. I slide one hand around, high up on her thigh. "Thank you for making me dinner."

"I hope you like it."

I look down at the portion she scooped onto my plate. It doesn't look right. The pasta is all clumped together and burnt. I take a mouthful, expecting the worst.

But holy shit. "This è deliziosa."

"Are you just saying that because of the bet?"

"No." I stuff another overloaded forkful in my mouth. The bet we made makes me want to lie and say this is awful so I 'lose.' But I won't do that to her. Not when she was so excited to cook for me. "Told you you can do anything, angel."

"Maybe I should get a job in a restaurant?"

I look up from my bowl to see if she's joking. "Really?"

She shrugs her shoulders. "Yeah. I mean, I'm going to need to find something at some point."

"I told you I'll talk to your manager. She'll beg you to come back after. With a raise. Guaranteed."

After listening to the voicemail Paige got from her boss, I was two seconds away from having *a special chat* with her boss anyway. Only reason I didn't was that Paige wasn't upset about getting fired and I like not having to share her with her co-workers. But if she wants to go back, I'll make it happen.

"Please don't. I wasn't quite ready to quit, but I'm glad I don't have to go back. It's a relief, actually. I'll find something else."

I take another forkful of this spicey, chewy, almost bitter but in an insanely delicious way, pasta. "You don't have to get a job at all."

"Yeah, well, tell that to my landlord."

"I told you, I'll pay your rent." I've gone to her place twice now to check it and to get some of her things. I was tempted to pack up all her shit and bring it here, but that wasn't an option on my bike. Didn't look like anyone had been in there and her neighbor from the down the hall said she hadn't seen anything unusual.

But even though Joey's guys don't seem interested in ransacking her place, I still want her here with me. "And anyway, you're not going back there anytime soon."

"Leave the dishes. I'll clean up later." Dom stands up and stretches, his dark happy trail drawing all my attention. He reaches for my hand, then leads me to the living room, collapsing heavy onto the couch then pulling me onto his lap. He presses my head against his chest and then pets my hair slowly.

I know he has a bet to pay up and that he's good for it—so good for it—but I also think he may be heading for a food coma since he never eats carbs but demolished two full plates of my spaghetti all'assassina.

As soon as I heard of the dish, I knew it would be perfect—you're actually supposed to burn it, so I knew I wouldn't screw it up. I think I could have even burned it *more* and it would have been even better.

"You should cook for me more often, no?"

"What else do you like to eat?"

"You."

I nuzzle deeper into him, hiding my smile against his warm chest, a patch of soft, dark hair tickling my cheek. "What else?"

"I'm easy."

"You are anything but easy." I rest my hand on his rippled abs.

"When it comes to you, I'm easy. You tell me what you need, what you want, and the answer will always be 'yes.'"

"Is that so?"

He kisses the top of my head, and I can feel him nodding.

Maybe I should test this. "In that case..." I slide off his lap onto my knees on the floor. I grab a mouthful of his pants and tug on the fabric.

Dom reaches down, cups my chin. "What are you doing, angel?"

Something I've wanted to do for a while now, but he never lets me. "Checking to see how easy you are."

"I won the bet. I should be the one on my knees." He rubs his thumb across my lips, presses against my bottom lip.

"You being difficult already, Mr. E-Z?"

"Fuck no. You want easy? I'll give you easy." Dom stands up and pushes his sweatpants and boxer briefs all the way down, steps one foot out, then flops back onto the couch. He leans all the way back and laces his fingers behind his head. "All yours, angel. Have at it."

I shake my head and smile. His dick looks even bigger up close like this. That's going to be a lot to take. I plant a gentle kiss on the tip and glide my hand up and down his burning hot shaft.

He looks from my eyes down to his dick, back up to my eyes. Tips his head to the side a little. I can read the *well?* in his expression.

I lick my lips to wet them. Rub them up and down his shaft.

"Yesssss," Dom hisses low under his breath.

I wrap my lips around Dom's fat head, opening as wide as I can. His salty tanginess hits my tongue. I grasp his dick at the base, exactly the way I've seen him grab it, and hold it steady while I give him a few shallow bobs.

Dom's hand lands on the back of my head, stroking gently, then steering me to where he wants me. He may think he's being all easy and laid-back, but the man can't help but take control. And he clearly wants me to go deeper.

I twirl my tongue around his slit. *Alright, gorgeous penis friend, you and me are in this together. Same goal: blow Damiano's mind. I'm going to go whole hog and you're going to not choke me to death or make me gag all over the place. Deal?*

Of course Dom's peen doesn't answer my silent prayer, though he does sort of twitch a little in my hand, which I take as a sign he's got my back on this. *Here we go, baby.*

I take as much of Dom in my mouth as I can, angling to the side a bit to take more. He pulls me deeper until I gag a little. I've never done this on such a big boy before.

Is he disappointed I can't take him deeper? I look up. He's staring at my mouth, watching me struggle. His eyes dart to mine for a split second, but then go back to my mouth.

I try again.

"Fuck, angel. Look how good you take my cock." He cups the back of my neck, pulling me deeper onto him.

"Still taking me deep even when you gag." He brushes my hair out of my eyes. "Tu sei perfetto."

I readjust myself, inching closer on my knees. I try to do that 'open your throat' thing Gina brags about, even though I'm not exactly sure what that means, but maybe it's just a swallowing motion?

"*Fuck, baby. Fuck.* Suck me just like that."

Ooh, he liked that. I swallow again and cup his balls, giving them a firm squeeze.

"Take it. Take every inch. Fuck, Paige." He thrusts his hips up at the same time he presses on the back of my head.

I started this adventure, but now he's taking control, which I know he can't help. I'm making these weird porno blowjob noises that sound like a sea lion barking for a treat. I hate making any noise, and I definitely hate making this noise, but I can't help it.

Damiano, on the other hand, seems to love it. "Jesus Christ. I want to blow my entire load straight down your throat when you take me like this." He threads his fingers into my hair and gently pulls me off him, then pulls me back down. "I could watch you do this all night. Fucking gorgeous." He pulls me off and back on a few more times, grunting and cursing each time I take him.

I swallow hard to take him deeper.

Dom tries to say something. It's not an actual word. But it is the encouragement I need to take him deeper, to suck even harder. I'm still making weird slurping sounds that he definitely doesn't mind. The way he's tangled one hand in my hair above my ear, holding my head against his thrusts. He's so into this.

"Like that." He's leaning forward, practically wrapped around me. His grip on my neck tightens, not letting me go. "I'm close, angel. I'm going to come straight down your throat. Can you swallow every drop for me?"

I nod and look up at him. He's staring down at me, his mouth open, his upper lip snarled.

I squeeze his balls one more time as I take him as deep as I can, gagging but not backing off. My other hand slides up to his happy trail, gripping at his skin to pull him closer.

Dom's back arches and groans as his salty mess pulses down my throat. I couldn't pull away if I wanted to.

After a few seconds, his grip loosens but he doesn't let go. He's still holding me close to him as his body collapses back onto the couch. He takes a few deep breaths in and out, rubs my lip with his thumb again. "Open your mouth, angel. Show me you swallowed every drop."

The command in his voice sends a shiver down my back. Of course I do as he says and stick out my tongue.

"Such a fucking goddess when you take me like that. Get over here." He pulls me up onto his lap, kisses me deep, then collapses back into the couch. "I need a few minutes to recover from that."

I bury my face against his chest, the soft hairs against my cheek.

Dom pets the back of my hair. "This isn't temporary."

"What? You being so drained you're about to pass out?" Plus the food coma that's probably catching up with him again.

"No. Us. You and me, angel. This."

IT'S POURING OUT AND I'm soaking wet because I'm stubborn as shit when it comes to umbrellas. Now I'm dripping all over my front hallway.

I hang my wet coat, slide off my shoes and socks, step onto the heated tile floor. Paige is somewhere in the apartment, but I can't see her from the entryway. "I brought you pizza, angel. From Gino's."

"Aww, thanks, sugarplum," a *man's* voice answers. "I avoid carbs, but it's the thought that counts."

I freeze. The hairs on the back of my neck stand on end. That's not Salvo, the only other person who has the access code for my apartment.

"Come, paisano." *Countryman.* "Come join our party."

Massimo. Definitely Mas.

What the fuck?

No fucking way he should be here. Not in Galliano territory, not in my apartment. I take a few seconds to figure out how this is going to play out with Paige here.

"Una mattina," Massimo sings, slow and deep. "Mi son svegliato. O bella ciao, bella ciao, bella ciao ciao ciao. Una mattina, mi son svegliato. E ho trovato l'invasor."

'Bella Ciao.' An Italian folk song. *One morning I woke up, O beauty bye, beauty bye, beauty bye bye bye. One morning I woke up, and I found the intruder.*

I have my Glock 41 on me and Bianca. I unholster my gun and pull my knife from the clip on my waistband. I hold both in my right hand, Paige's pizza in my left hand, and I walk into the room.

Mas is sitting at the table, still singing. He's leaning back, his hands laced behind his head. His Glock is set down on the table in front of him. The extractor LCI on its muzzle is protruding, signaling that there's already a round in the chamber.

Paige is next to him, sitting up perfectly straight, her hands folded neatly on her lap. She looks so small sitting there, staring at his gun. Afraid.

I lay my gun and knife down on the table next to his.

Mas smiles. Smiles his big shit-eating grin. He leans forward, elbows on the table. He looks at Paige as he sings the refrain, "O bella ciao, bella ciao, bella ciao ciao ciao." *O beauty bye, beauty bye, beauty bye bye bye.* It's the song our people sing to protest oppression.

He turns back to me, tipping his head toward Paige. "Are we doing this with your girl here?"

"She's not my girl."

Paige's eyes snap up to mine, her nervousness quickly morphing into confusion. Her lips part slightly.

I shrug my shoulders and exhale, try to apologize with a look. It's instinct to try to protect her at all times, including trying to keep a bull's eye off her back. The words rolled off my tongue without thought, but they didn't feel right.

Mas looks at Paige, tips his head to the side. "Alright," he very obviously checks out her tits, then smiles even wider. "Are we doing this with *some girl* here?"

I shake my head. This isn't for Paige to witness. I'd send her on a walk, but I don't know if the Bagliateri capture order covers her or not. "È sicuro per lei uscire?" *Is it safe for her to go outside?*

He shakes his head. Cazzo. Well at least that's confirmed now.

I turn to Paige. "Go wait for me in the bedroom. I'll come get you in a few minutes."

"But, Dom—"

"Massimo and I need to talk. Privately."

"I don't think he's here to talk." Paige looks genuinely concerned. And scared.

But she doesn't need to be. "It's fine. He's not going to hurt you. Go in the other room."

Massimo is watching her like a hawk. I am too. Paige slides her chair back and stands up.

She's wearing a pair of my boxer briefs with the waist rolled over a few times. Inches of her tan skin are exposed, the palest baby fuzz on her tummy. The outline of her sharp hip bone is showing. Sexy as fuck, looking like a wet dream.

Mas is thinking the same thing, I'm sure.

"Paige, please go. I'll handle this."

"But..." She's looking around the room, looking between the two of us. "Okay, I'll go. I'll—*Oh my god, what is that?*" she yells and points to the far corner of the room.

Neither of us flinch. It was an adorable attempt to distract Massimo. A failed attempt, but a fucking adorable one.

"What the hell is wrong with the two of you? Are you two robots? Normal people turn and look when someone yells, 'oh my god, what's that' and points. You're supposed to turn and look."

"Paige, please." I beg her with my eyes.

"Ecco perché hai bisogno di una ragazza Italiana. Uno che ascolta." *This is why you need an Italian girl. One who listens,* Massimo tells me.

"Come va per te?" *How is that working out for you?*

He shrugs, smiles. "Piu 'o meno lo stesso per te." *About the same as you.*

"Whyyyyy?" Paige bellows, far more dramatically than the situation calls for. She sits back down and flops herself forward, her long golden hair flying forward over her head that's now resting on the table.

Fuck. Don't do this, Paige.

A second later, she jolts upright, big smile on her face. She's got my gun in her hand, has it pointed at Massimo. "Run, Dom. I've got him covered."

"E' una fottuta pazza?" *Is she a fucking lunatic?* Mas asks, his eyes glued to her.

"Penso che stia cercando di salvarmi la vita." *I think she's trying to save my life.*

He tips his head to the side, eyes focused on the extractor LCI on the side of my gun, which is *not* protruding, indicating there is *not* a bullet in the chamber ready to fire. "Allora forse dovresti dirle di armare il martello, lo sai?" *Then maybe you should tell her to rack the slide, yeah?*

"Paige," I plead.

She shifts her eyes to me for a second, giving Massimo the opening I know he's going to take no matter what I do or say.

In a heartbeat, he slams her hand down to the table like they were arm wrestling. With his other hand, he grabs his gun—*with* its LCI extractor protruding—and points it at her.

"Think you can you chill the fuck out?" he asks her.

Paige doesn't know Mas. Doesn't know whether he's a threat or not. She knows people are out looking to hurt me, and she knows he broke into my apartment—I'm assuming he didn't knock and she didn't let him in.

How the fuck did he get in? The front door wasn't jimmied.

Paige nods her head like she's going to do what he says.

He squeezes her wrist until she lets go of the gun, he moves it to the chair next to him, the opposite side from her. "Jesus," he says, "you're a loose fucking cannon, aren't you?" Mas hasn't put his gun down. He's not pointing it at her, but he hasn't put it down.

Honestly, I have no idea what she'll—

"Dom!" She grabs my dagger off the table and throws it to me.

For fuck's sake—I leap out of the way just in time for Bianca to plant herself *pointy end first* into the back of the couch behind me. *Exactly at the height of my dick.*

I cup my junk, even though the imminent danger has passed. "What the fuck are you doing?" My voice is two octaves higher than normal. "Don't throw a fucking knife. Are you fucking nuts? I can't catch a flying knife. No one can catch a flying knife."

No way I'm moving my hand away from my dick anytime soon. I swear he felt the breeze of Bianca whizzing by.

"I'm helping. I'm saving you."

"Stop trying to save me. And stop risking your own fucking self."

I look to Mas, expecting his gun to be pointed at her again. Instead, he's rubbing the muzzle across his lip, smiling, watching with absolute delight in his eyes. "Questa è una custode, sì?" *This one's a keeper, yes?*

"L'aiuto di questo qui si è avvicinato di più a uccidermi di quanto lo abbia fatto chiunque dei vostri ragazzi." *This one's 'help' has come closer to killing me than any of your guys have.*

Mas turns to Paige. "Listen, sweetheart. I need to talk to our guy here. I'd prefer it if you beat it while we talk. But if that's not happening, I need you to sit there very, very still. Can you do that?"

She shrugs her shoulders, like she sincerely isn't sure whether she can.

"Do I need to tie you up?"

"La tocchi di nuovo e ti farò del male in modi a cui non hai ancora pensato." *You touch her again and I will hurt you in ways you haven't thought of yet.*

"Not your girl, huh?"

Paige interrupts our stare-off. "I'll behave. I promise." She spreads her palms flat on the table. She looks back and forth between me and Mas. "I promise. Really."

Mas nods at her then stands. He tucks his gun into his shoulder holster. That's a nice fucking holster. I want one like that. Now's probably not the time to ask where he got it. But where did he get that?

Mas pushes the chair with my gun on it further away from Paige, then takes a step toward me.

I have no idea what he thinks went down with his brother. Word on the street is that I shot him. *In the fucking back.* Like a slimy fucking coward.

Mas takes the last step to me. We're the same height. He's a little leaner, but only slightly. We're toe to toe. He's searching my face. Reading me.

"Mas, I—"

He shakes his head slightly. Doesn't say a word. Just lets out a long, slow breath.

He looks so fucking lost.

I reach out, wrap my hand around the back of his neck. I pull him into me, kissing one cheek, then the other, like we're still in Old Italy, then I pull him closer for a full-on hug. "It's been too fucking long, man."

He exhales a shaky breath, eventually relaxing most of his weight onto me.

"Too fucking long."

After a long minute, a minute where I worry he'll collapse to the floor if I let go, he pulls back, my hand still cupping the back of his neck.

"How's Davide?"

"Don't fucking know." His eyes are wet. "*Best* case scenario, he'll have to learn to walk again. His wife's a fucking mess over it all."

"Cazzo." I squeeze the back of his neck then let go.

Mas sits back down at the table. I take the seat next to Paige, pulling her chair closer to mine. The pizza on the table smells so fucking good, I'm tempted to say fuck all to the protein shake and salad I was going to make for myself.

Paige tips her head to the side, her brow tightly knitted. "He's *not* here to kill you?"

"No. I told you that. I said he was here to talk."

"I thought 'talk' was code for 'kill you.'"

"Why would 'talk' be code for 'kill me'? And why would I put my weapons down if he was here to kill me? And if he were here to kill me, I would have killed him first."

"You would have *tried* to kill me first," Mas adds, leaning back in his chair, smiling.

"Gina said that the Baglios want you dead."

"The *Bagliateris*," Mas corrects, "*do* want him dead."

"Aren't you a Bagliateri?"

Massimo gets a disgusted look on his face for a split second, then covers it. He better keep that shit under control before other people start noticing.

I answer for him. "Massimo's the enforcer for Johnny Gianmarco, *the nephew* of Joey Bagliateri. His allegiance is to Johnny, not Joey."

"Okay. But doesn't that make you a Bagliateri? Or a Bagliateri-by-association? Bagliateri adjacent? A Bagliateri once removed?"

I let out a long breath. Massimo stares at Paige like she has two heads.

Massimo's secret beef with Joey is a story for another day. No doubt Mas would put a bullet between Joey Bags' eyes if Johnny would green-light it, but Johnny actually loves his uncle, thinks the world of him. And Mas respects Johnny, so he swallows that shit down deep.

"Non ho tutto il giorno, amico. Nessuno sa che sono qui." *I don't have all day, man. No one knows I'm here.*

And no one can know. No one in the Famiglie knows the history between Mas and me, that we served in GOI together, that we would take a bullet for each other. Hell, Mas did take a bullet meant for me in Sardinia.

Lucky for me, I know exactly how to distract Paige enough so she'll stop talking and Mas and I can get to what we need to get to.

Plus, seeing her in my boxers, acting all brave, trying to defend me, has me all kinds of worked up. If it weren't for her throwing my knife at my dick, I'd be hard as steel right now. I reach down under the table and cup my junk again, letting the boys know they're safe.

With my other hand, I pull Paige's chair the last few inches so it's up against mine. She startles at the sudden movement. I wrap my hand around her neck and pull her close, whisper so only she can hear, "Can you sit quiet for a few minutes? Just sit there and listen?"

I bite her earlobe and don't let go, breathing heavy so she feels it. My other hand slides up her thigh, not stopping until my fingers slip inside the boxers and find the lacy edge of her panty. "No more talking. No more questions. Can you do that for me, angel? Do that, and I'll explain everything later, with my head between your legs. Yeah?"

She wriggles in the chair.

"Say 'yes, Damiano. Whatever you say, Damiano.'"

"Yes, Damiano. Whatever you say, Damiano," she whispers, her eyes closed. She spreads her legs a little, giving me better access. She tips her head closer to me, leaning on my shoulder, her mop of golden hair covering her face.

"That's my good girl."

I turn back to Mas. "So what the fuck happened to Davide? He wasn't even at the park that night."

He shrugs. "He was in the car. Him and Vinnie."

"*Vinnie* was there, too?" I lean back in my chair while that bomb sinks in. Wasn't expecting that. But it does explain how a guy with a bullet in his leg was able to drive away so fast.

Vinnie is Joey's consiglieri, practically his right hand. No reason—no *good* reason at least—for someone that high ranking to come to a bag exchange.

I have no clue what to make of this. "Well, then, him and Vinnie never got out of the car. I never saw either of them. Paulie Vitale shot me, then he swallowed a bullet before I could ask him what the fuck was going on. I hobbled Joey's *one* guy when he started shooting at me. He crawled away and the car took off. Never saw Davide or Vinnie."

Mas shrugs his shoulders. "When they rolled into my warehouse, Davide was in the back of the SUV bleeding out. The other guy was tits up with a shot to the leg *and* one in the back."

"And Vinnie?"

"Not a scratch on him. Said he stayed in the car while the *two* of them went to meet with you."

I shake my head. "What does Johnny think?"

He shrugs. "What Vinnie told him—that you opened fire then took off with the bag of cash. He doesn't have any reason to doubt Vinnie."

"Vinnie said that? He actually said I opened fire on them?"

Mas nods.

"Ed è per questo che c'è una taglia sulla mia testa." *And that's why there's a price on my head.*

Mas nods again. It's fucked up, but it makes sense. Joey blames me and maybe someone takes me out or maybe it starts the war he's wanted for a decade. Solid plan, since him and Vinnie have no clue that Mas would know I'd never hurt his brother. They have no clue Mas would know their story was utter bullshit.

"E poiché uno dei ragazzi è *mio* fratello, è un ordine di cattura." *And because one of the guys is my brother, it's a capture order.*

I nod. They want me delivered to Mas's doorstep so Mas, a true master in the art of torture, can exact whatever revenge he sees fit. Rob would do the same for me if the roles were reversed.

Paige fidgets like she's about to say something, so I slip one finger into the edge of her panties to stop her. She curls her entire body toward me, tucking harder into my side. Feels so fucking good. I kiss the top of her head, breathing her in.

I completely ignore the 'what the fuck' look on Mas's face. He's never seen me affectionate with a girl. No one has. Fucking around with a girl, sure. But cuddling? Never fucking happened before.

"So then Vinnie shot them," I add, trying to keep Mas's attention where it belongs.

"Either he did, or he knows who did. I know it wasn't Johnny, and I know it wasn't you. Beyond that? Who the fuck knows? But it does seem like a huge fucking coincidence that Vinnie—who hasn't gotten his hands dirty in a decade—happens to go to a bag drop the night Paulie decides to take you out."

"Paulie's girl is saying that Falco offered to open the books for him if he changed Famiglie."

"No shit?" Mas leans back in his seat.

"Claims Paulie didn't tell her specifics, but I could see taking me out as the buy-in. Not sure what me dead gets Falco, but not sure how else Paulie would prove his allegiance."

"Falco's a prick, but he doesn't have a death wish. No way he'd move against the Gallianos without Joey's nod."

I was thinking the exact same thing. "Think they're working together?"

He shrugs. "Entirely possible. Joey's always stirring the fucking pot. But I haven't heard anything."

"But why involve Davide?" I met him once in a big group setting. I don't know him beyond that, but I know Mas thinks the world of his baby brother. "They could have come after me without dragging him along."

He looks away. He stares out at nothing for a long minute. "Penso che Joey l'abbia fatto per punirmi." *I think Joey did it to punish me.* His voice cracks, the guilt crushing him. "Le uniche due persone a cui sa che tengo sono Johnny e Davide." *The only two people he thinks I care about are Johnny and Davide.*

Two weak spots. It makes Mas vulnerable for something exactly like this happening.

I'm positive Joey knows about Mas's third weakness—that Mas is completely fucking obsessed with Joey's youngest daughter. Mas is in complete denial about Joey knowing, but Joey's too fucking cunning not to notice how Mas—the smoothest, coolest cat there is—is a bumbling fucking idiot around that girl. Can barely talk, trips over his own two feet around her. Dropped his gun once and shot one of their own guys by accident when she walked into the room wearing a short skirt.

But Joey would never hurt Carly. Not because he's some amazing father or even a half-decent one. He's not, he's a complete piece of shit. He won't hurt Carly because she's promised to Riccardo Falco next year.

And no way Joey knows Mas and I have a blood oath deeper than any oath either of us made to our Famiglia. So he wouldn't come after me to hurt to Mas. He might come after me, but that would be to undermine the Galliano Famiglia, not for anything personal.

And I doubt any of Joey's guys could best Mas unless they shot him from behind. Plus going directly after Mas would hurt Johnny, which means the only way to hurt Massimo is to go indirect. To go after his biggest vulnerability—Davide.

The guilt over Davide is obviously killing him. Exactly how Joey intended it.

"You calling in a chit?" I ask.

He's looking straight at me, but I'm pretty sure he's deep in his head, running scenarios. He knows I'll kill Joey for him if he asks me to. It will start an all-out war among the Famiglie and will most likely betray my loyalty oath to the Gallianos.

But I would do it for Mas in a heartbeat. No hesitation whatsoever. I'll walk out the door and head straight at Joey this minute if he asks me to.

He shakes his head. "We're not there yet."

I nod. I don't want Paige to hear this next part. "Qualcuno dovrà prendersi la colpa per Davide e l'altro uomo." *Someone's going to have to take the blame for Davide and the other guy.*

Having the Bagliateris on my ass and a price on my head is annoying as fuck. I'd rather not kill every low-level guy who thinks he can come at me for a payday. Plus no matter how well I wrap a body in plastic, I still get blood in my trunk. And I fucking hate the smell of bleach. Makes me want to hurl every time, then Rob gets on my case when I trade out Rovers too often.

But most important—it puts Paige at risk whenever she's out of my sight.

"How about Riccardo?" Mas asks.

With Riccardo being the prick Carly's promised to, Mas's reason for picking him to take the fall is obvious.

"Does he have *anything* to do with Davide?"

Mas smiles and shrugs.

"If we're starting a war, I'm going for Joey, not Riccardo. Joey is the root of every problem. Always. Mark my words."

He nods, leans back in his chair. "It's not time for war. Not yet."

"Fine. Vinnie, then. All signs point to him shooting Davide anyway. Vuoi che me ne occupi io, così non si mettono dei guai tra te e Johnny?" *You want me to take care of this so it doesn't fuck shit up between you and Johnny?*

He smiles the widest I've seen in a long time. I can practically see the gears turning, a plan forming in Mas's head. I've almost forgotten what a happy Mas looks like. "Naah. This will be my pleasure. Lo renderò un casino da morire." *I'm going to make it messy as fuck.* "Anyway, you've got your hands full here."

Damiano

"You shouldn't come out here all alone." I force myself to take a deep breath so I don't lose my shit over the risks Paige takes.

"I'm not alone. You're here."

"I'm here this time. But you usually come out here alone."

"It's fine. It's perfectly safe here. Families picnic here, people jog with their dogs here."

"Strange men climb into your unlocked car here."

She smiles at me, bites her lip. "I seem to recall dragging that strange man home, tying him to my couch, then making him do unspeakable things to me. So maybe it's those strange men who shouldn't be out here all alone."

"I happen to enjoy those unspeakable things and want more of them." But that's not the point. "Promise me you won't come here without me ever again. I mean it, Paige."

"I promise. Plus it's nice to have someone else to carry the box."

Paige decided that Tango is ready to be released. I'm actually surprised she isn't trying to keep him. But she insisted he'd be happier here, with unlimited dirt and grass.

"We're here. This is my usual release spot."

I look around. It's a small clearing, a couple of boulders surrounded by some trees. There's a stream a few meters away.

"Looks like a nice spot."

"I released Charlie and Sierra in this tree." Paige walks over to a pine, leans against the trunk and looks up, like she expects to see them. She blows a kiss up the tree. "And I released Oscar in that one." She points to the next tree. She stares into its canopy.

She stands there a long minute. Pretty sure she's stalling.

"I don't think Tango can climb trees." I want to lighten her mood.

She smiles, but it's a sad smile. She walks over to take the box I'm holding. She sits on the boulder with it on her lap. "I like to sit here with them for a few minutes. Are we in a hurry?"

I shake my head.

"Thanks." Her voice cracks. She sounds so sad.

"You don't have to release him today."

"He's ready."

I'm standing here, doing nothing except watching Paige whisper into the box, tears gliding down her cheeks.

I need to make her happy. "Maybe his shell needs more time to finish healing? I don't think it's fully knit back together."

She looks up at me, her lips puffy and swollen. "It's fully knit, Dom. I just need a few minutes to say goodbye to him."

She's sad. My Paige is sad. I need to fix it. "Another week wouldn't hurt."

She shakes her head. "He's ready. He deserves to be happy." She sobs. "He deserves to find a mate and eat bugs. He can't do all that at your place. It's time."

I have no fucking idea what I'm supposed to do.

"Uh. I'll wait over there." I motion with my head to another clearing, but she doesn't look up. I tuck behind a tree. What the fuck am I supposed to do?

I dial Salvo.

"You're on speaker. Rob's here, too."

I speak quietly so she won't hear. "I need help. It's an emergency."

"Fuck," Salvo mutters. "Where? We're on our way."

Rob laughs. "Sit the fuck down, man. No way he's asking us for that kind of help. He never asks for that kind of help. What's going on, Dom?"

"It's Paige."

"Something happen?" Rob sounds genuinely concerned.

"She's crying. What do I do?"

"Why is she crying?"

"Because she's sad. What do I do?"

Salvo chimes in. "Did you make her sad?"

"No. Of course not."

"So then hurt whoever made her sad."

"If a person made her sad, they'd be dead already. It's her turtle. She's releasing it, and now she's crying."

"So tell her not to release it."

"I tried that. Didn't work. What else?"

Silence. Just the quiet gurgle of the stream and Paige's soft sobs.

"Rob, what do you do when Lyndie's sad?"

"Usually just buy her some shit to cheer her up. Or send our mom to go visit her."

Neither of those will help here. I peek around the tree to see Paige putting Tango down on the ground in front of a bush. "What else you got?"

"Uh... Fuck, I'm drawing a blank, man. Can you ignore it and wait for her to stop crying?"

"Her being sad is making me want to do recklessly violent and irrational things, but none of that will make her less sad. So no, I can't ignore it or I'll go insane. Salvo? You know women. What do I do?"

He exhales loudly. "They're never sad around me. My mere presence fills them immeasurable amounts of joy."

"Fuck you."

Salvo laughs. "What about... could you tell her a joke?"

"A joke?"

"Yeah, like, I don't know. Something funny to make her laugh?"

"Maybe. But I don't know any jokes."

"How about, 'knock-knock' then she says 'who's there' then you say 'Brittany' and then she says 'Brittany *who*' and then you pause and then you say 'oops, I did it again.'"

That doesn't make any sense at all. "I don't get it."

Rob agrees. "I don't get it either."

"Chicks will get it."

"You've used this on a girl?"

Salvo makes a sort of noncommittal sound. "Do you have any better ideas?"

"No. I have no fucking clue what to do." I say the joke back to him to make sure I got it right. I take a deep breath. "This better work." I hang up the call.

I step out from behind the tree. Paige is sitting on the boulder again, her head in her hands. I take a step toward her.

She looks up, red and puffy and crushed and sad.

"Kno—" I stop. No fucking way I'm telling her a knock-knock joke.

Paige is looking up at me, waiting for me to say something. Anything.

Anything other than a fucking knock-knock joke.

I hold up one finger, signaling for her to wait a sec. I take slows steps backward until I'm back behind the tree.

I call Salvo again.

"That was quick. She like the joke?"

"I can't tell her a joke right now."

"It might have worked," Rob says.

Pretty sure it wouldn't have. This time of day, Rob and Salvo are definitely at the Cat. "What girls are around? We need their help."

"Uh... Hey, Megan? Come here, babe."

"Hey, guys. What's going on?"

"What can Damiano do to cheer up his girl?"

"Did he make her sad?"

"No."

"Then that's easy. Just hold her."

"Hold her and then what?"

"Hold her, and that's it." She says it like we should understand what the fuck she's talking about.

Rob must be confused, too. "How does that solve anything?"

"Are you being serious or are you guys fucking with me?"

"Dead serious."

"He doesn't need to *solve* anything. He just needs to hold her. Let her cry. Let her sniffle into his shirt."

"That's it? Just hold her? That doesn't fix anything."

"Sometimes that fixes everything."

"Just hold her and nothing else?"

"Guys, you're overthinking this. Women are easy. A hug. That's it."

I let out a relieved exhale. "I can do that. I can definitely do that. Thanks, Meg."

I end the call and walk back to Paige.

I step over the back of the rock to sit behind her wrapping my arms around her tight. The rock is cold as fuck and jagged. I have no clue how she's managed to sit here for this long, but as soon as she leans back into me, her silky hair pressing into my face, I forget about the rock poking my ass.

"We should get going." Her voice catches on her breath.

I rest my head on her shoulder. "If you want to stay longer, we can."

"Okay, yeah."

Damiano

PAIGE IS WATERING HER plants. I repotted all of hers, splitting a few into two pots. Then I cleared a ledge off for her, right in front of a window. After we moved all her full-sun plants there, Paige snapped a few photos of the shelf saying it was 'Insta-worthy.' Every one of them has sprouted new leaves, turned brighter shades of green, and is in full bloom.

Paige finished watering her shelf, and I can tell she's eyeing some of my plants, trying to decide if she should water them. I'd rather she didn't since she still doesn't know what the fuck she's doing.

And I have a better idea anyway.

A fan-fucking-tastic idea. Brilliant, actually.

"Angel?"

She looks over and smiles at me. Fucking brilliant smile.

"Can you do something for me?"

Anything, she'll say *anything*. Because of course she will.

"Anything."

This girl will do anything to make me happy. Fucking blows my mind.

"Come talk to my little friend." I stroke my dick over my pants.

"What?" She looks away, instantly blushing. She bites the tip of her finger.

Does she think I don't hear her when she whispers entire one-sided conversations to him?

"Come here. I love when you talk to my dick."

She puts the watering can down and walks over. Slowly. Drags her fingers across the back of a chair as she passes it. "Are you making fun of me?"

"Angel." I lean back, unbutton and unzip my pants. I push them and my boxers down to my ankles, stepping one foot out. "Does this look like I'm making fun of you?" I'm already rock hard. Have been since she walked into the room in those tiny shorts that hug her perfect ass. No way I'm letting her out of the apartment in those. "Come tell him all your secrets." I'm gripping him at the base, pointing him toward her.

Paige lowers down to her knees at my feet, pulls her shirt up over her head, tossing it on the coffee table. My fucking goddess *and her goddess nipples* and her complete comfort being half naked.

She rests her hands on my thighs, looks down at my guy. "Hey, baby."

I fucking *love it* when she calls my dick 'baby.' She calls me Dom or Damiano. Never any nicknames. But my dick gets baby.

She leans forward, places a little air kiss to the right of him, then the left, her cheek brushing against him on each side for il bacetto, the Italian hello kiss on each cheek.

"Come stai?" *How are you?*

For fuck's sake, a drop of cum leaks out of my dick as he's revving the fuck up. "Are you talking to my uccello in Italiano?"

"Give us a second," she says to my dick, then turns her face up to me. "Do you mind? We're having a very private moment down here."

"In Italiano?"

"Yes. I'm learning *Italiano* so I can speak to mio caro." *My darling.* She points to my dick.

This girl. "And what about me?"

"What about you?" Paige holds my dick at the base and rubs the tip across her lips.

I grunt. "Tell me you're learning Italian for me, Paige."

She tips her head to the side, purses her lips as she thinks. "Nope. Just for tua minchia." *Your cock.* "Now, if you don't mind."

Fuck me, I definitely don't mind.

She whispers more to my dick. I can't make out what she's saying, but I can feel her lips moving against him, little butterfly kisses up and down my rod.

"You're not going to tell me what you're saying?"

She huffs like she's annoyed, but she's smiling a mile wide. "We are trying to get to know each other better down here."

"Yeah?" I fucking love it when she gets bratty with me. "In that case, think he can get to know your tonsils, too?"

She giggles. The girl is glowing, smiling up at me.

I guess she reached the end of her Duolingo lessons because she leans forward and starts full-on sucking my dick now. Taking more of me each time. Every time she does this, she goes deeper and deeper, just like every day I'm near her, I fall deeper and deeper.

I slide my hand into her silky hair. Gather it into a ponytail, pile it all on top of her head. I swirl it around and around, all gold and white and silky. Feels so good in my hand, but more than anything, I'm moving it aside so it doesn't block my view of Paige's lips stretched around me, her sunken cheeks. Her occasional gag as she takes me too deep.

My hand goes to the back of her head on instinct. Not to push—okay, to push a little—but there mostly because my body needs to surround this girl. Needs to envelop her. Needs to consume her. Meld into her. I'm tempted to wrap my leg around her head, but before I make up my mind, she grabs my balls. Rubs them.

"Such a good girl."

She pulls off me. "Do you like that?"

"Oh, now you're talking to me?"

"Damiano," she scolds as she licks up and down my shaft slower than humanly possible, using her tongue like a paintbrush of pleasure and teasing.

I need more. "Come here." I reach down under her armpits, pull her up onto the couch, onto her knees hovering over me. "My *minchia* has a message for your *dolce figa*. It requires special delivery."

I slide the fabric of her shorts and panties to the side and pull her down onto me, plunging right in. I knew she'd be soaking wet for me.

She tries to lean back as she moans, but I pull her close against my chest. One hand is tight on her hips, the other slides up her smooth, warm back. Her pussy's burning hot surrounding my cock, sucking him. My arms surround her, pulling her tight.

I whisper in her ear, knowing full well she won't understand me, "Questo è tutto il mio dannato mondo. Giusto qui." *This is my entire fucking world. Right here.*

I HAVE NO IDEA what Damiano just whispered in my ear. But I *felt it* deep inside me. And it felt big.

It felt like he's giving me a part of him he's never given to anyone else.

And maybe I should do the same.

I whisper back. "Do you have lube?"

He's buried in my hair, sucking hard on my neck. Probably going to leave a mark. And his fingers might leave bruises on my hips as he grinds me into him, making me hit the exact right spot each time. *Right there.* He's tender and affectionate, but not gentle. Not at all. "Hmm?"

I swallow hard between pants. "Lube?"

"You're soaking wet for me already. But if you need more, come sit on my face until you're drenched." He starts to shift our positions.

"We don't need lube *there.*" I grab his hand and reach it behind me, down to my ass. "We need it *here.*"

Dom's head tips back, he exhales heavily out his nose, nostrils flaring. "For fuck's sake, angel."

He grabs the back of my head and pulls me in for a deep kiss, grabbing a handful of my hair, holding my head where he wants as his tongue dominates mine.

"Hold onto me. Tight as you can." Dom stands up, lifting me along with him like I weigh nothing. He carries me... *into the kitchen?*

"You keep lube in the kitchen?"

"*Lube* lube? No. I don't have actual lube in the apartment. I've never had a girl here and never intended to. So no real lube. We're going Old Italy here, angel."

Before I can ask what the heck that means, Dom grabs a bottle of olive oil off the counter and turns us toward his bedroom.

"You're kidding, right?" I can't help but laugh.

"Laugh it up now, angel, but neither one of us is going to be laughing in thirty seconds."

"Won't that stain your sheets or something?"

"I can buy more sheets."

"Maybe we should wai—"

"Do not finish that sentence." The backs of my legs hit the edge of his bed. "Get on all fours."

I take a deep breath, give him one more kiss, then unwrap my arms from around him. I trust him with my life, so I guess I'm going to trust him with this too.

The second I'm on all fours, I'm pushed forward by his face burying into my ass. His rough, prickly stubble surrounding his soft, warm tongue as it teases me. He backs off only long enough to pull off my shorts and toss them across the room.

Dom's hands grip my ass, spreading me open as he licks and laps at my ass and *oh sweet Jesus* is that his finger or his tongue or—I *actually do not care one bit* what part of his that is because it feels *marvelous*.

"You taste like fucking heaven."

I moan deep and loud into the pillow. *Holy hell.*

"You like my tongue in your sweet ass, angel?" Dom licks my no-no while he tugs on my clit, and I swear I'm going to lose my mind. "Answer me. Tell me you like it, Paige."

I nod my head into the pillow.

"Nuh-uh." Dom stops. "Words, Paige. Tell me you like my tongue pushing into your tight little hole."

"Dom."

"Tell me." His finger teases me *there*, rubbing around the outside.

"I love it." I huff out a heavy breath. "I really love it."

I hear the jostling of Dom opening the bottle of oil, feel the cool drops land on me. I must tense up without meaning to.

"Relax, angel. I'm going to get you so ready you're going to beg for my cock. You're going to take my finger, then you're going to take two."

He lays us down on our sides, him spooning me. One hand prodding my ass, his other hand rubbing small circles on my clit, and I swear I'm about to see stars. I've never gotten so close so fast before. My toes start to point hard. I'm definitely going to explo—

He pulls his hands away. "Not yet, greedy girl. Not until I stuff this sweet ass full of cock."

"But... I was about to... *please*, Dom. Just another few seconds of what you were doing."

"La mia ragazza perfetta."

My perfect girl. That one I learned this morning.

"Kiss me, angel."

And of course I do. I twist as much as I can and kiss him. Deep. Passionately. With everything I've got.

"Don't stop kissing me. Even when it hurts, yes?"

I nod my head and keep kissing him. He moves one arm up, wrapped around me, hugging me in close. His other hand is lining his big dick up with my ass. I'm just going to focus on his lips and his tongue and his—

Ho-ly fuck-ing hell, that burns.

I turn away from his kiss and bury my head in his pillow while his cock slides deeper in my ass.

"Shh, shh, angel. That was the worst part. I'm in. I'm so fucking *in*. You took every inch of me like I knew you could." His voice is deep and breathy, like he's losing his mind. "Take a deep breath. I promise it gets better."

It can't frickin' get worse, so it'll either keep hurting like I'm being stabbed by his huge fricking dagger directly in my ass or, like he promises, it will start to feel better. There is no third option.

I mean, I guess this *is* the third option, technically. I giggle at my own stupid mental joke.

"See, angel. I told you." He leans down and kisses between my shoulder blades, licks a line up to my neck. Dom starts to move in and out, just a little, while nipping at my ear.

I reach down to play with my clit. Maybe that will help.

"Uh-uh. Hands on your ass, spreading your cheeks wide open for me, or hands above your head, in complete surrender. Pick one."

"But... I need more, like... before."

"I've got more for you, angel. Put your hands where I said."

I move my hands up above my head because I'm not sure how I feel about spreading my ass cheeks.

Dom starts pinching my nipple. Hard. It's the distraction I need. His other hand reaches back down and rubs little circles against my clit the way he almost made me explode before. "Grind against my hand. Take what you need."

I push forward, smashing my clit against his fingers, pressing against them. Yes. Yes. This is getting better.

"Such a good girl." After a few seconds, Dom spanks my clit hard.

I pull back in shock, unintentionally grinding down onto his dick.

"Again."

I do it again. Grinding forward against his fingers then pulling back when he spanks my clit. And again.

"That's it. *Fuuuuck*. Fuck. Ride my cock with your tight ass. Just like that. *Just* like *that*."

He tricked me. He tricked me into bucking back and forth, riding him.

But honestly, he tricked my body too because while this still hurts like hell, it's not as bad with me controlling the pace while he plays with my clit.

In fact... I might actually... Yeah, it's very possible...

Oh, it's so possible. There's a volcanic explosion building up inside of me.

"Tell me I can blow deep inside your ass. Beg me to fill you up with my cum."

I nod.

"Use your big girl words and tell me you want this. Say it."

With Dom whispering in my ear, biting me gently and holding me so tight, it's definitely going to happen. My eyes are practically rolling in the back of my head. He's thrusting deep and steady. Not hard and fast like when we're doing this the normal way. This is an entirely different rhythm that's hitting just right.

"Tell me to come deep in this ass as it chokes the life out of my cock. Show me what a good girl you are."

That's it. That is it.

My body explodes inside and out, actually convulsing and spasming against him. "Oh fuck... Dom." His name has five syllables as my ass pulses around him. I am literally shaking and panting.

What the hell kind of orgasm is this? I'm still quivering.

"Fuck, Paige. Fuck. Fuck. Tell me to come."

I take a deep breath in so I don't pass out. "Come inside me, Dom. Back there. Please."

One last thrust, yanking me hard up against him, his heavy grunt right at my ear. His entire body goes stiff as he pushes in deeper and erupts inside me.

I'm going to need a minute.

Or like, five. That was...

Dom pulls out slowly, then wraps himself around me like an anaconda, throwing his leg over mine so I'm completely surrounded by him. He plants tiny kisses on my neck and shoulder. "Un giorno mi sposerai, bella. Non esiste un cazzo di modo in cui io possa vivere senza di te."

"What does that mean?"

He hums against my shoulder.

"Dom? Tell me what you said."

"Shit, I forget already."

I turn in his big warm arms to face him. "You forgot what you just said, like, three seconds ago?"

"Your body just sucked every brain cell out of my head. I couldn't even tell you my own name right now." Then he smiles. A huge, gorgeous Damiano smile that makes his green eyes sparkle like gems.

Damiano

ROB IS SITTING IN our usual booth at the Cat, on the phone. He looks up and sees me approaching. "He just walked in. Yeah, I'll call you back." He puts the phone down. "Look who decided to show the fuck up."

I slide into the booth. "Miss me?"

Rob picks a pistachio nut from the pile in front of him and throws it at my chest. It bounces off me and falls to the floor.

"What?"

"What? Fuck you, that's what. There's a fucking price on your head. No one's seen you in two days. And your one-word text responses are pissing me off more than usual."

"I was... busy." When I wasn't hanging out with Paige or sliding into her warm, wet, death-gripping figa, I was busy staring at her from across the room. All higher priorities than coming here.

Rob scowls at me. Literally scowls like he's about to rip my head off. "I thought Johnny and Massimo caught up with you and you were bleeding out in Massimo's warehouse."

"Aww, you care."

"Fuck you. Of course I care." He throws another pistachio at me, this time with a little smile, and this time aimed at my forehead. "How is it you notice the slightest twitch on some fucker's face 200 yards away but you have no clue about what's right in front of your face half the time?"

I let out a long breath. "Well, clearly I'm fine."

"And last night? Were you fine last night?"

Last night, Gli Azzurri beat France with a penalty kick, and I celebrated balls-deep in Paige, her arms wrapped around me not letting go, so I'd say I was substantially better than fine. But pretty sure that's not what Rob's getting at.

"Last night?"

"Yeah. Last night." He cracks open another nut and eats it, watching me. "Last night when Vinnie Ricci confessed to shooting those the guys from the park."

"Huh."

Mas actually got a confession out of Vinnie? Fuck, I trained him good. I have to fight a smile, so I lean forward to grab some of Rob's pistachios. "That's interesting."

He stares at me a long minute, trying to see inside my head. "'That's interesting?' Don't you want to ask me why he did it?"

"Not sure I give a shit why he shot some low-level Bagliateri errand boys. But sure, enlighten me."

"I don't mean why he shot them, dickhead. I mean why he confessed."

I nod. That would make more sense. I shrug my hands for him to continue. "Did he say?"

"Apparently he made a video saying he felt guilty as fuck for offing those guys and grabbing the bag of cash." Rob goes back to his pistachios. "Then he actually apologized to Davide *and* to Davide's wife. Then said he was taking off for a while."

Well, fuck. The apology might have been overkill, but I get why Mas would want to hear it.

"So what's happening to him now? Joey won't give a shit about the two runners or the money—not where Vinnie's concerned—but Mas will want recompense."

Rob shakes his head. "He's gone."

"Gone, like..."

"Gone, like into the wind. Johnny went to his place as soon as they got the video. No Vinnie, no bag of cash. But also no sign of him leaving on his home security. Security showed him getting home around nine, then not a single thing until Johnny kicked open his front door at midnight. Poof."

Of course Mas would fuck with Joey by leaving him hanging—wondering if Vinnie ran or was taken out. If Joey knows the truth about the shootings, which I'm positive he does, he'd know the guilt and the cash grab were a lie, that the whole confession and disappearance was a setup. But he'd have to admit the truth to Johnny to point any fingers.

"Good riddance. Guess that means the price is off my head."

"Oh yeah? That's what you think it means?"

"What?" I grab another handful of pistachios, concentrating hard to avoid too much eye contact.

"Some people think it's awfully convenient."

I pop a nut into my mouth. "What are you saying?"

"*I'm* not saying anything. But Joey isn't buying it."

"Not buying what? That Vinnie was racked with guilt or that he split."

"No clue. All he said was, 'This is fucking bullshit, and you know it.'"

"So what did you tell him?"

"I told him I don't give a shit that Vinnie shot some low-level Bagliateri errand boys."

I smile. Rob truly is the best boss a man could have. My shoulders relax.

"Then I told him this better mean the price is off your head, unless he's calling Vinnie a liar *and* has some proof of who actually shot those guys. That shut him up fast."

"And?"

"And then he said the price was off your head *for now* and that we can both go fuck ourselves. Then I started to worry that Johnny and Massimo doubted the cover story too and came after you."

"I was home all—" *Cover story?* "What do you mean, cover story?"

Rob squints at me. "The cover story. Vinnie taking the blame. You staging it like a confession and him running. You definitely made him make that video."

I shake my head.

"You're shitting me."

I shake my head again.

"This has you written all over it. This is exactly your style. The obviously fake confession. The melodramatic apology to Davide's wife. Getting in and out with a body *without* cameras picking anything up. How was this not you?"

"Maybe Vinnie actually shot them and actually felt guilty and maybe he has a shitty security system? Why don't you believe it?"

"Because I'm not a fucking moron. And neither is Joey." He tries to stare into my head again, folds his arms across his chest. "If it wasn't you, who was it? I can account for every one of our guys last night except for you. Plus none of them would act without running it by me first. So what the fuck?"

If people believe that I didn't do it, they're going to start looking around for someone else with a reason to go after Vinnie. Mas has the most obvious motive after me because of Davide. I can't let anyone start looking in his direction.

"Naah, man. It was me. I was trying to see how convincing I could be."

Another pistachio aimed at my head. "I have no fucking clue if you're lying now or if you were lying two minutes ago."

I smile at him and leave it at that. Rob is cunning as fuck, and people rarely pull one over on him, so I better change the subject before he digs in, looking for details.

I make eye contact with Megan across the room and motion with my head for her to join us. She swishes her fine ass over and whispers something into Rob's ear. He pulls her down onto his lap. Pretty sure he's already forgotten about me.

Which is perfectly fine with me. Now I can go home and stare at my Paige some more.

"DO YOU KNOW THE code to unlock this one?" Gina's tugging on the doors of the cabinet that Damiano pulled his guns out of the other day.

"No. And stop snooping through his stuff." She's gone through his kitchen and most of the living room already. She found his drawer full of knives and another full of souvenir grenades from his military time.

"Of course we can snoop. When a guy leaves you at his place alone, it's allowed. It's expected. It's actually super weird not to."

"No, it's not."

"It absolutely is. Snooping shows you want to know more about him. That you're interested in his life before you came into it. It shows you care."

"Or it shows you're deranged."

She stops and looks at me. "You really don't go through a guy's things?"

I smile. "I'm screwing with you. Of course I snooped through this whole place. I did that, like, day two that I was here. Want to see his closet? It's massive and insanely organized."

We stumble through the bedroom and into his closet. The original layout for this apartment was as a two-bedroom, but Dom told me that, since he was going to live alone and was going to 'live Italiano,' he'd had it reconfigured into a one-bedroom with a huge closet for all his suits, designer clothes, and shoes.

I plop down onto the comfy chair in the middle of the closet, my wineglass almost sloshing over the sides. After my first week at my new job—my new job courtesy of Damiano—I'm exhausted and need this drink.

After I was sad saying goodbye to Tango, Damiano had the idea that instead of rescuing wildlife that I'm going to release back into the wild and never see again, why didn't I get a job at a veterinarian's office so that I can help animals that I will see again when they come back? He took me to the vet in his neighborhood. Damiano talked to the guy in the back for a few minutes alone, and then the guy offered me a tech job without bothering to look at the application I'd filled out. He's even paying me more than what I made as a paralegal.

Gina places her wineglass on the bureau and spins around. "Oh my god. You have got to marry this guy. This is like a magazine closet." She opens a drawer, then another. "He organizes his socks? I didn't think he was so anal."

Do I tell her that we... I don't know. Maybe it's weird to talk about that.

She opens another drawer. "So do you live here permanently now?"

I take another sip of the delicious Barolo Damiano bought. He doesn't drink much because he likes to stay in control of his environment, but he went out and bought six bottles of wine, plus olives and cheeses, when I asked him if Gina and I could have a girls' night in while he went to work. "I'm not really sure."

"What's going on with your place?"

I shake my head. "I still have it, but Damiano doesn't want me to go to that part of the city without him, and I don't know, I'm not sure I want to go back. And Dom bought me all new clothes." I motion over to the part of the closet he cleared out for me.

She's too busy flipping through his hangers to notice me point. "This is an insane number of suits. He must have thirty. Forty? Does he wear a suit every day?"

"When he goes to work, yeah. And sometimes around the apartment too."

"So fucking hot."

I bite my lip and nod. I love him in a suit. "But sometimes he goes casual." I motion to the other side of his closet. Stacks of Gucci trackpants, Prada shirts, Luca Faloni sweaters.

"Do you care that when he 'goes to work,' half the time that means going to their strip club?" Gina is holding up one of Dom's shirts and looking in the three-sided mirror.

I take another drink. A huge gulp this time. "I don't know how to feel about that." I really don't. "He says the girls are just in the background and they all know not to approach him. Apparently, that's how it's always been there."

"That he's never fucked the girls there? No fucking way that's true."

"No, I don't think that's what he meant. I think he meant like, *they* didn't approach *him*? Like, he would approach them when he wanted to... to do whatever?"

"And now he isn't going to approach them?"

I nod.

"Do you trust him?"

"I do." I really do.

Gina starts taking her jeans off.

"Uh, what are you doing?"

"I'm trying on one of his suits. You grab one too."

"What? Why? Is that creepy?"

"Come on. It'll be fun. Let's be gangsters for the rest of the night."

"Oh my god, yes!" I grab one too. The pants are too long, and the waist is too big, but he has a whole rack of belts.

"Do you know how to tie a tie?" Gina's holding two up, trying to decide which goes better with the shirt she has on.

"No, but let's YouTube it. Oh, I totally forgot. If you want to be a gangster, look in that cabinet, to your left. You'll love it."

Damiano

LAST NIGHT I CAME home to find Paige and Gina passed out drunk on the couch, each dressed in one of my suits. They were also each wearing a leather holster loaded up with knives in each loop. Gina had live flashbang grenades clipped to hers, and Paige was wearing brass knuckles.

It was hot as fuck finding them like that.

I disarmed Gina and left her on the couch to sleep it off. Then I carried Paige into my room and undressed her from everything except the holster, brass knuckles, and her pink panties.

First thing this morning, I had a guy from my crew drive a very hungover Gina home. Then I grabbed a bagel and orange juice for my sleeping angel's hangover. But it turns out, Paige wakes up horny after a night of drinking, so sliding back into bed with her was an excellent bonus.

Morning sex. Morning sex with Paige. Who the fuck knew that reaching over to find an almost naked Paige, with her skin burning hot from being under the blanket and her sighs soft and her legs spread just enough for me to slide in, was abso-fucking-lutely worth blowing through every no-sleepover boundary I'd ever set.

It's hours later now. My bed is huge, plenty of space. But me and Paige are using the same third of it, her head resting on my abs, my hand resting on her lower back, fingers tucked into the back of her little panties. Half the time we're home, that's all she's wearing.

Or those teeny-tiny shorts with a tight little tank top, nipples on full display.

Right now, she's telling me about growing up near the beach in San Diego. I'm half listening and half admiring the different shades of blonde and the lightest brown in her hair.

I can't remember ever taking an afternoon nap before, but after Paige rode me on the couch, then we showered together with her soaping me up, which led to another round in the shower, our warm bodies collapsed onto the cool, crisp sheets. I could drift off easy.

But I have an even better idea.

I slide out from under her, roll her onto her back.

She gasps from the sudden movement.

"Keep talking, angel."

I kiss her tummy.

"What are you doing down there?"

"Mangerò la tua bella figa mentre mi racconti qualcosa in più sulla California." *I'm going to eat your pretty pussy while you tell me more about California.*

She giggles. "What did you say?"

"I said, 'tell me more about California.'" I lick a line along her hip bone, suck in a mouthful of her skin letting go with a loud, wet squelch.

"Okay. Yeah. Or just, you do your part, and I'll just... Yeah."

I run my hand down her long, smooth leg, admiring my olive skin against her tan thigh. I hitch her leg up, place it over my shoulder as I shift into place.

I nuzzle right up against the cotton, take a deep inhale of her tang. "Keep talking, angel." Press my nose against her clit, her smell lighting me up.

"Uh... something? I was... saying something... Words?"

"Words?"

"I think I was saying words. Maybe?"

"Yeah, baby. You were saying words. Say some more."

I push the cotton to the side, latch onto her shiny little clit. She's sloppy wet already and I can still taste my jizz from finishing deep inside her in the shower. I squeeze her thighs like I'm never going to let go.

I'm thinking we—

Click. Woosh.

Did my front door just open?

Thud.

It slams closed. What the fuck?

Paige sits up. "What—"

"Shh. I'll handle this," I whisper. "Go into the bathroom and lock the door. Nod your head so I know you understand."

She just stares at me, her eyes huge.

"Paige?"

She nods.

I grab my pants off the floor, pull my dagger out of the clip. I'd rather not shoot someone in my apartment if I can avoid it.

Even though it's afternoon, my living room is dark. The window shades are on timers to allow the ideal amount of light in for the plants depending on the season. I edge into the room so I can catch whatever asshole broke in off guard.

The lamp on a side table flicks on, illuminating Rob. "You come at me with that fucking knife, and I'll punch straight through your skull."

I exhale, then twirl my dagger a few times. "What the fuck, man? Why'd you break into my place?"

"I didn't break in. I used the code."

There was a time not too long ago that I actually thought my apartment was a fortress. Now I have to revisit my entire security scheme. I still don't know how Mas got in. "Since when do you have the code?"

"Since I asked Salvo for *his* door code. What the fuck, Dom? You have your own code for my loft. Why don't I have a code for your place?"

I tilt my head to the side. Is he busting my balls, or is he really offended? I honestly can't tell. "What are you doing here, man? You came in like a fucking bullet train."

"Check your phone once in a fucking while, and I won't have to come all the way the fuck over here." Rob picks my phone up off the coffee table and tosses it to me. I haven't looked at it in hours. Once Paige started whispering sweet nothings to my dick, I forgot about the rest of the world.

The screen shows seventeen alerts for texts and missed calls. That many alerts and an amped-up Rob tells me something has gone way fucking sideways.

"You want to tell me what's going on, or you want me to read all this?" I toss my phone onto the couch, making it clear I'm not reading any of it.

"I'll tell you on the way. Get dressed so we can go kill some people. A whole lot of people need to die tonight. It's going to be a huge fucking blood bath, so grab your shit and let's go."

"The fuck, man? Keep it down." I tilt my head toward the bedroom.

Hopefully Paige actually listened to me and went into the bathroom and closed the door so she didn't hear that. "Alexa, play white noise on the bedroom speakers, level six." I step closer to Rob. "*The whole world* doesn't need to hear any of this."

Rob's mouth opens like he's going to say something, then he closes it. He definitely wasn't expecting me to have anyone here. Honestly, until recently, Salvo was the only person who'd ever been in my apartment.

Rob lowers his voice. "The rabbit girl still here?" He looks toward the bedroom. "Bring her out. I want to meet her."

Paige was mostly naked five minutes ago, and Rob's shouting about killing people. No way they're meeting right now. I ignore his question.

Instead, I get back to the business that forced me to get out of bed. I lower my voice and lean in, hoping he takes the hint and keeps his voice down too. "Why are we hurting people, and how many?" I need to know what gear to grab.

"Get this. My *dad* was just *arrested* for killing those three Bianchi brothers."

"*What*? He didn't have anything to do with that." Three low-level Bagliateri guys were found beaten to a pulp in an elementary school playground a few weeks ago. We didn't give a shit because they weren't our guys and they weren't in one of our neighborhoods. We assumed it was a drug deal gone wrong.

"Chief Brisbane is saying otherwise. Put on a whole press conference about it."

"Roberto hasn't gotten his hands dirty in years." That's what I'm here for. Rob, too. If Roberto wanted those brothers taken out, I would have done it, not him.

"Yeah, well. They're booking him as we speak."

"That's fucking ridiculous."

"Yup."

"So what now?"

"Now we go grab every Bagliateri soldier we can find and beat the piss out of them until they tell us who actually killed those guys and who's setting up my dad."

Rob loves getting his hands dirty. I fucking hate when he does. My entire job is to keep him safe. But I also get that he's not the type of leader that sends troops out to fight while he stays inside a bubble. I hate it, but I respect the hell out of it.

"So grab your shit and let's go hurt some people."

"It's going to be a long night."

Rob puts his hands on my shoulders. "Long. Reckless. Violent. Messy. Me and you, man. Our kind of night."

Our kind of night.

In fact, spending the afternoon with Paige, then *this* as my evening entertainment, then coming home to Paige in bed in her tiny panties? Might be the perfect day. I'm smiling ear to ear.

"Give me a minute." I motion toward the bedroom.

"Just one?" He shakes his head as I walk away. "Don't I get to meet your—" I slam the bedroom door closed before I hear the end of his question.

Paige is sitting quietly on the bed, not far from where I left her. She switched off the white noise at some point.

"Hey, I overreacted. It was just my boss, Rob."

"Okay." She's avoiding eye contact, seems a little shaken up by the threat of a break-in.

"I've got to head out to take care of some work stuff. Do you want to call Gina and invite her back over to hang out again? I can send someone to pick her up."

She shrugs one shoulder. "I'll probably just watch some TV or something."

"I'll be gone a few hours. You sure?"

She nods. "Yeah. I'll be fine."

I kiss the top of her head. I've never left for a job knowing a girl would be waiting for me after.

I could get used to this.

Paige

THE FRONT DOOR KEYPAD chimes. How is Damiano back already?

Shit. Crap. Dammit.

He walks into the living room. "Hey, angel. I didn't think you'd still be up." His face lights up, his Adam's apple rising as he smiles. Lips parting. He looks genuinely and thoroughly happy to see me.

Until his eyes drop down to the pet carrier and the cardboard box filled with my plants that are sitting in the middle of the room.

The smile falls from his face.

His shoulders stiffen. "You going somewhere, Paige?"

I shrug, avoiding eye contact.

He tosses his phone onto the table. Unholsters his gun and places it there, too. Takes off his knife, drops it onto the table.

He stares at the carrier for a long minute, his mouth closed, jaw clenched. He finally looks at me. "What's going on?"

"You changed your clothes. While you were out. That's not what you were wearing when you left." I can tell he showered too.

He lets out a long, slow breath of air.

"What do you want me to say? I'm not going to lie to you. You know who I am. You know what I do. You know what that means."

I shrug. "It means you were out killing people."

He pulls his lips in, eyes closed. Pretty sure he's thinking before he speaks.

Dom tips his head back, lets out a long, loud breath. "Don't do this, baby."

"What else am I supposed to do?"

He doesn't answer. He just looks at me. Searches my eyes.

"You knew this about me. Gina told you about my role in the Famiglia, and you asked me to deny it and I didn't. I told you it was true."

"I didn't understand what it meant until tonight."

"How could you not understand what 'hurting and killing people' meant?" He looks so confused, his brow furrowed. "There are guns and knives and explosives all the fuck over my apartment."

I wrap my arms around myself and shrug my shoulder, talking down to the floor. "I didn't want it to be true."

Dom walks over and rubs my arms. "Sit with me. Let's talk about this." He kisses my forehead, lingering there.

I swallow hard. "My mind is made up."

"But you waited for me. You're still here. You want to give us a chance to figure this out, yeah?"

I turn away. I can't meet his eyes right now. I shake my head, just a little.

Dom takes his hands off me, steps back, taking away his warmth. "Then why are you still here?"

I hesitate before answering. "I can't find Romeo." I swallow hard. "And I can't find the keys to Jolene." I look up at him.

His upper lip twitches as he folds his arms across his chest. "*That's* why you're still here? You *weren't* waiting to talk to me? You weren't waiting to see if we could figure something out?"

I shake my head. I know that's shitty, but it's true.

"You weren't even going to say goodbye?" Damiano's lips close.

I shrug.

He nods slightly, shifts his jaw. "Fine."

He disappears into the front hallway and comes back with my car keys. Tosses them to me kind of hard. I barely manage to catch them.

"Thank you." I use my polite and mature voice. We can be adults about this. "Can you please help me find Romeo?"

Damiano goes into the kitchen and gets himself a glass of water. "Romeo probably senses you're all stressed out and needs time to calm down. Why don't you come back later?"

I make full eye contact for this. "I don't need time to calm down, and I'm not coming back, Dom."

"Well." He stares at me a full thirty seconds, nods slightly. "Then it looks like you're shit out of rabbit."

And there we go.

I've got nothing left to say, so I just huff, then continue looking for Romeo. Under the couch, behind the chair. In the closet, even though the door was closed. I've already been looking for two hours.

Damiano is leaning against the kitchen door frame, watching me. Not helping, just watching.

"Can you just do that clicky mouth thing so he comes running to you?"

"Romeo is happy here. Why would you take that away?"

I stare at him long and hard. And blink.

"I mean it, Paige. Romeo isn't trying to go with you."

I roll my eyes. "He doesn't understand what's happening. He doesn't know I'm leaving."

"You sure about that?" Damiano motions toward the pet carrier sitting in the middle of the room.

I ignore him. I have no clue whether rabbits see a pet carrier and know that it means they're going somewhere like a cat does. I click with my tongue against my teeth, trying to do it the way Damiano does. No dice. "Maybe he's trapped in a closet or stuck somewhere?"

"Maybe Romeo's hiding from you on purpose."

"Why would he hide from me?" I look in the corner behind a built-in planter where Damiano set up a whole litter box area for Romeo that he's actually been really great about using, although I did notice him eating some of the hay he's supposed to be using for the bathroom.

"Oh, I don't know. Maybe Romeo did the math. Figured the odds of surviving increase by staying. The rabbit stays here, and it's one less rock on that shelf of yours."

It's like a punch in the gut.

I do *everything I can* to save the little critters. Sometimes I'm not enough, and he's throwing that in my face. I stare at him, my mouth open. "Would you just call my damn rabbit so I can leave?"

Damiano stares at me.

I stare back.

Damiano mouth-clicks two times.

Romeo cannonballs out from under the couch *that I checked twice*, practically climbing up Damiano's leg.

Damiano scoops him up.

Finally, I can get out of here. I pick up the pet carrier and unlock it. I take a step toward Damiano.

He walks around me to the refrigerator and takes out a celery stalk. Feeds it to Romeo, tiny green bits falling to the floor. The only sound in the room as Damiano stares at me is Romeo's crunch-crunch-crunch-crunch.

Damiano takes a step *away* from me. Away from the pet carrier.

"Where are you going? Give me my rabbit."

"No. And Romeo's a stupid name. She's called Ginger now." He walks toward his bedroom.

"You can't... *rename my* rabbit. And Romeo is a boy."

"*This* rabbit is not male."

What? "Of course he is."

He shakes his head vehemently. He seems absolutely sure about this.

I *thought* I was sure that Romeo was a boy.

"Whatever. Male, female. It doesn't matter. It's *my* rabbit."

Damiano slams the bedroom door closed in my face.

"I'll call the police. I mean it, Dom."

He opens the door a few inches. "Go ahead. Call the police. Give them my full name when you do. Ask them to send Lieutenant Baker." He throws me a chin lift. "He and I can have a nice long chat all about your illegal animal rehabilitation operation."

Huh? He wouldn't.

"Operating without a license." He shakes his head, tsk-tsking.

I stare at him, completely unable to form words, my mouth opening and closing.

He lifts Romeo higher, gives him—*her?*—a kiss on the top of his head, between his ears. Romeo purrs like a racecar.

Damiano takes a long breath. "Paige. If you want to stay and figure this shit out, go unpack then come talk to me." He reaches out, tracing his finger up my arm. The warmth of his touch zings up my spine.

But there's nothing to figure out. I slowly shake my head.

He pulls his hand away. "Then leave already."

"Give me my rabbit and I'll go."

"Just get out." He slams the bedroom door, twists the lock.

TWO WEEKS LATER

Damiano

No surprise I find Rob sitting in his private booth, his favorite Cat girl in his lap. She's whispering in his ear, he's whispering to her tits.

I drop down heavy into the booth. "No one knows a fucking thing about who clipped the Bianchi brothers."

Rob looks over Megan's bare shoulder at me. "How is that even possible?"

"No fucking clue."

"Give us five, babe?" Rob leans back to give Megan room to climb off.

She grinds in one slow circle on his lap before climbing off and walking away, her hips swishing back and forth.

Rob's eyes are glued to her ass while he speaks. "Someone knows something. Look harder."

"I've interrogated every junkie, every degenerate gambler, and every Bagliateri dealer I can get my hands on. No one knows a fucking thing."

Salvo slides into the booth on the other side of Rob, muttering, "I'd hardly call that an interrogation."

Rob looks confused.

"Ignore him." I flash Salvo a shut-the-fuck-up glare.

The two of them exchange looks in one of their weird fucking silent conversations. I'd roll my eyes if I wasn't too busy glaring at Salvo.

Salvo is immune to my glares, though. "Dom. You didn't even give that kid a chance to answer any of your questions. You said 'talk' and when he didn't answer in the first two seconds, you beat him unconscious."

"And?"

"And how could he tell you anything if he was knocked the fuck out?"

"He didn't know anything."

"And *twice* this week you've had to replace the garbage disposal in your floor drain. Twice."

"And?"

"And the rest of us are looking for information, not looking for punching bags to get out our pent-up aggression."

"I don't have pent-up aggression. I have overt, very out in the open aggression. Aggression solely related to Roberto sitting in jail. That's it. Now can you fuck off about my mental state?"

Rob tilts his head to the side a bit, looking at me, trying to see inside my head. But screw that. I turn fully toward him. "If you don't think I'm up for this job, send me back to Rome. I'll go. I'll get on a plane tonight."

They look at each other again. Rob is two seconds away from pitying me. I'm two seconds away from leaving.

Maybe I should go back to Rome. Pack up my plants, pack up my rabbit, get the fuck out of here.

"When was the last time you got your dick sucked?"

I look at Salvo like he's got two heads. "Back when it was none of your fucking business. Oh, look." I look down at my watch—my watch that Paige left on the counter when she walked out of my life. "It's still none-of-your-fuck-ing-business o'clock."

"You need to relieve some stress." Salvo looks around the room, then signals two of the girls standing by the bar. Of course he signals Mandee and Candy. Those two together can *do things*. Things that get stuck in a man's head and play on repeat *for weeks*. Things that make a man stupid until their black magic wears off. If I wanted to get my mind off of something, those two are exactly the way to do it.

Mandee approaches, leading Candy by the hand behind her. Mandee is looking right at me, wicked smile on her face. Candy's looking down at the floor, shy, subservient. Waiting to be told exactly what to do. It's like they're already slipping into their bedroom roles. Two months ago, I'd be hard as steel before they even reached the table.

But today, nothing. My rod barely even notices them, barely stirs to quarter mast.

I shake my head slightly, enough to stop Mandee while the girls are still two tables away. "I don't want my dick sucked," I say so only Rob and Salvo can hear. No reason to insult the girls. This has nothing to do with them.

"You need it, man. Rob, make him get his dick sucked."

"He can't order that." I turn to Rob. "You can't order that."

Rob's eyeing me hard, like he's trying to decide if he can order that or not. "I need you on point, man. It's been two fucking weeks, and we still don't know dick about who's setting up my dad."

"You think I'm not on point?"

"I think you usually gather intel with surgical precision. You usually find out whatever the fuck I need to know before I even know I need to know it."

"You're welcome."

"Yeah. But now? Right now? Right when there's something I need to know more than anything I've ever needed to know before?" He looks me dead in the eyes, his nostrils flare slightly. "I need you back, man."

I let out a long breath. Fuck. Letting him and Roberto down is the ultimate failure. "I know."

"So..." He chin lifts toward the girls. Mandee's whispering something in Candy's ear, they're both looking at me, smiling. Waiting. Ready to play.

I shake my head. "Naah, man. Too soon."

"Fine." Rob stands up. "Then let's go up to the loft. If you're not going to get all that frustration out with the girls, let's get it out in the ring."

There are three places Rob likes to be—at this booth with a girl in his lap, at his mom's dinner table on Sunday nights, and in his boxing ring where he's pretty much undefeated—and it's not because any of us let him win. It's because he's got a jab that can make a grown man cry.

And honestly, right now? A couple of rounds in Rob's boxing ring against the biggest motherfucker I know? Might be exactly the distraction I need.

"I SWEAR, IF YOU say 'pivot' one more time, I will actually kill you." Gina wipes her long bangs away from her face.

I bite my lip. It's all I can do not to blurt it out again.

My soon-to-be-*former* couch is wedged onto my building's luggage cart at a weird backward-reclining angle. It took the two of us twenty minutes and most of the strength we had just to get it onto the cart. Another ten minutes to get it out my front door.

Now the cart is stuck at the turn in the hall between my apartment and the elevator. The couch has locked itself into place, and only the cart moves under it while we push and pull and try to move it around the turn.

I'll admit we probably could have moved the couch out more efficiently if we started moving it *before* polishing off three-quarters of the box of wine Gina brought over, but that ship sailed several mugs of wine ago.

"We could just take it back inside?"

"No!" Gina climbs over the armrest, slipping but landing on her feet, to join me on my side of the hallway. "No steps backward. This couch is the hotbed of deceit and criminal activities and hurt. It needs to go."

It's also where I've slept every night since I left Damiano's apartment, but I'm not admitting that out loud.

"Clearly, it doesn't want to go."

"It's a couch, Paige. It has no wants. It has no needs." She plops down onto the couch, sitting at a backward-tilted angle, her feet up in the air. "But you do. And what you need is this beast out of your life."

She reaches her hand out for me to hand her the Garfield mug she's using as her travel wineglass. I grab it from the floor a few feet behind us and hand it to her. I grab my Ziggy one and plop down onto the couch next to her. I found this entire set of 80's comics mugs at Salvation a while back. Ziggy and Garfield definitely get the most use. Pretty sure Tom took the Hagar one when he moved out. No one ever reaches for Family Circus.

I join her and kick my feet up in the air. Huh, why don't they make couches angled back like this? It's like a cocoon. I snuggle my face into the back cushion and take a deep inhale.

"Oh no, you don't." She pushes my head away from the cushion. "Do not try to find him in the couch. You made your decision."

"I know."

"If you want to change your mind, change it. But otherwise, don't slip back."

"I know."

"And getting rid of this couch is Step Two in the Gina Stratham Break Up and Move On Plan."

Here we go again.

"First, ditch the guy." She holds up one finger.

"Check," I say with no enthusiasm whatsoever.

"Second, get rid of something that represents him or your relationship. Burn it, toss it, destroy it."

"Donate it. Check."

She gives me a look. Gina thinks the couch should go on the curb, not back to Salvation. But she raises a second finger anyway.

"Third, drink copious amounts of alcohol with someone who gets you."

We clink our mugs and take a drink.

"And last—"

"Do not say 'have sex with some other guy.'"

"Have sex with some other guy. It doesn't even have to be a new guy. Text Spencer. He'll be over here before you can shave your legs."

I am nowhere near close to hooking up with someone else. But I also know Gina won't drop this. "Yeah. Soon."

She gives me a look.

"I mean it." I don't mean it.

Gina sips her wine, staring at me while she bottoms up her mug.

Gina hops up off the couch and tries giving it another push. It doesn't budge. "We're not getting this unstuck, are we?"

"No. I guess we need to unwedge it enough to get it back into my place."

"I have a better idea. Your hot new doorman."

"What about him?" Is she back on the hooking up thing, or is she still on the moving the couch thing?

"Or the other new guy at the reception desk? Let's get them to help."

"They're not going to move my couch. They're busy with their actual jobs."

"Their jobs are to help the building tenants. Just ask nicely, and they'll do it. Use your magical pretty-please powers on them."

"I do not have magic powers."

Gina gives me a look. She regularly gives me crap because guys usually do whatever I ask if I ask nicely. She calls it my magic power, but it seems conceited to admit it, so I deny it whenever Gina brings it up.

But it does work pretty much every time, especially if I touch the guy when I ask. Like touch his arm or something. And it does come in really handy, like when Gina and I got stopped by two police officers while we were day drinking out in the open or when I needed to talk my way out of a parking ticket for Jo-Jo.

"I don't want to bother those guys."

"Okay, fine. I'll go ask."

"Don't—"

She's already on her way to the elevator. I'm stuck, trying to climb my tipsy ass out of this tilted-back couch. But I give up when the elevator door chimes to take her down to the lobby. I sink back into the cushions. Truth is, Gina and I aren't moving this couch forward or back without some help.

I tip my head back, eyes closed. Another deep breath—his cologne, his sweat. Him. Gina's right, I need this thing gone. But another deep whiff first.

Less than five minutes later, Gina's back with two tall, muscular, dark-haired guys. Since when is Chicago swarming with Italian stallions everywhere I look?

"That the couch?" one of them asks.

I fully expect Gina to make some snarky comment since it's the only couch currently stuck in the hallway, so of course this is *the couch*, but she doesn't.

"Paige, this is Matteo, and this is Angelo. Guys, this is Paige."

I get a "hi" from one and a nod from the other.

"So are they moving this with you on it or what?" Gina asks.

Oh, right. It takes me two drunken attempts, but I manage to climb off this thing without falling.

Gina and I stand out of their way. "Kudos to Sheila," she whispers, referring to the manager of my building. "These two are fucking fire. Let's invite them to your place when their shifts are over to thank them for helping."

"Absolutely not. Don't you dare."

"Don't I dare? I love a good dare. You know that."

"Please don't."

The two of them very easily lift the couch off the luggage cart and unwedge it. They're walking it down the hall like it doesn't weigh all that much. Pretty sure I could have stayed seated on it and they still would have moved it without breaking a sweat.

The four of us, the couch, and the two mugs Gina refilled with the last of the boxed wine while the guys were unwedging the couch step into the elevator and head down.

Gina is eyeing these guys hard. "You guys want to come back up for a round of 'thank you' drinks?"

Their eyes dart to each other. One shrugs. "Uh. No-fraternizing policy." The other one nods aggressively.

"Says who?" Gina is relentless.

"Uh. Our boss wouldn't like it."

"Sheila? Sheila used to hang with us all the time. She won't care."

Gina's right. Sheila came to my apartment once because a neighbor made a noise complaint. She found Gina and me having a drunk dance party, and Gina convinced her to join us. She'd hang every so often until she went off and had a kid.

The two of them look at each other like deer in headlights. "No one's watching the door. I really need to get back."

"Me too. To the, uh, desk."

"Really?" Gina calls after them as they step off the elevator.

She may be disappointed, but I'm relieved.

I say a quiet goodbye to the couch as I push the button to go back upstairs.

ANOTHER WEEK LATER

Damiano

I FINISHED GIVING ROB an update on the most recent intel we've been gathering. It isn't much, which is fishy as fuck. People in this town like to talk, but no one seems to know a damn thing.

Rob, of course, shifted the conversation from *that* problem to 'his other problem,' meaning me. "I need you here, man. When you're not out in the streets looking for information, I want you here. Not holed up all alone at your place."

This again.

Salvo walks over, eating his afternoon butterscotch pudding cup. He places a second unopened one on the table as he sits.

Rob barely pays him any attention. He's too focused on me. "You can't keep people safe just by keeping away from them."

"Of course I can. Paige is safe now. No reason to go after her if we're not together."

"Yeah? Try telling that to them," Salvo chimes in, taking another spoonful of pudding.

Rob's eyes dart to Salvo. "Shut the fuck up, Sal."

Rob only calls him 'Sal' when he's pissed at him. And now Rob's glaring at him. What the fuck?

"What are you talking about?" I ask Salvo, who just shrugs and licks his spoon. I turn to Rob. "What is he talking about?"

Rob huffs out loud. "Nothing. Everything's under control."

"What's 'under control'?"

Rob sits back in his seat, folds his arms across his chest. He looks at me for a long minute before answering. "Paige's security. It's under control, like I said. Nothing for you to worry about." He stares hard at Salvo. "Nothing for you to even know about."

"The fuck are you talking about? Why does Paige need security? That's obviously something for me to know about."

"You're not trying to get back with her, right? You're staying locked up in your self-imposed solitude, not letting anyone get close. Not letting anyone be there for you. You're good, she's good, it's all good." Rob leans back and spreads his arms across the back of the booth.

"The fuck are you talking about? Salvo, what the fuck is he talking about?"

Salvo points at me with his spoon. "Right now, he's talking about you shutting him and me out because you think we're safer that way, which is complete bullshit. But a minute ago, he was talking about the Bagliateris going after Paige even though you're not together."

I stare at him like he's got two heads. Then snap back to the matter at hand. "Who the fuck went after her?"

"Relax. I've got three guys on her at all times. They're neutralizing any threats."

"The fuck, Rob? Perché cazzo non me l'hai detto? Sta bene?" *Why the fuck didn't you tell me. Is she okay?*

The room is tilting. I might hurl all over our booth at the Cat.

I grab hold of Rob's beer, needing something cold in my hands. I take a slow breath in.

Rob puts his hand on the back of my neck, squeezes, bringing me back. "Paige is fine. She's going on with life. No disruptions. She doesn't even have a clue she's got security."

"Who's on her?"

"Dante's in charge of her detail. He's got Enzo and Angelo."

Dante?

Well, shit.

Dante covers security for Rob's sister when she's in town. I trained him myself. He's not quite as good a shot as I am, but he's related to her by blood, which is one of Rob's requirements for Lyndie's personal security detail. Rob trusts me with *his own* life but barely trusts anyone to be alone with Lyndie. And I get it. His sister is a fucking goddess now that she's all grown up. And that's no exaggeration. The girl's best friend is an actual swimsuit magazine cover model and when the two go out together, *Lyndie* gets all the attention. She'd be walking runways if she weren't Famiglia.

When Lyndie's in Rome, which is pretty much all the time, Dante runs security for Rob's twin ten-year-old brothers. Rob taking Dante off the boys and putting him on Paige is a big fucking deal.

And it tells me two things. First, Rob really fucking cares about what matters to me, and that makes my chest hurt in a way I don't recognize but also don't have time to deal with right now.

And second, he is seriously concerned for Paige's safety.

"How close did Joey's guys get to her?"

He looks at me funny, sits back in his seat again. "Don't you mean *Johnny's* guys?"

I stand up, jolting the table and spilling Rob's drink, which says a lot since the table is bolted down. "*Johnny's* guys went after her?"

"No. They've been Joey's guys. But how the fuck did you know that?"

I ignore his question and sit back down. No way we're discussing Massimo right now. I lace my fingers and lean forward. "How close did the guy get?"

"The first time, one—"

"The *first* time?"

Rob shoots me a look. He hates being interrupted when we're talking business. "The first time, the guy was waiting in the backseat of her car. Did you know the locks on her piece of shit don't even work? I only had Angelo on her then. He was mainly covering the lobby of her building, following her when she left. Just in case. He went into the garage for a cigarette and saw movement in her backseat. He handled it just fine. That night I pulled Dante off the boys to oversee things."

I know Paige loves that fucking car, but it's unsafe, it doesn't have an alarm, and she can't charge her phone in it. The girl needs to be in an armored car.

Or I should drive her around. Be at her beck and call 24/7. Wherever she needs to go. Rest my hand on her thigh when we're cruising. Sometimes have her ride on the back of my Ducati, arms wrapped around my stomach, tits pressed against my back.

Except none of that is what she wants.

I pull my phone out and dial Dante. Rob's only telling me half the story, I can tell. Dante will tell me everything.

Rob's watching me, arms spread wide. Cool as a fucking cucumber.

Dante answers on the first ring. "Damiano, hey, man."

"What's the PPD for Paige?"

"A twenty-four-hour post in her building lobby, one man parked on the street next to the garage entrance to monitor motor traffic in and out. I have three guys cycling eight-hour shifts on those posts—Matteo, Angelo, and Mike V. They stay at their posts even if she leaves. Then between Enzo, Jimmy, and me, we're on rotation with two of us trailing her when she leaves her apartment, the other one stays. Everyone's unmarked and going in and out in plain cars, not the Rovers."

I hold the phone down and look at Rob. "You said three men. Dante has *six* on detail, Rob. *Six*. How big of a fucking threat is there?"

He nods his head slowly, looking deep at me.

The pull to go to her is insane. So is the need to puke all my guts up. No one can keep her as safe as I can. No one can. Dante's good—Dante's great—but he's not good enough for Paige. I can kill or maim anyone at 100 meters and slit the throat of anyone who slips in closer.

But she doesn't want to be with me.

I put the phone back to my ear. "How much action has there been?" I ask *Dante* since Rob clearly isn't telling me shit.

"Four attempts."

"*Four*?" I glare at Rob.

"But the last forty-eight hours have been quiet. Pretty sure she's in for the night tonight, so expecting another quiet one."

It's right on the tip of my tongue to ask what visitors she's had, or about anywhere she's gone, then to hurt anyone she's spent time with that isn't Gina.

"If you need more manpower, let me know."

"Will do. Rob already authorized as much muscle as I need." Of course he did, because he fucking cares even though I put up thick fucking walls. "Right now, six is the sweet spot. It's hard enough getting us in and out of Bridgeport unnoticed. We get too many men here, and the Bagliateris are going to claim we've declared war."

I'm ready to declare fucking war, but I know I'm being completely irrational on that.

"Shift your reporting to me, not Rob." I stare at Rob to see if he's going to give me shit about this, but Megan walked over and started rubbing his shoulders, so he's pretty much forgotten about me.

"Uh... Yeah, okay," Dante reluctantly agrees. I outrank Dante, so he better fucking agree with me. I hang up and toss my phone down.

I'm staring at my hands, trying to figure shit out.

Salvo stands up, starts to walk away. "Well, looks like my job here is done. You want my other pudding, man?"

Damiano

FUCK IT. I CAN'T be without her.

I miss her dark blue eyes, the way she smiles biting her lip. The way the rest of the world fades out of existence when she looks my way.

I miss her nails scratching up and down my back, lulling me to sleep. I miss her hopeless optimism and the entirely outsized confidence she has in her own abilities. How awful she is at so many things.

I miss her calling my dick *baby*. And the way she tastes, the way the slightest whiff of her sends electricity up my spine and shooting down into my plums.

I miss being the man keeping her safe.

Not seeing her every minute of every day is doing nothing to ease the beast inside of me. The beast that devours every rational thought. The beast that overflows with panic that something might happen to her. The beast that rages because, even setting aside my irrational overprotective instincts, there remains one simple truth—she's in actual danger because of me, whether we're together or not.

So we should be together.

Then I can keep her safe, and she can keep me so warm.

I'll make whatever changes she needs me to make. I'll quit being enforcer. Rob will fucking murder me, especially with his father's shitstorm in full effect, but he'll understand. Eventually.

Or he won't.

I'll figure that shit out later. Right now, I need to convince Paige that I'll do anything, *give up everything*, for her.

I pull up at her place. I should have brought Romeo with me, but sneaking into Bagliateri territory is hard enough without worrying about a three-legged rabbit getting lost in the city. Plus, if things go according to plan, Paige will come back to my place with me, so she can see Romeo then.

I brought her one of my mom's plants instead. The vanilla orchid. It might take some time to change Paige's mind, for her to believe me that I'll change however she needs me to. So I'll leave the orchid at her place, next to her bed.

Or more likely in her living room by the window so it gets enough light. But she'll still see it all the time and think about me until she comes home.

I'm using Salvo's idea of taking an Uber, since my Rover and my bike stand out and since I'm hoping we'll load Paige's shit into Jolene and drive back to my place together.

The driver tried making conversation, but I shut that down quick. Promised him five stars and a $100 cash tip if he stopped talking at me. I set the drop-off location as two buildings away from Paige's so I can recon before I get out to make sure there aren't any Bagliateris lurking around, hoping to find me here.

I spot Dante's lookout parked across the street from her building. He's well-hidden, and I might not have noticed him if I wasn't looking. But I make him easy since he's exactly where I would've placed someone.

Same thing as I head into the lobby—if I wasn't looking for him, I might not have noticed Matteo acting as door-man. He doesn't even nod to me as I walk in.

Good. Maybe Rob will promote Dante to enforcer when I give it up for Paige. He'll do a good job. I can probably still train him for a few months, give him ideas, help him set up his own workshop. Or I guess I'll give him my workshop since I won't need it anymore.

I let out a loud breath as I push the elevator call button.

The thing is slow as fuck, but eventually arrives. I step in, press the button for the fifth floor.

"Hey, hold the door," a guy in a polo shirt hollers. "Thanks, man."

"No problem."

"That for your girl?" The guy motions to the plant I'm holding.

I nod.

"Damn. I should have thought of that. Plant's a good idea. Better than wasting money on flowers. Then again, nothing beats a you-brought-flowers blowie, you know what I mean?"

I nod and smile as if I do. But I've never brought a girl flowers.

"You trying to get out of the doghouse?" he asks while texting.

"You could say that."

"Good luck, bruh. I just got out of there myself. This girl"—he points up—"is so fucking fine. Complete smoke show. Finally letting me hit it again."

"Time to lock that down?"

He shrugs. "I probably should. I don't know, though. She's hot as fuck, but she's also a headcase. But fuck it, the hot ones always are, right?"

I smile. Paige is a bit of a headcase, too. It drives me crazy about her. Unpredictable as hell. Whatever I think she's going to do or say next, I'm completely wrong. Keeps me on my toes. Brings me to my knees.

The guy checks his teeth in his phone camera. "I don't know, bro, maybe I should lock it down. The girl blew me off for the last few weeks. Put me in the penalty box for only texting her late at night, you know? She started playing hard to get, wouldn't let me come over. And what do you fucking know? It worked like a fucking charm. I want back in so bad now, might actually commit to her for the next couple of weeks until I get her out of my system."

"She sounds like a handful. Good luck with that, man."

"You too, bro." He motions at my plant.

The elevator stops. I let the guy get out first, since I hate people walking behind me.

He turns *right* and heads down the hall.

The fuck? The cute redhead in 5B should be a left turn, not a right. But he—

No.

He walks past 5E.

Past 5F.

No.

I stop where the hall takes a hard right. I lean against the wall, tip my head back to stare at the ceiling. There are only two apartments after the turn, and there sure as shit isn't a smoke show headcase in 5G.

No fucking way she invited that prick over. No fucking way.

I close my eyes. I hold the orchid up, take a deep inhale to calm down. Like a summer morning in Roma.

He knocks. An irritatingly chipper knock.

She's going to send him away. She's going to answer the door and send him away.

You've got to, angel. Please, baby.

"Hey, Spence."

"Hey, beautiful. I missed you."

The door to her apartment thuds closed.

I count to ten. Slowly. My hands squeezing into fists.

The pot I forgot I was holding shatters, dirt and plant fall to the carpet.

I slide down onto the floor, sit my ass next to the shards of terracotta and soil.

I could bust the door open, grab that prick by his face, end him. Eight seconds from door to dead. Or drag him to my workshop and end him slowly, taking hours, days.

But I'm not going to do either.

Adrenaline isn't surging though me. It's draining out. My hands aren't tingling, they aren't itching to take action. They're numb and heavy as fuck.

My vision isn't focusing, isn't sharpening. Everything's blurred and cloudy. My heart is slowing down like it wants to stop beating altogether.

She moved on.

To a guy who's better for her.

A guy who looks like he works in an office and who sends emails and gets on conference calls. And has a 401K, whatever the fuck that is. He won't go down on her, but he also won't come home with some guy's toe in his pocket because he forgot it was there.

She deserves a guy like that. A regular guy who keeps her safe by not dragging her into trouble in the first place.

My phone vibrates with an incoming call. I want to ignore it, but it's either Rob or Salvo, and neither will leave me the fuck alone if I don't answer. I pull my phone from my pocket. Rob. He's the last fucking thing I need right now.

I try to answer but no sound comes out of my mouth.

"Damiano, we don't hurt civilians."

"I know that."

"So then what the fuck are you doing?"

"Nothing. Sitting."

"Sitting fucking where? Matteo just called and said you're at Paige's but that some dude-bro also showed up. If you're sitting in a pool of that guy's blood, we're going to have a huge fucking problem."

"I'm not in her apartment. He is. I'm in the hallway."

"And what are you doing in the hallway, man?"

"Sitting."

"How about some walking? Come on. Stand up, man. Walk to the elevator, push the button, and get your ass to the Cat."

"Yeah. Something like that. After I sit some more."

"No, Dom. *Right now.* If I don't hear the elevator call bell in the next ten seconds, I'm sending Matteo up to drag you out."

"Matteo couldn't drag me out on his best day," I say with no conviction whatsoever. Honestly, I wouldn't put up any fight right now, but I still need to say it.

"True. But better you hurt him while he tries to pull you out than you try to get into that apartment."

I get up, surprised my legs work. It takes all my energy to move. "I'm not trying to get into that apartment." I drag myself to the elevator.

"Good. Come to the Cat."

"Naah. I'm just going home."

"No, man. Be at the Cat in thirty minutes. That's an order, Dom."

"I'm not messing around with any of the girls tonight. I'm not in the mood."

"Screw you, asshole. I'm not telling you to come here to fuck the girls. I'm telling you to come here because I'm here and Salvo's here. You need us, man. So come the fuck here."

I don't want to be near anyone right now. "I'm going to lose the signal in the elevator. I'll call you later."

"No need to call me later, you'll see me in thirty fucking minutes when you get your ass over here. I mean it."

I hang up.

The elevator doors slowly close. I look down the hall in the direction of Paige's place one last time.

Mamma's orchid is in a broken pile on the floor where I was sitting. I should go save it.

I lift my hand to stop the elevator doors from closing. But then, fuck it. I cannot walk back down that hall.

I lower my hand and watch the doors close.

TEN MINUTES EARLIER

Paige

I'm not ready for this.

Gina

yes you are

I'm still too sad

My phone rings immediately. "I know you're sad. But if you and Damiano can't be fixed, you've got to move on."

"I know."

"You know, but..."

"I wish we could be fixed. I like so many things about him so much."

"So get over the one thing you don't like."

I shake my head. "I can't."

"Then move on."

"I guess."

"We both know Spencer sucks. But you don't need perfect. You just need to move on. Spencer is good enough for that."

"I guess."

"And he can be good practice. Practice telling a guy what you need. Tell him you want him to take you out before you'll bang him."

"Yeah, maybe."

"And tell him you want to meet his friends."

"Maybe."

"And tell him to go down on you. For like twenty minutes, *minimum*."

"I'm not asking him that. He should only do that if he wants to."

"No, he should only do that if you want him to. And you do."

"How do you even ask a guy to do that?"

"I mean, quality guys just do it on their own. But since Spencer isn't, just push his head down in that direction. Or, you know, use your words."

Damiano just did it on his own. All the time. An image of Damiano's face between my legs while I stroked his velvety head flashes into my mind. Him leaning back a little, staring at my kitty like he was in awe, licking his lips like he was starving for a taste, then diving back in, his hands wrapped around my thighs, pulling me into him. I squeeze my eyes closed so I don't cry.

"Maybe I can do the push-his-head-down thing."

"Push him down and then hold him down there until you get exactly what you need. If five minutes is all it takes, good for you. If you need twenty, thirty, just hold him in place till you're all set. Wrap your legs around his neck if you need."

"Uh, maybe."

"No maybe. If you don't get what you need from your fuck buddy, then you need a new fuck buddy."

Knock-knock knock-knock-knock.

"He's here. I'll call you tomorrow."

"Get it, girl."

I toss my phone on the chair, fluff my boobs up in my bra, and head to the door.

"Hey, Spence."

"Hey beautiful. I missed you." He steps in, drops his hands to my hips. Pulls me close while also walking me backward. He kicks the door closed without taking his eyes off me.

That was pretty frickin' smooth. Okay, tonight might be exactly what I need.

He squeezes my ass and lifts me up, nibbles on my neck as he walks us toward the couch.

My new IKEA couch. It's functional, but boring and stiff.

Spencer sits and pulls me tight onto his lap.

I adjust myself so I'm not sitting directly on his hard-on. "I'm glad you texted."

"I'm glad you invited me over. How's your raccoon?"

"My raccoon?"

"Your... What were you rehabbing this time?"

"Oh, my fox. He's all patched up. Released back into the wild where he belongs. Turns out he didn't need that much of my help after all."

"So now you can spend all your time taking care of me?" He smiles wide. I never noticed his dimples before.

Maybe now is the time to channel my inner Gina. "Or maybe you can take care of me?" I run my finger along his bottom lip, hoping that's a good hint.

"Yeah, I can." His hand slips down to my ass and squeezes. He leans in and kisses me. After a minute, he slips his hand up under my shirt.

It feels nice, and my body is definitely reacting the way it's supposed to, but...

But I'm not ready for this.

I need a breather.

I pull away, lean back.

Spencer pulls me back toward him, his hand pressing against my back.

"Wait." I push against his chest.

"Huh?"

"Can we... I don't want to just..." Oh god. I'm going to start crying. That's the last thing I want right now.

No. Actually having sex with Spencer is the last thing I want. I deserve more.

"What's going on, babe?"

I shake my head. Why is it so hard to say this? "Can we slow down?"

"Slow down?"

"Yeah, I..." I close my eyes. I need to say it. Deep breath. "I don't want to just have sex. I want more."

"More than sex? Like sixty-nining too?"

What the?

"Relax, beautiful. I'm joking." He smiles. "I get it. You don't just want me for my body. You want my mind, too. I don't blame you." He's clearly messing with me now.

"Is that... okay?"

"What do you mean 'is that okay?' Of course it's okay. You want to go out for a bit? You hungry?"

He's not mad or annoyed.

I nod.

"Sounds like we have a plan. We can get to know each other better." He tips my chin to look at him. "I can tell you how awesome I am, and then you can tell me how much you agree." He breaks into a huge, playful smile.

"What about how awesome I am?"

"I already know that part. But we are coming back here after, right?" He adjusts himself underneath me.

I bite my lip and nod again.

"Go change. A few of my buddies are over at Bernie's Tavern. We can meet up with them." He squeezes my ass. "I'll get to show you off."

I can't hide my smile. I like that. I like that a lot. We're going out *and* meeting his friends.

And when we get back, he's definitely going down on me.

"Give me two minutes." I climb off his lap and head into my room.

Maybe this can work. Maybe he can be the guy I need.

I change out of my tee and yoga pants into a cute V-neck sweater and my favorite skin-tight jeans. I slip on a pair of ankle boots I borrowed from Gina and have no plans to ever return. I touch up my mascara, swipe on my Fresh Sugar lip balm and voilà.

Ten minutes later, Spencer is right where I left him, texting away. He looks up and sees me, looks me up and down. "Fuck, we are definitely coming back here after." He walks over, grabs my hand and leads me out the door.

Maybe I can have it all with a guy who doesn't kill people.

We head to the elevator. "You been to Bernie's before?" Spencer asks.

"A few times. Do you go there a lot?"

"Yeah, my buddies—aww, shit." Spencer stops walking. "Looks like my guy didn't make it out of the doghouse."

"What?"

He points at a broken flowerpot on the floor. "I rode the elevator up with a guy who was trying to get back together with the redhead in 5B. He brought her that plant. I guess she sent him packing. Tough break."

He tugs on my hand, pulling me toward the elevator.

I've been sitting on this sun-drenched bench outside Damiano's apartment for two hours, waiting for him to get home.

My phone was almost dead before I even got here, so I've been people watching. I saw a teenage boy shoot his shot with a girl while a group of their friends watched. They were holding hands a few minutes later, a huge, goofy smile on the kid's face.

Then an orange tabby cat strutted by carrying half a cinnamon roll in its little mouth. He had icing in his whiskers and looked incredibly proud of himself. Lady Luck is lurking around here somewhere—hopefully she saved some good fortune for me.

A huge gorilla of a man plops down onto the bench next to me, the wooden slats shifting under his weight. "So you're Paige."

"Uhhmm..."

He's tall, tan, and extremely good-looking. His arms are bigger than my thighs. He's wearing sweatpants and a tight T-shirt, Gucci slides that I know cost a couple hundred bucks. He's got tattoos on his arms and hands. I'm guessing he works for Damiano.

"He's not coming back here anytime soon." The guy motions toward Damiano's building.

"Damiano?"

He nods. I'm waiting for him to say more, but he's focused up the block. Two little old ladies are stopped, hollering at each other. A wheel on the shorter one's granny cart is wedged in a crack in the sidewalk. She's pushing on the cart, and the other is tugging on it, trying to break it free.

The wheel snaps clear off.

"Stay put. We're not done here." The guy jog-walks over to the ladies. They stop bickering as he approaches. He's speaking to them in rapid Italian, his voice loud even though he's not yelling.

He wolf-whistles, and two teenagers come sprinting over, though they walk the last few steps like they're nervous. They look up at him like he's a celebrity. He hands one of the kids some cash and the kid runs off at full speed. The other kid nods at whatever he's saying.

"Grazie, Signore Galliano, Dio ti bendica," the two ladies say over and over. They walk away, with the other kid following them, carrying the broken cart.

The guy walks back to my bench and sits again, one arm stretched wide across the backrest. "Where were we?"

"Do you know those women?"

"Me? No."

"But they knew who you are."

He smiles. "People from here know who I am."

"So you're Rob."

"See? You're catching on. Maybe you can be from here someday too."

"Did that one kid take off with your money?"

"That kid?" He tips his head in the direction the kid ran off. "Naah. I sent him to Ace to buy the lady a new cart then take it to her apartment."

A good one of those carts is, like, $100. It's why I haven't gotten one yet, though Gina told me I'm too young. She joked that when you turn fifty, one magically shows up on your doorstep.

"You're not worried he'll just run off and keep your money?"

"Fuck no. Not at all."

"You always help strangers like that?"

An old man walks by and tips his hat at Rob. Rob nods back.

"This neighborhood—this community—it's my job to take care of the people here. That crack in the sidewalk, the one the cart got stuck in? That sidewalk will be fixed tomorrow. Maybe later today."

"So you guys kill people and help little old ladies?"

He lets out a long breath of air. "We keep the community safe. Sometimes it's as easy as helping a little old lady with her groceries. Sometimes it's not. Same goal though."

We sit in silence for a few minutes. He seems perfectly comfortable with the quiet, but I'm not. "Why are you here? Outside Damiano's apartment?"

"I was going to come by later today to water his plants. Then a little birdie told me you were sitting out here waiting for him. I waited an hour to see if you'd give up. Then I figured I'd save you from wasting the rest of the day."

"Why are you taking care of his plants?"

Rob's sitting with his legs spread wide, his hand on his thick thigh, his thumb tapping. "Dom's staying with me until he gets his head back on straight. I don't want him off on his own, all alone. He doesn't trust any of the guys to be in his apartment except for me and Salvo, so it's my turn to water the plants."

"Funny that the big boss would be watering plants."

"I'm more than his boss."

We sit in silence for another minute.

"I really need to talk to Dom. Can I come to your place?"

Rob shakes his head.

"Can you give me his new phone number at least?"

"Not going to happen."

"Why not?"

He shrugs his shoulders like the answer is obvious.

"He wants to talk to me, Rob. He came by my apartment last night."

"Yeah? And what did he see while he was there?"

I swallow hard. Rob clearly knows what Damiano *thinks* he saw.

Or, really, he did see what he saw. But he didn't see the rest.

He didn't see the part where I didn't go with Spencer to meet his friends, where I didn't invite Spencer back inside with me.

He didn't see the part where I knelt on the hallway floor and carefully—*reverently*—scooped up Damiano's mom's orchid and all its dirt, brought it inside, and spent twenty minutes reading online about repotting an orchid.

"He saw me trying to move on. But he didn't see the rest. I need to talk with him, Rob."

"What's changed?"

"What do you mean?"

"I mean, three weeks ago, you broke his heart because his job involves hurting people—and for the record, so there's absolutely no misunderstanding about this part—he loves his job. I'm not going to sugarcoat that shit for you. So three weeks ago, accepting him for who he is was a nonstarter. You good with that side of him now?"

"No. How could I be good with that?"

He shrugs, then goes back to tapping his thigh.

I guess I thought maybe Damiano would give that up? I thought that's why he came to my apartment, to tell me he'd change. I really need to talk to him.

We sit in silence.

Time to ask nicely. I turn my body toward his, put my hand on his forearm. "Please let me talk to him, Rob." I hold his eye contact and smile. "It would mean a lot to me."

He looks at me, his eyes dropping to my mouth then, for a split second, to my tits. Of course. His eyes move to my hand on his arm. He stares at it. "My little sister thinks saying pretty, pretty please and throwing a sweet smile will get her anything she wants too."

Caught. I smile wider, then pull my hand away. "Does it work?"

"For Lyndie? Fuck yeah. The girl has every one of us wrapped around her finger. For you? You bat your eyelashes and ask me to buy you a new car? Yeah, I'd give in. But you ask me anything involving Damiano? Sorry, sweetheart, but absolutely not. I've got to look out for his best interests."

"And I'm not in his best interests?" Ouch. I shrink into myself.

He shakes his head. "Look, I'm trying to be nice here. He's finally getting back to normal. Being around people who accept him for *exactly* who he is—spending time with me and Salvo, spending time with the Cat girls—people who don't ask him to change. He deserves people who accept him completely."

I look away. That is exactly what Damiano deserves.

"You figure out a way to accept him for who he is—who he is *without* him having to change into who you want him to be? Then you can come find him at the Cat. Otherwise? Leave him alone."

"But—"

"No buts, Paige. And don't try finding some other way to track him down. Damiano may think he's the big swinging dick around here, always watching my back to keep me safe. But don't doubt for one second that I watch his back twice as hard. You hurt him again, and you answer to me. I'm giving you two options. Accept him *completely* and I will welcome you into my Famiglia with open arms. Otherwise, leave him the fuck alone so he can move on or I will personally make you regret it."

With that, Rob gets up and leaves.

THERE IS ONE PLACE I go when everything feels off. When nothing makes sense.

Not a place literally. To Brian. *Home.*

When I texted Gina about my bench-chat with Rob yesterday, I also told her I needed to cancel our brunch plans for today because I desperately needed some brotherly love. She texted back right away, saying no need to cancel and that she'd tag along.

Then she texted me four times in rapid succession, then called me, to make sure the new plan worked. Then she made me go over the naval base visitor dress code rules with her.

Then, this morning, she was actually ready on time. When I pulled up outside her apartment, I was about to text her that I'd go grab us lattes while I waited the usual twenty minutes for her, but she was already standing on the curb, holding our drinks.

Now, we're here, on base, being driven by two sailors to the field where they said Brian is training some of the newer recruits.

"Here you go, ma'am, ma'am." The driver tips his head toward me and toward Gina. "Lieutenant Commander McAfee is over there." The Jeep pulls onto the grass.

I see my brother in all his uniformed glory, talking to a group of sailors. His back is to us.

"Would you like us to wait for you, ma'am?"

"We told you, it's Paige and Gina."

He smiles wide. "Yes, ma'am." No way he's calling us by our names. These guys are absolutely adorable.

"Brian will get us back to the gate." We climb out of the Jeep. "Thanks, Jordan. Thanks, Bobby."

"No problem. We'll wait here anyway, in case you change your mind about that ride back."

Gina *isn't* recklessly flirting with them. She's on her best behavior. Pretty sure it's because of my brother. She's a docile little kitten around Bri, not her usual stir-the-pot self. I swear she has a thing for him even though she won't admit it.

I don't shout his name to get his attention as we approach since we're not really supposed to be back here. He's told me that before. Top-secret stuff happening, though honestly it looks like they're just standing around playing with their guns. I'd sneak up behind him and cover his eyes and make him guess who, but he's holding a firearm, so I know better.

Before we get within ten feet, four of the dozen or so guys he's talking to snap to attention like synchronized swimmers and salute Gina and me.

Brian looks over his shoulder, confusion instantly melting into a smile. Then he turns back to his guys. "Why are you saluting civilians, Marshall?" He's using his big Navy voice.

"I, uh..." The poor kid swallows hard, lowers his arm. "Sir, I, uh... uh..."

He shakes his head. "Sanchez, why did *you* salute civilians?"

"Sir, it seemed appropriate, sir."

"It 'seemed appropriate, sir'? Why did it seem appropriate?"

"Uh... I..."

"Is my *baby sister* in uniform, Sanchez?" The sudden panic on all the guys' faces is clear.

"Sir, no, sir."

"Is her friend an officer?"

"Sir, no, sir."

"Do you—"

"Hey." I put my hand on Brian's arm. "Give them a break. They were just being polite."

He shakes his head at me, as he's done since we were little. But he also can't really say no to me. Never could. "Marshall, Sanchez, Jones, McGee—three miles. *Now.* Make 'em fast or do 'em again. The rest of you, at ease."

They all bark in unison, "Sir, yes, sir." The four that saluted us take off on a jog.

"Walk with me." Brian motions to the left with his head. He holsters his gun, and we start walking. "Do you really think those guys were just being polite, or are you fucking with me?"

"All the guys here are very polite." I motion over to the Jeep. "Jordan and Bobby drove us all the way out here so we wouldn't get lost."

"You know you're not allowed back here, right?"

I shrug. "Yeah, but I told them you were probably really busy and it would be better if we came to you instead of you coming to us."

Brian's eyes pop out of his head. "And that's it? That's all it took? They escorted you onto secure training grounds where there's live ammo present and in use because you said it 'would be better'?"

"And she said 'pretty please,'" Gina chimes in while staring at the ground.

I nod aggressively and with a big smile. I can tell this is annoying Bri, so I'm loving it.

"Stay here a minute." Brian strides over to the Jeep and starts barking at the guys. A minute later, they get out and start jogging the same path as the first four.

Brian shakes his head as he walks back, muttering something about national security and protocol and busy schedules, but stops when he gets to us. "Come here." He squeezes me in a big hug, lifting me a few inches before he puts me down. He's wearing the same cologne as always, the same cologne our dad wears too. All the tension eases out of my body as he puts me down.

"Don't I get a hello?" Gina's biting her lip, finally looking up at him.

He stares at her for a long minute, his nostrils slightly flaring. He leans in and kisses her on the cheek, lingering a few long seconds. "Hello, Gina."

"Hello, Commander." She's totally blushing. I am so going to give her crap on the drive home.

Brian smiles, then hides it. He turns back to me. "Why are you here?"

"Can't we just come visit?"

"No. Talk to me."

I shrug. "There isn't really anything to talk about."

"There some guy I need to hurt?"

Brian was a senior when I was a freshman in high school. Any guy even looked at me, and Brian would get up in the kid's face. He was already six-foot-two by then and on the football team, so one look from him and most guys ran for the hills. It wasn't until he enlisted and shipped out that I could actually hang out with guys without them being too nervous to make a move.

"No. I just... I don't know."

Gina jumps in. "We wanted a guy's advice. A guy who would give us honest answers."

He tilts his head a little, suspicious. "Okay, shoot."

"Oh, speaking of shooting," Gina bats her eyelashes. "Since we're here, can you teach me how to fire a gun?"

"No."

She takes a step closer to him. "Can I at least hold it?"

"You want to hold my gun?"

She nods.

"No, Gina, you can't hold my gun."

She bites her lip and looks at him through heavy lashes. "Can I touch it?"

Brian's nostrils flare. "Gina." His voice is husky, scolding.

"Please may I, Commander?"

Gina slowly reaches for Brian's holster. She rests her fingers on the fabric strap securing the gun. She pauses, waits. She starts to open the top strap.

Brian grabs hold of Gina's wrist. He doesn't let go, but he doesn't actually move her hand away either.

He turns to me, still grasping Gina's wrist in place. "What do you need honest answers about?"

I wait for Gina to answer him. She was supposed to ask this part. That was our plan on the drive out here so Bri wouldn't freak out and try to track Damiano down. But now she's in a trance, eyes fixed on where Brian is gripping her wrist.

"So..."

"Spit it out."

"So, I'm asking... for a friend. She's not sure about this guy she likes and she doesn't know what to do."

"A friend, huh? And this *friend*—does she actually think she's found someone good enough for her?" He glares at Gina. Gina, whose wrist he's still clutching, maybe pulling a little closer to him. Gina, who's still in a complete trance.

"I mean, sort of. She's found this guy who treats her great and is gorgeous and makes a good living and she really wants to be with him. But—"

Brian drops Gina's wrist like he touched a hot pan.

Shit. He thinks I'm asking for Gina.

She realizes it too. "Paige has other friends. You know that, right?"

He folds his arms across his chest, his stance wide. "Does she though?"

"Ouch. Don't be a jerk. Maybe if *the Navy* didn't move us around every few years when we were little, I'd have a whole gaggle of besties."

Brian's expression softens and he gives me his 'I'm sorry' look. He knows I'm sensitive about how much we moved. How it meant my friendships were always temporary. How it meant we couldn't have a dog or a cat or even a fish because we never knew when we were going to move again. Even when we moved back to San Diego when I was twelve, we didn't know then that would be a permanent assignment for Dad.

"You're right, there's no other friend," Gina says. "What Paige really needs to know is... why is it okay for you to kill people?"

"*What?*" Brian asks and I yelp at the same time. I really didn't want to get into what Damiano does. Also, wow, Gina really doesn't want Brian to think she's dating someone.

"That's a fucking pivot." He looks at her like she has two heads.

But she doesn't stop. "*You* kill people. You train all these guys to kill people." Gina points to guys on the field behind us.

Some of them seem to think she's waving, and they smile and wave back. Brian scowls at them and draws a little circle in the air with his finger. The two that waved take off on a jog.

Gina continues, "The entire purpose of the military is to kill people. Why is all that okay?"

He turns to me. "That's not the purpose of the military at all. You know that, P. We use the threat of force to keep people safe. Sometimes, we have to show force so that the next asshole country that wants to hurt someone knows what they're up against. Fewer people die because of us."

"I wouldn't mind a show of force," Gina whispers under her breath.

Brian turns to her, takes a step closer. "Is there some guy or not?"

I know he's asking *her*, I know there's something trying to brew between them. For all our sake, I'll come clean on this, that this is about me. "I was sort of seeing someone."

He looks relieved, which tells me just how into Gina he is, since finding out that I'm seeing someone always makes him tense up. When I told him that Tom and I were getting an apartment together, Brian had one of his former SEAL buddies who's now in private security run a background check on the guy. Then Brian and two of his friends made a point of helping move my boxes, shouting at Tom to pick up the pace when he was in front of them carrying one box and they were behind him carrying two or three each.

That was the day I met Gina, actually. She was walking by and saw three shirtless guys and one Tom carrying boxes. When she realized they were with me, she decided we were best friends now.

"What does this guy do for a living?" This is always Brian's and my dad's first question. It's exactly why I didn't want to bring Damiano up.

"You mean, like, for a job?"

"He better fucking have a job."

I don't want to get into that. I was avoiding it on purpose. Ergo the 'asking for a friend' thing.

I smile to myself for using 'ergo' in my stream of consciousness.

"He used to be GOI or GIO. I forget which way that goes."

"GOI? As in Italy's special forces?"

I nod.

He looks impressed, nods. "They're like the SEALs, but worried about getting mud on their boots."

"What?"

"Nothing. Sounds like he's a huge fucking improvement over that pansy-ass Tom."

"Yeah, but..."

"But what? Don't tell me you'd let someone being in the military stop you from being together." Wow. These former special ops guys stick together.

"No." Or at least, I don't think so. I hated the moving-around part as a kid, but I admire my dad's devotion to service. Brian's too. But none of that is the point at all. "He's not in the military anymore. But he sort of does similar work now."

"Black ops?" Brian asks suspiciously.

"No," Gina jumps in. "More like, security?" Her voice gets suspiciously high.

"Private security," I add in, hoping Gina follows my lead and doesn't elaborate.

"Must be boring as fuck for him after special forces. But what's the problem? Sounds like he's just making a living."

I shrug.

"Paigey, no one's going to be perfect. This guy treats you right? And has a job? I'm sure he's good-looking—"

"Oh, he's hot as fu—" Gina starts to chime in, then looks up to see Brian scowling at her. "I mean, if you're into that big, strong, demanding military type."

"Ex-military," I correct.

Brian keeps staring at Gina, then turns more toward me. "I don't know this guy. But I've met most of your exes. If this guy was good enough for GOI, he might actually be good enough for you. Or as close as a guy can get to being good enough for you."

"And what about for me?" Gina asks.

Brian leans in close to Gina's ear and whispers. She closes her eyes and takes a deep breath. I can't hear what he's saying, but I swear if he doesn't wrap an arm around her, she's going to collapse on jelly legs.

Finally, he pulls back.

Gina's stunned, speechless, and a deeper shade of red than I thought humanly possible.

I better get her out of here before she starts dry humping his leg. "We should get going." I have a lot to think about.

"Get in the Jeep. I'm driving you to the gate myself."

I wave to the group of guys assembled behind him. A chorus of "bye, Paige" and "come back and see us again, ladies" echoes as we walk away. They are so sweet.

Brian jog-walks toward us, shouts over his shoulder, "I swear to God, if a single one of you even thinks about wanking off thinking about my little sister, I will end you. Understood?"

"Sir, yes, sir."

An especially brave one asks, "What about the friend, sir?"

Brian stops dead in his tracks. "Burpees. All of you. *Do not stop* until I'm back. And for the record, I'm leaving the Jeep at the gate and walking back. Leisurely." He jogs back toward us with a self-satisfied grin, mumbling to himself, "Good luck even lifting your arms tonight, motherfuckers."

We've been in my car for ten minutes now. Gina hasn't said a word since Brian clicked her seatbelt in for her.

I haven't either. At first, I was quiet because the road out of that place always confuses me and I needed to focus so I wouldn't go the wrong way. But I've stayed quiet because Brian made everything more confusing by making it sound so simple.

Like, maybe I actually could get past the one bad thing about Damiano in exchange for all the good? Or that the bad isn't as bad as I was thinking because they do the bad for good reasons? Am I naïve to believe that, or am I heartless to reject Damiano for it?

Okay, Gina needs to snap out of her daze and help me figure this out.

But first, I need to give her shit. "So what was all that?"

"That, my friend, was Brian telling you it's okay to be with Damiano."

"No, not *that* part. We'll get back to that part. What was with you and Brian? What did he whisper to you?" I glance over quickly, waiting for her response.

She sighs. "Nothing a sister should ever hear."

My eyes back on the road, I smile. "You know I'm totally good with you two going out, right?"

"I know. But it's not going to happen. We just joke around with each other."

"Brian doesn't joke around." He doesn't. It's not his nature. It's also not his nature to shamelessly flirt. He's super private with his relationships. I haven't met any of his girlfriends since he was in high school. Not even Hailey, and they were together for three years—every time he'd show up somewhere without her, he'd claim that she couldn't come because she was tied up in his dungeon.

Gina shrugs. "*Anyway*, you can be with Damiano now, right?"

My turn to shrug. "To be honest, I thought Brian was going to shut it down. I thought he was going to say some magic words to help me to move on, that there's no way it could work out."

"But instead, he gave you permission. He told you to get down on your knees, crawl across the floor, and beg Damiano to take you back."

"He didn't say anything even close to that."

"Hmm. I swear he said something about crawling and begging, being gagged. Maybe that was just when he was whispering to me."

"Gina!"

She sticks her tongue out and shakes her head at me, giving me an evil grin. "Anyway, explain this to me again."

"Explain which part?"

"Explain the part where you really like Damiano and he really likes you and he's got abs for days, has a job, is a fully legit actual bad boy but treats you like a queen, and he—"

"Are you going somewhere with this?"

Out of the corner of my eye, I see her giving me a look. "*And* he can be the partner you need. He's loyal, he's intuitive, he actually likes your petting zoo. He even stole your rabbit so you'd have to go back to him. This guy is everything."

"Except that his job is to kill people. *Kill them*, G."

"Granted, that's a check in the 'not ideal' column, *but* let's say he had a different job. Let's say he's a dentist and—"

"He *is* a dentist." I wiggle my eyebrows.

"He's a wha—? Ooooh."

I turn and look over at her and nod. Luckily we're stopped at a traffic light.

"Finally! Good for you. So that's a check in the 'hell yeah' column. You know what? That's two checks."

"Three checks, G. Give him three checks for that."

"Okay, three in the plus col—"

"Honestly? Count it for four." I shift Jo-Jo into gear as the light turns green. "I mean, it's like glitter bombs exploding in my va-jay-jay."

"So what the fuck are you even stressing over? Why aren't you with him?"

"You think I should completely ignore that he kills people?"

"I think Tom and Spencer were mostly shitty guys who didn't give you the attention and respect you deserve. Tom cheated on you. Spencer completely used you. I have no clue how those two are more acceptable options than Damiano."

"Because they don't kill people, that's why."

"You want to know what I think? Here's what I think. *You* didn't grow up here, I did. North of 63rd Street used to be a frickin' war zone. The Famiglias were at each other's throats and regular people got caught in the crossfire *all* the time. The family in the apartment across from ours when I was little? Their son was one grade above me. He got killed in a shootout walking home with his mom."

"Exactly the life I don't want a part of. You've made my point for me."

"No, that's not my point. My point is that everything changed. The next generation of Famiglia guys took over. The violence ended. It ended, Paige. They figured out a way to make peace with each other. They made the neighborhoods safer."

"Uh-huh."

"There's still violence, but they keep it within their world. Innocent people aren't getting killed anymore. You read the news, when was the last time you saw a story about... You don't read the news, do you?"

I shake my head. "Local news makes me sad, and national news makes me mad."

"I don't really watch much either, it's boring as fuck. But you don't need the news to get my point. Chicago is safer now because of them."

"I guess."

"You're still looking for excuses for things not to work out. Quit that. Close your eyes and imagine what it would be like to wake up next to Damiano every day."

"I can't close my eyes, I'm driving."

"Close your *mental* eyes. Picture it. Stop focusing on why it shouldn't work out, and imagine what it would be like if it did."

"And just accept that he kills people?"

"Well, first off, let's not use the K-word anymore. Let's say he... 'immobilizes threats.' Second, yes. You should just accept that he *immobilizes threats*. Remember when I thought I was getting serious with Martin and then he said I should quit my job? He got super weird about how much I had to travel and how much time I spent with the team?"

I nod. "He wanted you to give up what you'd been working toward for more than a decade."

"And what did you tell me?"

"That if he respected you, he'd trust you to make good decisions while you were apart."

"Did you mean it?"

"Of course I meant it."

Gina has a smug look on her face because she just made me make a point against myself.

"*But* in my defense, I don't know what I'm talking about half the time and just make things up as I go."

"No, Paige. You speak and act from the heart all the time. That's what your heart was telling you then. I bet it's telling you the same thing now. Can you trust him to make good decisions while you're apart? And I don't mean good decisions in the eyes of the law, or right and wrong, or artificial social constructs, or—"

"Not killing people is not an artificial construct."

"Ah, ah, ah."

I roll my eyes. "Sorry. Not *immobilizing threats*," I wait for Gina to give me a nod acknowledging my correction, "is not an artificial construct. It's a real thing."

"Is it though? Cavemen ki—*immobilized* other cavemen. Dominance is in our genetic makeup. It's only illegal because the law says it's illegal. And anyway, the point is this—do you trust him to make good decisions related to you and your relationship?"

"Absolutely. But—"

"No buts. You need to balance those two things."

"Balance the fact that he immobilizes threats with the fact that he'll treat me amazingly and would never cheat—"

"And would go down on you for an hour every night."

"Be serious."

"I never joke about muff diving, you know that."

I huff out loud. I need a few minutes to think. Everything Brian said and everything Gina's saying all seem to make sense. And seeing Rob taking care of the neighborhood and taking real care of Damiano, seeing them as a community—I can get behind all those things.

And I really like Damiano. I don't want to be without him.

We're stopped at a light. Gina holds up her phone, showing me a map. "If you turn left here, it's only four minutes to the Cat's Meow."

"WHAT DO YOU MEAN, we can't come in?" Gina challenges the guy sitting on a stool outside the Cat's Meow.

"Sorry, sweetheart, this is a gentlemen's club. Only women allowed in are the dancers."

"That's ridiculous. We have rights."

"Not here."

I can tell Gina's about to let loose on this guy Gina-style, and I'm pretty sure that is not going to help. I elbow her so she drops her fight. "We don't really want to go in. I'm just looking for Damiano Zucco. Do you know if he's here?"

The guy looks me up and down. "Damiano's not here. How about you let me help with whatever you need, sweetheart?"

"What she needs is to find Damiano. Duh," Gina adds in.

I throw her a look. Her attitude isn't helping us. "Do you know where I can find him?"

He shrugs at me. It's not a yes or a no.

"Can you call him for me?"

He shakes his head. "He doesn't answer his phone."

"Can you text him?"

He shakes his head. This guy is useless.

"I really need to see him. Is there any way you can help me find him? Please?"

He shrugs. "Tryouts are tomorrow at 2:00 p.m. All the top guys come in for that."

"Tryouts?" I say with horror at the same time Gina says it with absolute glee.

He nods. "But the only way you're getting through these doors is if you make the first cut."

"Tell me about these tryouts," Gina says, finally being friendly to the guy.

"Are you going to wear a one-piece or a bikini?" I ask Gina as I yank swimsuits out of my bottom drawer. I brought a whole bunch with me from California. *You can swim in the Lake,* Brian had said when he asked me to move out here to be closer to him. He didn't mention that only diehards actually go deeper than their ankles because it's zero degrees.

"Lacy bra and matching thong."

"The guy said bathing suits are okay."

"I know."

I turn away from her before I smile. At first I was thinking that Gina offered to try out with me for moral support, but now I'm thinking she might actually be serious about it.

"Probably thigh highs, too." She's laying on her back on my bed, scrolling through her phone, playing a few seconds of a bunch of different songs, trying to pick one.

She's been looking for a new job for a few weeks. And dancing is her thing. She'd be amazing at this. And apparently, the Cat is the premier strip club in Chicago, paying dancers more than a lot of lawyers make and not charging the dancers crazy fees for every little thing like the sleazy clubs apparently do, according to Gina's online research.

"I'm going swimsuit." Spending my teen years in San Diego, I practically lived at the beach. I'm just as comfortable in a swimsuit as I am in regular clothes. Honestly, sometimes I'm more comfortable in a swimsuit because I don't have to worry about styling and accessorizing. Top and bottom, flip-flops, lip gloss, done.

"What about this one?" She plays a Brittany classic.

"For you?"

"No, for you. I'm already set."

"Oh, I'm already set too."

"Then why am I picking out music?"

I shrug. "What's your song?"

"I'm going with an old school mafia don classic."

I blink hard for a minute. "I have no clue what that would even mean."

"It's got to involve guns and killing but also be desperately romantic. And it's got to be Sinatra, obviously."

"Obviously," I agree, though I have no clue why. "Wait—why?"

"Sinatra was practically in the mafia. But I'm going Nancy, not Frank."

I'm utterly confused, but also I'm going to start freaking out if I don't start practicing my routine.

Gina rolls onto her elbows. "You know you don't actually need to try out, right? Once we get in the front door, you can just go find him."

I shrug. "I don't know. I think I need to show him that I can be what he likes."

"You are what he likes. He's been pretty clear about that."

"I mean, show him that I can accept his world. That I'm willing to fit into it."

"And you'll show him that by showing your tits to all his friends?"

"The guy said we only have to dance. I'm not *actually* stripping, are you?"

She shrugs, then climbs off the bed and starts swinging her hips in front of the mirror, running her hands along her hips and thighs. She drops low so her ass is practically on the ground, then swings back up, flipping her hair. This girl was born to dance.

"So what song did you pick? No, wait. Let me guess."

"Okay. But it should be pretty obvious."

She freezes in place and stares at me in the mirror. "No. No, Paige."

"Why not?"

"Have you ever even been in a strip club?"

I shake my head.

"It's a lot of rap, some Top 40s. Think bass-pumping, high energy."

"Dolly is high energy."

"Dolly is G-rated midline energy. She's, like, pump-you-up-before-you-go-to-the-club energy. She's not bring-him-to-his-knees energy."

I shrug. "She will be when I dance to her."

Gina smiles wide. "Well, then. Okay, Miss Thing. I like this vibe on you. 'Jolene'?"

No way I can taint 'Jolene' in case this doesn't work out. "No, '9 To 5.'"

"Alright. Maybe that can work. Show me what you've got."

Damiano

ALL THE TOP-TIER AND mid-level guys in Rob's crew gather at the Cat on Tryout Day. It's become a tradition.

Salvo likes a crowd to be there to make sure the aspiring Cat girls are comfortable dancing in front of a packed room. The guys like to be there because there's something about watching brand-spanking-new girls on stage for the first time.

Or so I'm told.

I never go inside on Tryout Day. If another Famiglia wanted to take down all of Rob's top brass at once, tryouts are like a big fucking neon sign advertising when and where to hit. So I stay out front, keep an eye on the parking lot, walk around back, make sure nothing goes down. Routine surveillance.

A couple of girls are standing around the parking lot when I arrive. Two of them are crying. Another's getting into a taxi, holding pole shoes in her hand. Those would be the girls that didn't even make it inside.

But it's still only a quarter to two. Tryouts don't start for another fifteen minutes.

I walk up to the bouncer stuck babysitting the door *outside* the Cat. "Jimmy." We shake hands.

"How's it going, man?"

I shrug. "Why the fuck are *you* out here?"

Jimmy's been with the Famiglia a long-ass time, longer than I have. He must have pissed Rob or Salvo off to be *out here* instead of *in there*. Usually low-level guys get stuck watching the door on Tryout Day.

Jimmy takes a long drag on his cigarette, the cherry end glowing. "I fucked up, man. Told Rob how ridiculously hot the girl he was Facetiming with was." He gives me a pointed look.

I cringe on his behalf, the poor prick. "There's only one girl Rob Facetimes with."

"Well, I did *not* know that. And Lyndie was a little kid with pigtails last time I saw her. I had no clue she grew the fuck up." He shakes his head. "The girl I saw on his phone, that girl—"

"Stop right there, man. I'm on strict orders to slice the tongue out of anyone who disrespects Lyndie. Even a little." I pat his shoulder so he knows it's nothing personal.

He nods, sparing us both the violence and mess any further commentary would bring. "So now I'm in the fucking penalty box and I miss Tryout Day." He flicks the butt of his cigarette into the parking lot. I'd give him shit for littering in front of the Cat, but he's already being punished.

"At least he didn't put you in the hospital."

"Yeah, but this might be worse. You should have seen the girls that showed up today, man. I didn't think there were girls in Chicago even close to as hot as the Cat girls, but a few of the ones today? I'd take any one of them. Any one of them, man."

Usual process is for the girls to line up out here. Rob walks down the line, making the first round of cuts based on looks alone since he thinks Salvo lets too many girls in. Once they get through the door, it's all on Salvo to make the final decisions since he manages the Cat.

"Rob start early or what?" All the girls should still be out here.

"Yeah. Didn't say why. He took one look at the girls in line, made his picks and sent the rest packing. A couple of girls hadn't even shown up yet." He points to the ones still standing around.

"How many girls showed up?"

"Thirty-one."

I let out a long whistle. Thirty-one girls vying for one, maybe two, spots at one of the few clubs that doesn't pimp out its girls. Our girls are friendly as fuck, but only with the top-ranked Galliano men, and only if they choose to be.

For actual customers, it's a look-but-don't-fuck-ing-touch-or-else-lose-use-of-your-hand lap dance. No side deals, no extras. Any customers who don't like that can go to the Tropicana and get anything they want, as long as they're okay getting it from girls that didn't make the cut at the Cat.

"How many made it inside?"

"Six. And they're fit, man. One of the blonde ones? Fuck me sideways, man, the girl was a fucking wet dream."

Six auditions means I can get out of here in about an hour. That's around the time the actual Cat girls will start showing up for their shifts. I'm still not in the mood for any of their attention, so I want to be gone before they get here.

"Alright, man." I shake Jimmy's hand, then head around the parking lot to make sure the back entrance is secure.

I don't know, maybe spending some time with the Cat girls is exactly what I need. Maybe it's time. I could grab a couple of them and head up to my room in Rob's loft. Blow off some steam. Try to get back to my old routine of working, then playing with a few of the girls, then working some more. Try to get back to norm—

Why *the fuck* is Paige's SUV here?

I stare at the old brown-and-white Blazer. There is no doubt in my mind that's Jolene. I check the license plate anyway, *praying to god* there's another beat-the-fuck-up old Blazer within city limits. But that's definitely Jolene.

Jolene is in the Cat's parking lot.

There's a tavern next to the Cat. Paige has got to be in there. Seems like a long way from home for a burger, but people do rave about this place.

I yank the tavern door open, storm inside.

"Oh. Hey, Damiano. How are—"

I blow past the hostess. She's actually a very nice girl, the sister to one of our soldiers. I'll probably owe her an apology for charging past her, but right now I don't give a fuck. I need to find Paige *in here*, sitting at a table, mouth stuffed full of food.

I stomp through the dining area, getting looks from the lunch crowd. I'm tempted to check the kitchen and the bathrooms, but it's clear she's not here.

I step back into the parking lot. There's a pizzeria, too. But I can see in its front window from the parking lot. No Paige.

Next to it's a pawnshop, but no way Paige is parting with any of her stuff, or if she did, she'd give it away, not sell it, so that place is out.

That's leaves...

There is no fucking way she's in the Cat. Not any day, and definitely not on Tryout Day. No. Fucking. Way.

I'm staring at Jolene, my shoulders tight. My chest rises with each breath I'm pulling in, forcing out. I'm *willing* Paige to appear from whichever shop she's in. I'm seconds away from losing my fucking mind.

My phone vibrates. Salvo.

I close my eyes as I answer, trying to regulate my breathing. My jaw is clenched, my nostrils flaring. My pulse surging.

"Soooo... What kind of mood are you in, man?" Salvo, as always, sounds cool as a cucumber.

"She's in there?"

"Depends."

"It doesn't fucking depend. It's a yes or no."

"Sure. But whether I'm letting *you* in *depends* on whether you can come in and sit down like a normal human being and watch tryouts with us, or if you're going to fly the fuck off the handle and break things."

"Depends," I tell him, being a jackass right back to him.

"No, man. I need a yes or no, and I need you to mean the fuck out of it."

I rub my forehead. "Just send her out here. She doesn't belong in there, whatever the fuck she thinks she's doing."

"I'm not going to do that."

"Yes you are."

"No, I'm not."

"Why the fuck not?"

"Well, for one, I already tried. I tried to kick her out, but she's really fucking convincing and, second, her friend—Gina? Holy fucking shit, bro, you were right about the friend. Why didn't you tell me she's a Bulls cheer-leader?"

"What? Really?" How'd I miss that?

"Bro, she's a Luvabull. I recognized her the second she strut that fine ass in here. Then she said *she'd* only try out if Paige gets to try out too, and you know I've got a thing for the Luvabulls. Plus I think the friend's got a solid fucking shot at being my new Cat girl. I mean, I'm rooting for her, and I'm the one who gets to pick, so it's looking really fucking good for her."

I have no fucking clue what to think of that. But I do know one thing. "You think for one fucking second that Paige is going to be a Cat girl, and I swear—"

"Relax, bro. And what the fuck are *you* about to threaten *me* for? *You* don't want relationships, remember? Maybe her being a Cat girl is the perfect solution? She seems to think so."

"The fuck are you talking about?"

"She obviously knows what the Cat is, she knows what the Cat girls are for you. Maybe this is her way of saying you two can just fuck around without all the strings. Seems like she's offering you exactly what you want. Win fucking win."

"No fucking way that's what she... Wait. What do you mean that 'she knows what the Cat girls are for me'? I never said a fucking word about the Cat girls to her."

"Huh."

"Huh? Huh what, motherfucker?"

He exhales loudly. He's stalling on answering me. I'm going to tear the door the fuck off the Cat and rip him in half. Literally rip him into separate pieces.

"What the fuck, Salv! What did you—"

"Damiano." It's Rob.

He either grabbed Salvo's phone or Salvo pussied out and handed it to him. Knowing the two of them, Rob was probably sitting next to Salvo and heard all of that.

"Rob."

"I need you in here, Dom. Stop at the front door. Hand Bianca, and your gun, and any other weapons you have on you, to Jimmy. That includes anything that isn't technically a weapon but that you're already thinking about how to use as a weapon. Do you understand?"

"Yes." The deep-rooted habit of adding 'sir' is there, but I resist it.

"Good. Now, what are the lap dance rules we tell customers?"

"Rob, I—"

"Tell me the rules, Damiano."

I huff. "Sit on your hands. Be nice to the dancers. Pay without bitching about it."

"Good. So you're going to come in here. *Unarmed.* And you're going to sit on your fucking hands. I see one finger even twitch, and you're answering to me. And you're going to be nice to everyone. And you're not going to bitch about any of it. Yes?"

"Rob, I—"

"Le mie parole sono dannatamente chiare e chiare? Non lascio qui alcuno spazio ad interpretazioni. Capisci? *Are my words crystal fucking clear? I am not leaving any room for interpretation here. Do you understand?*

"Sì."

"Now get your ass in here. We've got auditions to watch."

Fuck.

THIS HAS GOT TO be the most insane thing I've ever done. Somehow crazier than finding a man bleeding to death in my car and even crazier than being in a real live car chase *with guns*.

I blot my armpits with a paper towel and readjust my bustier. The bustier is part of one of Gina's team uniforms. Solid black, strapless, designed to stay firmly in place while cheering, thanks to built-in grippy strips. Gina's bustier and a black bikini bottom I already had that matched perfectly. A sliver of my tummy shows, which feels sexy as hell, but I'm way more covered up than on any trip to the beach.

Gina picked Nancy Sinatra's 'Bang Bang (My Baby Shot Me Down)' because of course she did. She strolled onto that stage in mile-high heels, hair curled into perfect big 1960s bouffant waves, smoky eyes, pale lips. The three girls that went before her each danced to high-energy, fast-paced music. Gina's song couldn't have been slower, sexier.

No one could take their eyes off her. I mean, of course she can dance. She's been dancing her whole life. But I'm used to her hyping a crowd up with kicks and splits to bass-pounding, ear-ringing group choreography.

This was slow, deliberate. Sultry. Drawn-out spins around the pole, intentional eye contact. The entire room in a trance, hypnotized. When she pretended to be shot and slowly slid down to the floor with her back against the pole, her legs spread, guys were getting out of their seats, yelling and cheering. She absolutely killed it, and the guys are demanding an encore.

She walks toward me. I'm holding out a water for her, but she barely broke a sweat.

"You were unreal out there." Her confidence in front of a crowd is insane.

"All in a day's work."

Salvo's voice over the speaker announces the fifth dancer. I'm up last, which now means next. Holy crap.

"Was Damiano in the audience?"

She nods while drinking from her water bottle. "He wasn't at first. But he came in near the end. Him and the guy that made the first cuts outside were arguing, but then they sat next to each other. Damiano wasn't paying any attention to me, by the way. He kept leaning over to the other guy to talk to him."

Rob.

Rob, who took one look at me standing in line outside, told me I better be here to cause the good kind of trouble, then sent Gina, me, and four other girls inside.

"Damiano looked pissed, P. Really pissed. At one point, he got up and started to walk out, and the other guy barked at him to sit his ass back down. It was loud enough to hear over the music."

"Where was he sitting? Like from up on the stage, where would I look?"

She moves to stand next to me, facing the same direction. "If you're standing in the middle of the stage," she points down and a little left of center, "he's right there. The guy that yelled at him is on his right—your left. There's a row of guys right at the edge of the stage, then there are a few rows of folding chairs set up behind those. He's in the first row of chairs."

They gave us a quick peek at the stage before tryouts started, so I have a good mental picture. The place is really nice inside, not at all what I pictured.

I let out a breath. Am I really doing this?

"And there are stairs from the stage down to the floor, over there," she points to the right, "in case you decide to go down to the floor."

"Wait—should I go down to the floor? I didn't rehearse doing that." I hope she doesn't hear the panic in my voice.

Gina turns toward me and looks at me thoughtfully for a minute. "If it feels right, yes, you should. I know you worked really hard on your choreography, and it's good, P—really—but keep an open mind about just letting loose and feeling the beat and going with the moment."

"I don't know how to do that."

She hands me the headband that goes with my outfit. "You do. You've got this."

"Do I?"

She shrugs with a smile. "Well, we're about to find out."

Damiano

THE LIGHTS ARE DARK, and there's a spotlight center stage.

Paige is going to walk out any minute, and I, most likely, will have to start killing people. It's too bad. I can tolerate most of these guys. I like a few of them. It'll be a shame to hurt them for putting their eyes on my angel. But quel che sarà, sarà. *Whatever will be, will be.*

Rob is sitting right next to me. Closer than a straight man should sit next to another straight man at a strip club. He's facing me. Breathing down my neck. He wasn't sitting this way during the last performance. I can't tell if he's turned toward me now to avoid looking up on stage when Paige comes out or if he's watching for some tell that I'm about to jump out of my seat to hurt someone. Probably both.

Rob's bigger than me—the guy's a fucking animal working out twice most days. He's fast too, spends hours in the boxing ring. If he gets a solid hit in, it's lights out.

But who knows, maybe it won't come to violence.

The room goes silent as Paige walks into the spotlight. She's wearing *big bunny ears*, one standing up, one flopped down, red high heels and a puffy little tail sitting high on her plump ass.

This will definitely come to violence.

"Alright, fam," Salvo's voice over the sound system. "Last tryout of the day. Little Miss Bunny, give me a nod when you're ready."

Paige looks straight at me and winks. She tucks her hands up next to her ear, like they're a pillow, resting her head on them. She takes a deep breath in then nods toward the sound booth.

Piano chords start pounding, Paige moves her hips to the beat, swishing side to side.

She does a little hop. Motions like she's pouring a cup of coffee.

What is she doing?

Big exaggerated yawn, pushing her gorgeous tits out. Now she's... fake showering?

Is she acting out the song? This is the absolute furthest thing from a stage routine I've ever seen.

And it's bad.

It's awful.

It's like a 9-year-old's choreography.

I swear if a single guy in here laughs at her or boos, I will slit his throat. Crack Rob's beer bottle on the seat of my chair, then use the sharp stump.

Leave all weapons at the door, my ass. I am the weapon.

I force my eyes away from her to the guys sitting along the tip rail to see who's about to say shit to her, to see who I'm hurting first.

But no.

Vinnie's jaw is dropped.

Tommy's leaning forward, eating her up. Ronnie's got his hand in his lap, gripping his dick.

They're into it. They're into her.

Into my Paige. My angel.

Fuck this.

I lean to my left, close to Eddie V. The guy wears way too much cologne, so this is going to serve two purposes. "I need you to take Ronnie out."

He's barely paying attention to me, entirely focused on Paige. "Huh?"

"Take Ronnie the fuck out. Now."

That got his full attention. "I can't do that. Salvo will kill me for starting beef in the Cat."

I don't take my eyes off the stage. Is Paige doing some kind of YMCA arm motion? Whatever she's doing, she's doing with a smile that melts my fucking core. So goddamn pretty. So fucking gorgeous.

I know Rob is watching me like a hawk, so I say this with a big smile on my face, still literally sitting on my hands while I explain Eddie's new situation to him. "Option one, choke Ronnie the fuck out, drag him out of here, and don't come back in. Option two, I show up at your apartment tonight and fuck you up so bad you'll be better equipped to try out as a Cat girl than to have your dick sucked by one."

I glance at him for a split second. He's looking at me, confused, horror in his eyes. He's trying to tell if I'm joking.

I'm not.

"811 Armitage, apartment 4B. You sleep on the side of the bed closest to the bathroom, Maria sleeps closer to the window." I glance at him again, then turn back to Paige. "And you snore like a fucking freight train."

"You're an asshole, Dom. *Fuck*." He launches himself out of his seat, wraps his arm around Ronnie's throat, pulls them both down onto the floor.

Ronnie didn't see it coming, so he's struggling against Eddie's chokehold just to take a breath. The guys on either side of Ronnie reluctantly stand up, half-ass try to pull them apart, but without taking their eyes off Paige. Salvo runs over, shooting me a dirty look while kicking all of them out.

Four down. Thirty-three more to go.

I feel Rob's glare burning into the side of my head, so I turn to him and shrug, as if I had nothing to do with that.

Paige has her hand on the pole now, bunny hopping around it in a circle. She's lucky her top is holding up to the motion, or we'd have an even bigger problem.

Mikey is sitting in the front row, laying a stack of bills on the stage in front of him. Tipping isn't usually a part of Tryouts, but it's not unheard of either.

He waves a twenty-dollar bill in the air to get Paige's attention, but she's ignoring him. I'm pissed he's trying to get her attention, and I'm furious that he thinks a dub would be enough for her. I should shove his stack of twenties down his throat.

"Don't," Rob says the second I stir in my seat.

Fine.

I pull out my phone and open my texts. I have to scroll really fucking far to find Dmitri's number. He's sitting on Mikey's right. The guy used to text me all the time, wanting to get more involved in the enforcement side of the business. Doesn't look like I answered any of his last ten texts.

Damiano

> I need a favor

Instant response.

Dmitri

> Name it

Mikey starts calling out "Here, bunny, bunny, bunny. Come to daddy, little bunny." Paige looks over at him but doesn't move toward him. In fact, she takes a step away from him. Good girl, you'll get a reward for that. That is, after you get punished for stepping foot on that stage in the first place.

> Dislocate Mikey's jaw and you can ride with me for 2 weeks

> Fuck yeah. I'd do that for you for nothing. But definitely taking that ride-along. Thanks man

Dmitri puts his phone in his pocket then leans toward Mikey and whispers something in his ear. Mikey stands up and swings at him. Dmitri dodges it and lays into Mikey twice as hard. The loud fucking crack is music to my ears, as I watch Mikey hit the ground.

"Motherfucker!" Rob jumps up out of his seat. "Fuck you, Dom." He's loud enough to command everyone's attention over the music. "Everyone, get the fuck out."

Paige freezes on the stage mid-hop, her hands held up in front of her like little bunny arms. She starts to turn toward backstage, like she's leaving the room too.

"Not you," Rob tells her. "You stay."

She freezes.

The room empties within seconds, including Rob and Salvo. Now it's just me and my bunny and Dolly Parton playing on loop.

So... What do I do now?

Do I go to Damiano? Do I stay up here? Do I keep dancing? The song is about to restart. I *could* take it from the top.

Dom's just sitting in his chair, leaning back. With the bright lights shining toward me I can't make out the look on his face. Is he happy I'm here? Is he pissed? Has he moved on?

I take a few steps toward the edge of the stage, but Dom shakes his head.

We stare at each other long enough for Dolly to get to the chorus. Damiano stands up and takes a step toward me.

My whole body relaxes, my shoulders release, I let out the breath I was holding.

But then he stops.

And turns around.

He walks away.

I'm about to shout to him, to beg for him to stay, when he reaches for the back of his folding chair, closes it. He walks to me, dragging the chair behind him. He slowly climbs the stage stairs, the chair thud-thudding two steps behind him.

Facing me, he starts at my feet and slowly works his eyes up my body. I feel his gaze so hard it's like he's touching me. He's no longer backlit, so I can see his face now. But his blank expression is almost worse. A minute ago, I could pretend he was smiling. Now that I can see him, I can't read him at all.

"Dom, I—"

He shakes his head.

He unfolds the chair, sits down. He looks up at me, but doesn't say anything.

I point with my thumb over my shoulder toward the pole. "Should I maybe do the dance again?"

He slowly nods his head.

"Gina said I should forget the choreography and just—"

He nods again.

I have to count a few beats before I can pick up my routine. It's the refrain and I'm supposed to shimmy down to the floor then shimmy back up.

He bites his lip, watching me.

I take a step closer and shimmy down to the floor again.

On my way up, his hands circle my waist, tugging me toward him. I should be hopping right now, but with his hands on me, I can't.

"What am I supposed to do?"

"Did you come here to be a Cat girl or to be my girl?"

I put my foot onto his thigh. "I'll be whatever you want me to be."

"Oh yeah?" He tugs me onto him. I'm not sure his chair is going to hold both of us, but he doesn't seem worried.

"Yeah." I nod, causing one of the bunny ears to flop down into my face. "And you can be whatever you need to be."

"And what if—" Dom pushes the floppy ear back. "What if all I want is for you to be you—exactly you—and for me to be me and *everything* that means? That going to work for you?"

I like that. I nod again.

He stares at me a long minute. "Kiss me, angel."

I lean in, and his lips meet mine, his hands immediately tangling in my hair.

It's familiar *and* new, it's sweet and aggressive. It's pure Damiano.

I claw at his shirt. I need to feel his skin against mine. I grind myself against his thick bulge.

I know how to show him exactly how *his* I am. I start to slide down onto the floor.

Dom gently tugs my arm, standing me up. "You will most definitely be getting down on your knees for me. But not here."

He's right. It's a bit gross, and anyone could walk in.

"Yeah. I guess your days of getting blowies in this place are over. Right?" *Please say yes. You better say yes.*

Dom looks around the room, his gaze lingering on one particular booth that's slightly higher than the rest. He eventually looks back at me. Smiles.

Dom stands, takes off his suit jacket. "Put this on." He helps me get my arms in.

I reach up to take off my bunny ears.

"Leave those on. And the tail. We're going to need those."

"Yeah?" I wrap my arms around his neck.

"Yeah. My naughty bunny is getting one hell of a spanking for setting foot on this stage. I want to watch your tail jump with every smack."

"Dom." My voice cracks.

He leans forward, bites my lip. "Then when you can't take it anymore, you're going to swallow my cock to make up for all those blowies I'm going to miss from this place."

I laugh out loud. Not quite the romantic sonnet I was expecting. "And what's in it for me?"

"Besides getting to suck my cock?"

"Yeah, besides getting to suck your delicious cock."

His nostrils flare. I love when he loses control for me.

"Well, let's see." He leads us off stage. "You get to sit on my face every day for the rest of our lives. For hours if you want."

"I want that. What else?"

"You get my time and devotion. My support, my protection."

"I want that too. What else?"

"You get everything I am, angel. And if that's not enough, I'll figure out how to be more."

"And what do you want from me?"

Dom stops, steps in front of me. He rests his hand over my heart and taps one finger. "This." He slides his hand over to my boob, pinches my already hard nipple. "And this." His other hand slides down to my ass. "And every so

often, this. But most of all, angel, this." Dom leans down
and kisses me, kisses me like he's never going to stop.

A FEW WEEKS LATER

SALVO TEXTED FIFTEEN MINUTES ago to say they had another guy down in Damiano's workshop. I wasn't kidding when I told them to grab every fucker we could get our hands on until we figure out who killed those brothers my dad's getting blamed for.

Dom's workshop is *not* my favorite place to go. It creeps me the fuck out. It's a weird fucking glimpse inside Damiano's head, and that's not somewhere anyone should want to be.

I jog down the first short flight of steps to a landing. Hard left turn to a steep ramp down, then another hard turn. Then it's *up* a few uneven, wooden steps that creak and threaten to snap under my weight, only to go back down a few more.

The hallway narrows as I go. This part is brightly lit. The next hall is almost pitch black but smells like fresh-baked cookies. The one after this has its own air-conditioning unit dialed down for a blast of sharp, subzero air.

Damiano likes his 'guests' to enter through this twisting, demented path up and down and around again, like a fun house hall of mirrors, pain, torment, and destruction. A mindfuck before things start to hurt.

There's a shortcut entrance that goes directly from the garage into a *perfectly normal* elevator straight into his workshop, but Damiano set the passcode on that door's keypad to 17-17-17, that motherfucker. Seventeen just happens to be the unluckiest number to Italians, basically meaning that death is right around the corner. Fitting for his workshop—but it's also a number my superstitious-as-fuck mom drilled into me as a kid to stay the hell away from.

So I go the long, twisty, fucked-up way unless someone else is with me to enter the code.

I enter the dull-green tiled workshop, expecting today's 'session' to be well underway.

But it's not.

There's a guy tied to a metal chair looking like he's going to piss himself, which I expect. And Salvo's sitting off to the side, texting on his phone, which I expect.

But Damiano isn't busy at work, as expected. Instead, he's off in the corner, *watering his fucking plants*.

The guy keeps a couple racks of eucalyptus plants down here under artificial grow lights. He claims the plants are here so their fragrance covers up the residual smell of sweat, piss, and blood, all of which gets washed away after each session with industrial-strength hydrogen peroxide from tanks Damiano had installed.

But I think they're more of him fucking with his guests. Case in point—the 'Hang In There' poster with the little kitten dangling from a rope that's on the wall opposite from where this guy is tied up. Right at eye level with the chair.

Something is definitely up with Dom since he hasn't gotten started yet. This is probably the real reason Salvo texted me to get down here. Must be my turn to deal with Damiano's recent mood swings.

"Damiano, man, your plants are looking good." I ease into the conversation.

"Thanks, Rob." He pinches a leaf between his fingers then smells them, smiles. "You want a few branches to take home, brighten up the loft?" He takes the big-ass dagger off the clip on his belt and saws off a branch, reaches for another.

"I don't know, Dom. These plants have seen some shit." He smiles.

I lean against the corner of the table next to the junkie. Arms crossed, ankles crossed. Relaxed and cool as a cucumber. The table is covered with various tools that *aren't* currently in use.

"Can I ask you something?" I wait for Dom to give me his full attention.

He turns toward me, leans his shoulder against the plant rack. "Of course. Yeah."

I'm trying to remain calm, which is a major fucking undertaking given that my dad is *still* rotting in a jail cell and we don't have a single fucking lead on who killed those guys or who's setting him up or whether it's the same people or whether the killings just created an opportunity for someone else to fuck with us.

"So I'm wondering, man, how come this fucker is sitting over here with all his fingers still attached, with all his teeth still in his mouth, and with all the fucking information I need still in his completely intact skull?"

Dom looks over at the kid, looks him up and down like he's confirming the guy is still in one piece. He lets out a long breath. "Can we talk for a minute? Over here." He motions toward the corner he's standing in.

The room isn't that big, so even though I'm stepping away from the guy, we're only a few away from him.

I put my hand on his shoulder, give him a light squeeze. Sometimes Dom needs reassurance, and I can be the guy to give it to him. Especially on the rare occasion he opens up enough to let me. "Yeah, man. What's going on?"

He rubs the back of his neck, looks down at the ground. Clearly, he doesn't want to tell me whatever he's about to tell me. "Paige doesn't want me torturing guys."

This shit again? "I thought she agreed to look the other fucking way." I told her that was a fucking requirement of being with him.

This is *exactly* why the Cat girls are so fucking over-paid—to keep my top guys completely satisfied. To keep my men from settling down with girls that make them question their priorities. "Your main job is torturing guys. You love your job."

He nods. "I know, man. But Paige hates it."

"And she asked you to stop?"

"No. But I can read her body language. When I get home from the gym, she's friendly as fuck. When I get home from the workshop, she keeps her distance for a while. And if it bothers her, my heart won't be in it."

"Does your heart need to be in it? I'm good with you just using your hands, maybe an occasional boot to the nuts."

He looks at me like I've got two heads. "Interrogations are an art, Rob. And like any art, it's got to come from here." He presses over his heart. "It's got to be pure."

For fuck's sake. "Wherever the fuck you usually pull this"—I wave my arms around the room—"from, you've gotta find a way to make *this* happen, man."

"It's killing me. I want to do right by the Famiglia—you know I do. But Paige is all about saving lives, you know? She thinks I should try positive reinforcement to get what I want out of the guy."

The dickwad strapped to the chair decides to join the conversation. "I agree with Paige."

Dom's head snaps toward him. In the blink of an eye, Dom's dagger hurls through the air straight at the guy, planting firmly into the chair, right between the guy's legs, ever so slightly pressing against his dick and balls.

"*What the hell?*" the guy screeches, four octaves higher than a minute ago.

"Say her name again and I'll slice your tongue off, motherfucker."

The guy struggles against the ropes to pull his dick back from the razor-sharp blade. "You just said your girl doesn't want you torturing anyone. That includes me. You can't hurt me and keep your girl happy."

"Hurting you right now wouldn't be torture. It would be punishment for you saying her name. Say it again, and see what happens." Dom cracks his knuckles.

Hal-le-fucking-lujah. There's what I need. I knew my most effective hurting machine hadn't become a complete pussy. "You know, Dom, you don't have to torture this guy if Paige doesn't want you to."

"Really?" the guy and Dom ask at the same time, looking at me. Even Salvo looks up from his phone with a what-the-fuck expression.

"Really." I walk over and tug his knife out of the chair. I'll admit it, even I find Damiano's crazy-ass dagger intimidating as fuck. I walk it over, hand it back to him. "Here's how this is going to go. Instead of you torturing him to get him to tell us why the fuck he's helping the police set up my dad, I'll ask him some questions. Every time he gets one wrong, you're going to punish him."

"That's the same, that's the same! That's the exact same thing!" the guy squeals, pulling against the ropes, spittle flying out of his mouth.

Damiano lights up. "No, yeah. That works, right? *Torturing* is to get him to talk. Future tense. *Punishing him* is because he didn't talk. Past tense. It's not the same."

I smile. "It's not even close, man. Right, Salvo?"

"Works for me," Salvo adds, his attention focused back on his phone.

I nod. "You good with this?"

Dom has a glimmer in his eye. Bites his lip, smiles. He slowly nods. "Let's test it. Ask him something really fucking hard."

My number one hurting machine is back. Thank the fucking Lord. Now maybe we can figure out why the fuck my dad is in prison awaiting trial for a triple murder he had abso-fucking-lutely nothing to do with.

**Check out <u>Rob's Struggle</u> (The Famiglia – Book 2)
to see just how far Rob is willing go to free his dad.**

THANK YOU FOR READING my book! If you enjoyed it, consider leaving a review on Amazon or Good Reads.

Huge thank-you to Adam Argot, story coach extraordinaire, for your feedback and encouragement. Colossal thanks to Gabriela Pereira, writing coach virtuoso, for keeping me on track (and for demanding more Gina). And I could not have gotten this over the finish line without Danika Bloom and the Author Ever After gang.

Thank you Angel S. for beta reading, Sarah D. for the idea of a second meet-cute, Pippa K. for help with the navy base scene, and Dr. J for writing and speaking about the thread of sexuality (I hope I tugged at it hard enough).

Thank you to my girls for pushing me through this journey. Here goes (in alphabetical order because I'm not telling you who I love the most): Allie, Alysse, Angela, Jessica, Kirsten, Kit, Lindsay (Hmm... a sexy blonde Cali girl with a certain last name and who falls for a hot foreigner?), Sara, and, of course, Shannon. Yes, you can read it now.

BIG LAW ATTORNEY DUMPS private jet pilot to sail off into the sunset with sexy firefighter... That's not the plot from one of my books. That's my life.

When I'm not at work or glued to my laptop writing, you'll find me skiing, sailing, or reading. I'll probably be wearing black and will almost certainly have a cup of coffee in my hand, and two or three mostly empty, day-old cups nearby. Like Paige, I'm pretty sure I can do anything and have a basement filled with enough almost-finished projects to prove it.

Find out more at www.redtenpublishing.com. Feel free to email me at LeahM@Red10Publishing.com, or to sign up for my newsletter at https://www.red10publishing.com/contact.